Avenging Skulls

Avenging Skulls

LM Terry

Avenging Skulls

Copyright © 2022 LM Terry

Published by LM Terry

All rights Reserved

ISBN-13: 9798353649847

No part of this publication can be reproduced or transmitted in any form, either electronically or by mechanical means without prior written consent from the author. Brief quotes are permitted in the instance of reviews or critical articles. This book is licensed for your personal enjoyment only.

This book is intended for readers 18 and older, due to adult content and language. This is a work of fiction. Any names, places, characters, events, or incidents come from the author's imagination and are used in a fictitious manner. Any resemblance to actual persons, living or dead, or actual events is purely coincidental.

Cover Design by Just Write. Creations and Services

Edited by Red Ribbon Editing Services

Dedication

This book is dedicated to my readers. You helped fulfill a little girl's dream of becoming an author. There is no way to convey how much you've filled my heart. I love you all!

"And then, over time ... The girl with all the books became the woman who wrote them." ~ unknown

Contents

Prologue 1

Chapter One 5

Chapter Two 9

Chapter Three 16

Chapter Four 22

Chapter Five 31

Chapter Six 39

Chapter Seven 45

Chapter Eight 49

Chapter Nine 52

Chapter Ten 58

Chapter Eleven 62

Chapter Twelve 66

Chapter Thirteen 73

Chapter Fourteen 76

Chapter Fifteen 82

Chapter Sixteen 88

Chapter Seventeen 99

Chapter Eighteen 102

Chapter Nineteen 111

Chapter Twenty 116

Chapter Twenty-One 126

Chapter Twenty-Two 131

Chapter Twenty-Three 145

Chapter Twenty-Four 149

Chapter Twenty-Five 156

Chapter Twenty-Six 164

Chapter Twenty-Seven 172

Chapter Twenty-Eight 176

Chapter Twenty-Nine 201

Chapter Thirty 205

Chapter Thirty-One 218

Chapter Thirty-Two 228

Chapter Thirty-Three 240

Chapter Thirty-Four 245

Chapter Thirty-Five 258

Chapter Thirty-Six 265

Chapter Thirty-Seven 268

Chapter Thirty-Eight 282

Chapter Thirty-Nine 299

Chapter Forty 307

Chapter Forty-One 323

Chapter Forty-Two 327

Epilogue 341

Main Characters in the Rebel Skulls Series

Sugar and Skulls – Book One:

Bill – President – daughter is Jesse

Dirk – Vice President

Raffe – Sargent at Arms

Katie – young friend of Jesse

William – friend of Jesse from foster care

Big Dan – Owner of Big Dan's Tattoos

Watercolor Skulls – Book Two:

Dirk – President – married to Jesse – daughter is Billie Rose

Bill – Retired President – married to Candice – father of Jesse and adopted daughter's Katie and Ally

Big Dan – Vice President – Owner of Big Dan and Little J's Tattoos

Raffe – Sargent at Arms – married to Rachel (Dirk's sister) – son is Jackson

Lily – daughter of Senator Ramsey

Roses and Skulls – Book Three:

Dirk – President – married to Jesse – daughter is Billie Rose

Bill – Retired President – married to Candice – father of Jesse and adopted daughter's Katie and Ally

Big Dan – Vice President – married to Lily (sister to Jackson) – twin sons are Carson and Cole

Raffe – Sargent at Arms – married to Rachel (Dirk's sister) – adopted son is Jackson (brother to Lily. They share same father, Senator Ramsey)

William – Friend of Jesse from foster care – married to Penny – son is Elijah

Avenging Skulls – Book Four:

Dirk – President – married to Jesse – daughter is Billie Rose

Bill (deceased) – married to Candice – father of Jesse and adopted daughters Katie and Ally

Big Dan – Vice President – married to Lily (sister to Jackson) – twin sons are Carson and Cole

Raffe – Sargent at Arms – married to Rachel (Dirk's sister) – adopted son is Jackson (brother to Lily. They share same father, Senator Ramsey)

Elijah – club member - married to Billie Rose – daughter Aurelia

Brody – club member – uncle to Lanie (deceased)

Petey – club member

Grandma Maggie – daughter is Jenny (deceased) – grandson is Jackson (Jenny is his angel mom)

Prologue

Willow ~ 12 years old

"Come on, Willow," my brother soothes gently. "It's only four years, and then I'll be back for you. I promise."

Ignoring him, I continue reading my book.

He pulls it out of my hands, carefully placing the feather I use for a bookmark between the pages. "We need to talk about this before I leave."

Sighing loudly, I finally sit up and turn to him. "Ash, I can't do this without you. I don't understand why you can't get a job here."

"I'm not smart like you." We both jump when the music suddenly starts blaring below us. "I'll send money. You'll have everything you need while I'm gone."

I lie back down on the attic floor, staring up at the photo of my father, brother, and me. "How? You know she'll spend every last dollar you send on drugs."

Ash lays down beside me. "I've got a plan for all that. I talked to the owner of the grocery store over on 5th Street. He said I can send him money each month, and he'll keep a running tab for you. He said he won't tell mom. You get to decide what you guys need."

I close my eyes, realizing my brother is really doing this. There's nothing I can say to stop him.

'It's within walking distance; you'll have everything you need. And the school knows I'll be taking care of all your expenses there. I've already talked to the superintendent."

With one last ditch effort, I whisper, "But you're all I have, Ash."

He looks up at the picture on the ceiling. "The Army is the only shot I have at getting us out of here, Willow. You'll be fine. You're a smart girl. Just remember everything dad taught us. That's what I'm going to do."

My head falls to the side, and his gaze meets mine.

'One day, we'll look back on this moment and be glad for it. This is the right decision, little sis."

I give him a tiny nod, sniffling. He pulls me into the comfort of his arms as the party downstairs gets louder.

'I am going to miss you, though," he says, brushing my hair away from my face.

I curl myself into a tiny ball, resting my forehead against his broad chest.

He kisses the top of my hair. "You just keep your head down and work hard in school. And you better do some research and figure out where you want to live once I get back. We'll go wherever you want."

'Let's go somewhere where there are lots of trees," I say, wiping tears from my eyes.

'And baby goats," he adds.

Avenging Skulls

I tip my head to stare up at him. "Chickens. We have to have chickens so I can make us eggs, sunny side up, every morning."

"With ketchup," he teases.

My nose scrunches, and I make an exaggerated gagging sound. "Yuck."

He laughs, pulling me close. "I love you, Willow. We're going to make dad proud."

Something shatters downstairs, and my brother tenses next to me. This is where we hide when mom is on a binge, which is most of the time. Ever since our father passed a couple of years ago, she's been on a spiraling path of self-destruction. Unfortunately, we've been on that journey with her.

My father died in a construction accident. It was so unexpected, none of us knew how to handle it. Up until then, I would say our family was normal. Whatever that really means. Is anyone normal? I was ten when he died; Ash was sixteen.

Ash graduates in a few weeks, and after that he's determined to enlist in the Army. Or I should say has … he has enlisted in the Army. My heart breaks in a thousand pieces every time I think about it.

"Just keep your head down, okay?" he says again. "It's better to fly under the radar in this world."

"I will."

He jumps up and rummages through the pile of books we have lined up along the wall. "I want you to keep this in your bag."

I sit up and take the book from him. "Ash, no. Dad gave you this."

Gently, he pushes it against my chest as I try to hand it back to him. "Just until I get back and then you can return it to me. I'll have a whole squad; you'll just have yourself for a while."

My thumb rubs over the cover of the survival guide my dad gave to Ash the Christmas before he passed. He used to give us a new book each year. Usually, it was something involving nature. Our father loved the outdoors. I lean over and carefully place it in my bag, along with my book about bugs that our father gave me that same year. When I zip the bag shut, my brother gives me a smile that reminds me of him.

"It will be okay. You'll see," he says, lying back and tucking his arms under his head and closing his eyes.

It doesn't take long before he's snoring quietly. He's confident in the decision he's made for us.

I spend the entire night staring at him, afraid that if I close my eyes for too long, he will disappear, too.

Chapter One

Willow ~ Fifteen years old

"Mom, can you get the door?" I holler over my shoulder as I'm washing dishes.

She grunts as she walks past me, tightening her bathrobe around her thin frame. I glance at the clock on the wall; it's a little early for her usual suitors to be knocking. I know it's not for me. I don't have any friends and even if I did, I would not bring them here. I'm doing my best to keep the house clean and to fix the things I can, but the house has seen better days.

When I hear masculine voices coming from the living room, I grab a dishtowel to dry my hands. Peeking around the doorway, I see my mom sitting on the couch with a military officer crouched in front of her, another standing quietly at his side.

I start to back away when my mother tells them they will have to talk to me. She isn't feeling well.

The uniformed man in front of her stands and helps her to her feet. My mom walks past me, not even giving them a second glance.

Before I know what is happening, I'm the one on the couch and one of the officers is sitting by me, his hands wrapped around mine. A casualty assistance officer he calls himself. I catch the words accident, beneficiary, remains ...

His mouth is moving, but I'm only catching every other word because my mind is trying to make sense of what is happening. There must be a mistake because my brother knows how to survive anything. Then I catch the word explosion.

Oh, how do you survive that?

'Do you have someone you can call to be with you and your mother?" he asks.

I shake my head, struggling to clear the ringing in my ears. "I'm, um, no, we'll be okay," I hear myself say.

He glances around the room, then gives the man with him a concerned look.

Standing up, I walk over to the door, opening it for them. "Thank you for letting us know." My eyes drop to the ground.

Both of them step outside. "I'll be back in a few days, after you've had time to process. I have a few things I need to go over with you and your mother. Would Thursday afternoon be a good time to stop by?"

I nod my head, forcing my eyes to meet his.

Slowly, I close the door, staring out the window as the two uniformed men make their way down the broken sidewalk toward their vehicle. They look so out of place here, all polished and prime. Most of the homes on our street have been abandoned. There are some squatters a few houses down, but most of the houses are no longer livable.

We were going to leave, too. That was before my dad passed.

Avenging Skulls

I turn away from the door as my mom comes out of her room. She looks at the couch before turning her glazed eyes my way.

Clearing my throat, I tell her what the COA told me. "He said he'll be back Thursday."

She runs her fingers through her messy brown hair. "I can't do this anymore. I'm sorry," she mutters and then walks out, the door banging closed behind her.

I follow her as far as the top step. She sways, tripping over broken concrete all the way down the sidewalk.

I continue to watch as she walks away from me, disappearing around the brick building on the corner. My eyes linger there as the hot summer sun continues to beat down on the top of my head. When it moves far enough across the sky to cast a shadow of our house over the street, I finally go back inside.

Sliding down the door after I lock it, my ass hits the floor with a thud. This isn't the first time she's left. In fact, she's left several times. Occasionally, I worried and wondered if I should call the police. But something tells me she's not coming back this time.

A piece of my heart just left with her. Your heart has four chambers; I think I'm down to one. Can it continue to pump with just one?

My eyes roam over the empty room. How did this happen?

Ash was coming home in a few months.

We were going to get out of the city and go somewhere beautiful.

With trees.

Now …

I don't know what to do. Ash was the only person I had, and now he's gone.

Gone.

Eventually, I pull myself off the floor and make my way to the attic where I continue to stare blankly at the photo of my father, brother, and me. Four years he had said.

Four years just turned into eternity.

I'll never see my brother again.

Chapter Two

Willow

Two days have passed. As expected, my mother hasn't returned. I don't know what I'm going to tell the military man when he shows up again. The thought of going to a foster home terrifies me. Maybe I'll be able to convince him she's still not feeling well. I'm going to have to try.

I kick a can as I make my way to the grocery store, sticking close to the buildings as I pass the makeshift tents set up along the sidewalk. This is one of the poorest neighborhoods in the city. No one can afford rent, and even if they could, most of the homes around here are falling in on themselves.

Keeping my eyes down, I manage to avoid the comments and unwanted attention from the men loitering on the street. When I get to the checkout with my items, the clerk tells me there aren't enough funds on my account to cover it all.

"I'm sorry, hun," she says, smacking her gum loudly.

My cheeks heat as I quickly do the math and set a few things aside.

"Maybe your brother will call today and add some money to your account," she says cheerfully as she removes the items from the transaction. The woman behind me sighs loudly, clearly annoyed I'm taking longer than expected.

"I'm sure you're right," I agree with a forced smile on my face.

When I leave, I have forty-three cents left on the tab. I take my two bags and make my way back to the house. It's starting to get dark; I silently scold myself for going out this late. A few men start jeering at me, so I pick up the pace. In my rush, one of the plastic grocery bags breaks, and the contents fall out onto the ground. I watch as a can of soup rolls under a van parked nearby.

I stand there, staring.

And suddenly it hits me.

My brother is dead.

He is dead.

Tears begin to spill down my cheeks as I quickly try to pick up my items, more falling from my arms as I lean over to retrieve the next thing. The men behind me laugh.

"Hey, here, let me help."

A man I've never seen before hops out the side of a blue van. He must be homeless too, but he doesn't look like the rest of the men on this street. He's well groomed. His dirty blond hair is cut short and styled to one side, but it's his crystal blue eyes that make him stand out.

He gathers my items and then goes back to his vehicle. I follow but remain a few feet away, leery of getting too close. He pulls out a plastic bag and carefully places everything inside as he sits down on the floor of the vehicle.

Avenging Skulls

"Are you okay?" he asks, his eyes darting between me and his task.

I nod and wipe my nose with the back of my hand. He notices me peeking inside his van. It's nice.

"Do you have far to go? I can give you a ride," he offers, his eyes trained on me.

If I were to guess, I'd say he's a few years older than my brother. His skin is tan, like he spends a lot of time outdoors.

Shaking my head, I stare at the ground. "I'll be okay. Thank you for your help." I hold my hand out for the bag without looking at him. When he doesn't give it to me, I glance up.

He's looking around the area, concern pulling at his brows. "How about I walk with you? It's getting dark, and I wouldn't be a particularly good human if I let you walk alone." He stands and slides the door to the van shut.

Extending his hand, he waits for me to give him the bag I'm still holding. Reluctantly, I release it to him.

"Lead the way," he says, pulling his shoulders back and scanning the area with those clear blue eyes.

I swipe at my cheeks, struggling to keep the tears from falling.

No one has offered to help me in a long time. I suppose it will be okay to accept his generosity. He looks nice. I'm sure it will be fine. Yeah, it will be fine.

As we get close to my house, I begin to slow my steps. "Thank you for helping me. I really appreciate it, but I live just up ahead. I'll be fine the rest of the way."

He stops and glances around. "I think I should take you all the way. I'd like to talk to your parents about how unsafe it is to let you walk alone like this. Especially at night. It's dangerous."

The man notices the look on my face before I can mask it.

"Come on," he says, walking ahead of me.

I jog to catch up to him. "My mom isn't feeling well." It's not a lie.

"Is that why you're doing the shopping?" he asks, his stride long and sure.

I point to my house. "I live right there. Really mister, I'll be fine. My mom won't like it that I let a stranger walk me home."

"Well, I don't like it that your mom *let* you walk alone."

Little bursts of energy skitter down to my fingertips at his words. His eyes continue to scan right, then left, his features hard and calculating.

He marches right up the steps and holds the screen door open as I fish my key out of my pocket. As soon as I have the main door unlocked, he pushes it open, waiting for me to step inside. His blue gaze takes everything in as he walks to the kitchen, setting the bags on the table.

"Tell your mom I'd like to speak with her."

He seems much bigger now that he's in my home. When I don't move, his intense eyes stop on me. "She isn't here, is she?"

I wring my hands together. "No, but she'll be back soon," I say quietly. "Thank you again for your help."

He grabs the little notepad I have stuck to the fridge and a pen, then slaps them down on the table. "I want you to tell me where she is. An address, directions, whatever. I'm not leaving this town until I've talked to her."

Suddenly, I burst into tears. Right here, in the middle of the kitchen, in front of a stranger.

His features soften as he sits down on one of the kitchen chairs, pulling me between his legs. "Don't cry. Do you have someone other than your mother?"

I shake my head. "My dad is dead and my brother too," I cry, the sobs coming harder and faster by the minute. He brushes hair away from my face with both of his hands, reminding me of Ash.

"Shh, little one. Shh, I'll take care of you. No worries."

He pushes me down into a chair and walks around the house, peeking in doors as he goes. When he finds the bathroom, I hear him turn the water on. He comes out, wiping his hands on a towel. He crouches down in front of me. "I've run you a hot bath; it will make you feel better. I'll make you something to eat while you're in there." He stares into my eyes, offering me a small smile.

I nod and make my way into the bathroom. When I get there, I lock the door. Is this guy for real? I know I shouldn't trust him, but I don't know how to get rid of him.

Pots and pans bang, and cupboards open and close as I settle into the tub, wrapping my arms around my knees. My mind runs through different scenarios of how I can ask him to leave until he knocks on the door.

"It's time to get out, sweetheart."

Sweetheart?

"Your supper is getting cold," he adds.

When his footsteps retreat, I finish cleaning myself and step out of the tub, wrapping a towel around me tightly. I open the door and dart down the hallway. Quickly, I tug on the rope to pull the attic steps down.

Scrambling up the stairs, I rush to dress myself. Just as I tug my jeans over my hips, I turn around to find the man standing behind me.

"Shit," I squeak, retreating a few steps.

He crouches down, running his hand over the blankets on the floor. "Is this where you sleep?" he asks.

"Sometimes," I answer quietly.

He nods, his fingers rubbing over his mouth. "Go on downstairs. Your food is getting cold."

I slide past him and hurry back down the stairs. When I get to the kitchen, I find a bowl of tomato soup and a grilled cheese sandwich sitting on the table. My stomach growls loudly as he comes up behind me. He pulls out a chair, then scoots it in for me after I sit.

He takes the seat across from me. "My name is Bradley. What's yours?" He pulls a business card out of his pocket and begins to flip it through his fingers mindlessly.

"Willow," I say quietly, covering my mouth as I speak.

"It's nice to meet you, Willow."

Anxiously, I tap my fingers on the table. "Thank you for everything, but I think you should leave now."

He pulls his head back but remains firm. "Willow, I want you to tell me where your mother really is."

I let my spoon fall into the bowl, soup splashing over the edge. "She's … she's in the hospital, but she'll be back tomorrow. She's going to be really pissed if she finds out I let a stranger in the house. So, no offence, mister, but you need to leave. I appreciate all you've done." I pause and look up at him through my lashes. "It's been nice."

Avenging Skulls

He nods slowly. "Okay, I don't want to get you in any trouble. But promise me you'll eat everything." He waits for my response, tipping his head toward my food.

I agree with a tiny nod, staring at the bowl.

"Okay then, Willow. It was nice meeting you." He stands, pausing beside me to run his hand down the back of my hair. Without another word, he walks out of the kitchen.

"Don't forget to lock the door behind me," he yells from the other room.

When the door bangs closed, I rush to the living room and turn the lock, breathing a sigh of relief. I make my way back to the kitchen and finish the meal he made. It's good, and I'm thankful I didn't have to cook anything tonight because I'm just so tired.

After I finish, I make my way out to the couch and lie down. I'll clean up the kitchen tomorrow. All that crying must have worn me out. My eyes blink closed as I think about asking the owner of the grocery store for a job. That's what I'll do.

I'll survive. I will.

Chapter Three

Willow ~ five years later

"Are you going to sit there and pout all day?" Bradley asks.

I turn away from him to stare out the window.

He weaves a business card through his fingers as he snaps his gum between his teeth.

Sighing loudly, I try to ignore him.

"Talk to me."

I hate it when he does this. He makes me feel like I'm being childish. "I'm fine."

He leans forward, his arm draped over the steering wheel. He tips his aviators down his nose, his glacial eyes scanning my face. "I told you I was sorry. It won't happen again."

Pulling my knees up to my chest, I stare out the windshield, watching a family walk into the truck stop. "Do you promise?"

He rolls his head on his neck as if he's thinking about it. Now, he'll pretend he is doing me a favor.

"Okay, it won't happen again. I just wanted you to see what it would be like with someone who doesn't care about you."

And here we go. It's time for him to turn it back on me. And don't think I didn't notice that he didn't promise me anything.

I bite at a hangnail. This is the game we play. And even though I hate losing every time, it's worth it. Swallowing my pride, I give him the words he's been fishing for. "You're right. It wasn't the same as being with you."

He smiles, his pride firmly back in place. His wide grin lets me know I got my lines right this time. Like I said, all part of the game. He likes games.

Bradley places a finger under my chin, forcing me to look at him. "It won't happen again. Okay?" He tips his head down, his eyes meeting mine.

"Okay," I say quietly.

"Can I get a smile from my girl?"

I swallow hard and nod, forcing the corners of my mouth to turn up.

"Good girl." He presses a soft kiss to my forehead. Then, he pushes his sunglasses back over his eyes, pulling the keys from the ignition. "Lock the doors when I get out."

Nodding, I lay my finger over the automatic lock button.

"I'll be right back."

He jumps out, pausing to listen for the lock. When he hears it click, he heads up to the door. He holds it open for a young woman, giving her that creepy smile of his. His eyes meet mine one last time over the rim of his glasses before he disappears inside.

I should do it this time.

Do it.

Willow, do it.

Move.

I grab my bag, shoving crackers and a few bottles of water inside, then I open the door and run.

I'm going to pay for this when he catches me. I know I am, but I have to try. When I get to the back of the building, I see a train stopped in the middle of a field. I run and run, then dodge between the cars of the train, shielding myself from the truck stop.

I continue to run alongside the train when it makes a loud clunking sound. No! It's going to leave and then I'll be exposed with nowhere to hide.

"Willow!"

A sob escapes me as I hear my name being called. The train makes another loud noise. I stop and look at the car beside me; there's a small space at the end. I could fit there. Carefully, I climb up the ladder and slide into the space in front of the grain car. When the train lurches forward, I grab my bag and scoot back as far as I can.

Bradley's calls are getting closer, but the train is finally moving. The noise eventually drowns him out.

This is stupid. This is stupid. Bradley is the only person I have in this world. I wrap my hand around the iron railing, debating whether I should jump off. I glance around the landscape as the train picks up speed. Slowly, I slide back.

I have myself. I can survive. I can.

The train is moving too fast for him to catch me, and it would definitely be reckless for me to jump off now. The decision is final. There's no turning back.

I hug my bag close to my chest, still struggling to catch my breath.

Oh my god, I did it. I really did it.

I'm scared but not nearly as terrified as I was the day I woke up in the back of his van.

The train continues to ramble down the rails as I watch the beautiful countryside pass by. After a few hours, I begin to get drowsy, but I don't dare fall asleep.

Just as my bladder tells me I'm going to have a new problem, the brakes on the train begin to screech. The train eventually slows to a stop, right in the middle of nowhere. It's starting to get dark, but I guess it would be okay to hop off for a minute. I really need to relieve myself and stretch.

Carefully, I climb down, my legs screaming at me in protest. Quickly, I dart away from the train, the fear of being caught by a railroad employee spurring me on.

Running through a patch of tall grass, I find a tree to hide behind as I shimmy down my shorts and squat to pee. When I'm finished, I scan my surroundings, wondering how long the train will be stopped here.

The bubbling sound of a stream pulls me away from the train. When I find it, I continue to follow its winding path. If I had time, I could start a fire and boil some water to refill my empty bottles. I cross the stream, hopping on a few big rocks to get to the other side. I hear the clucking of chickens, so I keep walking.

The trees begin to thin out, revealing a farm. A cute two-story farmhouse stands tall in the middle of a well-kept yard as chickens peck around on the ground. My gaze roams over all the buildings, pausing on a large red barn. There is a mural painted on one side. Dragonfly Farms, it says.

I slide my backpack off and crouch down, pulling out my book of bugs. On the front is a close-up photo of a large dragonfly. My eyes go back to the side of the barn.

A loud sound comes from behind me. The train is starting up again. I need to get back. Slowly, I rise from the ground.

My thumb rubs over the cover of the book. Maybe this is where I'm meant to be.

Suddenly, a door opens to the house and I jump behind a tree. An old woman appears with a basset hound at her heels. He lifts his nose, sniffing the air before walking down the stairs and plopping on the green grass. Following him, the woman drags a large bag over the lawn, struggling to get it as far as the chicken coup. She wipes her brow, breathing hard.

The train makes another loud clank as the cars begin to move. I should go.

"I'll just leave this right here for the night, and maybe some woodland fairies will be kind enough to move it for me," she cackles.

I'm not sure if she's talking to the dog or herself. Both, I suspect.

She shakes her head at the mutt. "You're right. That boy will show up tomorrow, and he won't be happy if he finds out I did it myself."

Avenging Skulls

The woman makes her way back to the house, clapping her arthritic hands for the dog to join her. He reluctantly gets up, yawning before he obeys. When the wooden screen door bangs shut behind them, I make my way back toward the train.

When I get to the tree line, I watch as it slowly begins to roll forward. There's still time to catch it.

A dragonfly buzzes past my ear as the breeze rustles the leaves hanging above me. Have you ever had a sudden feeling of familiarity? The wind, a smell, the sounds of birds singing, the sun on your face ... just something that reminds you of ... well, I don't really know. It's just something you can't put a finger on. All you know is it feels good, calm. I've often wondered if maybe these kind of feelings were small reminders from Heaven.

The train picks up speed, but my feet remain still.

I close my eyes as the cool breeze tugs at the ends of my blonde hair, whipping it around my cheeks.

The train chugs along without me.

And I think that's okay.

Yes, it's definitely okay. Bradley could be waiting on the other end of the line. I should stay.

I take a deep breath, listening to the familiar click of the wheels. Opening my eyes as the sound fades, I catch the last railcar slip around the bend and out of sight.

It leaves me behind at Dragonfly Farms.

Chapter Four

Jackson

I watch my cousin, Billie Rose, hold her daughter's tiny hands in her own and walk backwards. The look on Aurelia's face as she stares up at her mother puts a smile on my own. But as usual, my guilt quickly erases it.

It is wonderful things worked out for Billie Rose, but I'll never forgive myself for the part I played in it all.

Kelsie, my sister's newly adopted daughter, finally makes her way over to me, her eyes darting around the patio. I know she's making sure the twins haven't spotted her. The twins think they are her bodyguards, not just her new brothers. However, they do look the part. They're ginormous, just like their dad.

With the party going on around us, nobody notices when I nod my head toward the front of the building. She understands, disappearing around the left side of the warehouse while I head to the right. We meet up in the parking lot.

"Do you have him?" she whispers as we quickly make our way over to my truck.

Avenging Skulls

Laughing harshly, I answer, "Did you doubt me?"

She takes another quick look around before her eyes land on my tailgate. "No, but I didn't think you would find him this fast."

I grab the handle, jerking on it. When it's open, I hop up and sit on the edge. "I told you, I have help."

Tipping my head, I study her. She really is cute as all get out, but I'm staying away from the female population right now. Maybe forever. After what happened with Lanie, I can't risk it. And besides, she's now my niece, so no thanks.

"So, are you sure you want to do this? You don't have to. I can guarantee it's him. He'll never touch you or anyone else ever again."

She nods, her short blonde hair bouncing around her face. "I need to see."

After a quick glance around, I pull the tarp away from the dead man's bloody face. Kelsie sucks in a breath, jumping back a step.

I remain where I am, my eyes trained on her. When she's seen enough, I cover him up. Hopping off the tailgate, I slam it shut. "It's done. You can move on now."

"I have moved on, Jackson. But thanks to you, I only have to worry about him finding me in my dreams now." She lowers her head in thanks. When she lifts her face, tears are streaming down her cheeks. "You've given me something the law never could."

She rises on her tiptoes, places a soft kiss to my whiskered cheek, then spins around and runs back to the party. Hopefully before the twins notice she's missing. I'm surprised she got away for as long as she did. Between the two of them, you rarely catch Kelsie by herself.

Bringing my phone to my ear, I pull out my cigarettes.

" Hey. I'm just confirming I received your package," I tell the person on the other end.

"Glad I could be of help."

I take a drag, letting the smoke fill my lungs. When I release it, I glance up at the clouds. "Was that the last one?"

"Don't know. I just had another tip come in."

My dad pulls up, so I begin to make my way toward him.

"You can't get them all, you know." When I don't get a response, I decide to wrap up the conversation. "Hey, I'm going to have to let you go."

"I'll call you when I get another one."

I drop the cigarette, stomping it out with my boot. "Be careful."

A dog barks in the background. "Always." And then the phone goes dead.

My dad's smile falters a bit when he sees me.

"What's up, old man?" I ask as we meet at the door of the warehouse.

He holds it open, waving for me to go ahead of him. "I need to talk to you about something. Let's have a drink."

As the family chatter continues around us, my old man sits down on a barstool as I pull a bottle from the top shelf. "You're late to the party," I joke, but I can see he isn't in a teasing mood.

"I just came from your grandmother's."

"I know. I know. I'm headed over there in a bit. You don't have to lecture me. I called and told her I couldn't make it yesterday."

"Jackson, I think your grandmother is starting to show signs of dementia." He stares into his glass, refusing to look at me. "She hasn't been the same since your grandfather died."

"Dad, grandpa has only been gone a month. Give her some time. She's fine," I assure him. My grandmother is the toughest woman I know, and I know a lot of badass women.

"Jackson, I just came from there and I tell you, something isn't right with her. She thinks woodland fairies are stealing her eggs."

I laugh but reign it in when I see he's being serious. "Are you sure she wasn't just fucking with you?"

"I wish I was, Son."

Sitting across from him, I take a sip of my drink. "I'll go out there right now and talk to her. Do you think I should make her an appointment to see the doc?"

"Yeah, that probably wouldn't be a bad idea. I just want to do right by Jenny, so whatever Maggie needs, I'll take care of the expense."

Tapping my glass on the counter, I lean in close to him. "Dad, you don't owe my biological mother anything. I'll take care of it. Maggie is my responsibility."

"That's where you're wrong. We are a family. When one of us is down, we all step up. All of us."

I stretch when I stand upright. "Okay, but let me go check it out before we make an announcement to the whole club."

He stands with me, patting me on the back. "We'll meet up later?"

"I'll stop by the house in the morning. Tell Ma to have breakfast made, yeah?"

My dad thumps me on the back of the head with a finger, making me laugh. He knows I'm only joking.

"I'll see you later, old man."

When I pull into the farm, I drive around to the hog pen, backing up with an arm resting on the back of the seat. I slam it into park, slide my hands into my gloves and then hop out, quickly unwrapping the dead man. He hits the mud with a loud smack. The hogs grunt and immediately get to work on the latest delivery.

I walk over to the water pump, tossing my gloves onto the ground. As I wash my hands, I let my eyes scan over the farm. Grandma is already hobbling down the back stairs. I jog over to her, wiping my hands off on my jeans. When I get there, I offer my arm to help her down.

"You just missed your father," she says before settling herself in an old metal lawn chair.

"I saw him over at the warehouse." I squat down in front of her, watching patiently as she wraps wisps of white hair around the bun on the back of her head. "What do you need me to do this evening?" I ask.

She pats her hair and then points toward the chicken shed. "I hauled the feed down there a few days ago. I need you to put it in the tubs for me, so the critters don't get into it."

I stand up and salute her as I back away, but when I get to the shed, I can't find a bag of feed. I tip the lids on the containers, finding them full.

My heart falls to my stomach. Slowly, I make my way back to her. "It's already done. Maybe Dad did it?" I tilt my head, hoping that's the case.

She gives me a confused stare. "Raffe didn't come back here. It must be those darn woodland fairies. You know they've been stealing my eggs."

Avenging Skulls

My gaze scans the forest, and I swallow hard. "Grandma, you know fairies aren't real, yeah?"

"Well, then, Mr. Smarty Pants, where are my eggs going?"

I take a seat in the chair across from her, and she pushes a Tupperware dish full of homemade cookies across the little table separating us. Popping open the container, I grab a cookie before settling back in my chair. "Maybe you got coyotes."

She laughs. "Silly boy, if I have coyotes, don't you think they would eat my chickens first?"

I brush crumbs from my beard and lean forward. "You been feeling okay, Grandma?"

She rubs her hand over her chest. "I'm just fine. Don't you worry about me, Jackson." She leans forward and pats my knee. "I see you brought another delivery for my babies."

I chuckle at her reference to the hogs. She's always called them her babies. "There's an endless supply of deliveries, Grandma. But I'll take them somewhere else if it makes you uncomfortable, you know that."

She raises an arthritic finger and points it at me. "I don't care, boy. I just don't like the fact you think you have some debt to the world that you need to pay off. Your biological father will pay for his own sins when he meets his maker. You don't need to be paying for them here on this earth."

"That's not the only reason I do it," I grumble, reaching over to pour us each a glass of lemonade. I'd like to steer the conversation away from the dead men I feed to her hogs. "So, what else do you need me to do while I'm here?"

Her cloudy blue eyes roam over the landscape. She sighs loudly. "There's an endless supply of chores. Take your pick."

"Well, I better get started then. Thanks for the cookies." I grab the container and my lemonade, then head down toward the barn.

"You're staying for supper, aren't you?" she asks as I walk away.

"Wouldn't miss it for anything," I yell over my shoulder.

She chuckles. "Well, don't go spoiling it by eating all those cookies. I'll holler when it's ready."

I wave, letting her know I heard her. My grandmother is the world's best cook, hands down. I shove the door to the barn open and gather up the painting supplies I recently bought. I've been meaning to give the chicken coop a fresh coat of paint for a while now. Grandpa always preached to keep the wood sealed or it will rot.

Grandma's right though; there is an endless supply of work around here. She's never going to be able to keep up by herself. Maybe I should start coming every day instead of just once a week. Lily and JD can manage our business, Junkyard Treasures, without me. Kelsie is working there now, filling the void left by Billie Rose when she opened Black Rose Custom Bikes.

I can build things anywhere, I think as I set the cans out by the coop, along with my cookies. I slam my lemonade before heading back to the barn. I could even set up a workshop out here. That way I can still follow my passion and be around for grandma, too. I'll talk to Dad about it more tomorrow.

Grandma's old basset hound, Fred, sniffs the ground and then starts barking up toward the loft.

"What is it, boy? Is there a critter up there?" I pat his head before climbing up to check it out. "Something is stealing grandma's eggs. Could be a coon."

Avenging Skulls

My eyes scan over the area. Dust motes float in the sunrays peeking in from around the hay door. Grandma and Grandpa bought this place after they found out I was their grandson. My biological mother had been a runaway at fourteen, and they never saw her again after that. They named the place Dragonfly Farms because she loved dragonflies. In fact, that's how my sister, Lily, found me.

It's not a working farm anymore. Yeah, Grandma convinced Grandpa to get her some pigs, chickens, and a few other furry animals, but that's about as far as they ever took it. She used to plant a huge garden every year, but she said she wasn't up to it this year. It's sad, because the woman canned some of the best things. Pickles, salsa, you name it. She could store anything away for a rainy day. It's simple and quiet out here, and I like that. Sometimes my brain goes so fast it's hard for me to concentrate. But here, it's different.

I climb back down, finding nothing unusual. The old dog must be getting senile, too.

After several hours of painting, Grandma opens the back door and hollers at me for supper. I clean up, putting everything back in the barn before heading inside. I'll come back and finish tomorrow; a few more hours and then I can cross it off my list.

The wooden screen door squeaks as I step in. The smell of mashed potatoes and green beans makes my stomach growl. I give my grandma a kiss on the cheek as I stop beside her at the sink to wash my hands.

"Is there any paint on the coop?" she teases, her gaze roaming over my paint-stained clothes.

I laugh and take a seat at the table as she fills me a plate with all my favorites. Rubbing my hands together, excited to dig in, I notice the flowers on the table. "You didn't go and get yourself a boyfriend, did you?" I joke.

She sits down beside me, smiling at the colorful bouquet on the table. "The fairies left them on my step. They think it's a fair trade for my eggs, but when I catch them, I'm going to give them a good ear full."

My stomach does that weird sinking thing again. "Well, they sure are pretty."

Grandma stares at them. "They are. I guess if you're going to have fairies, it's good to have ones with good taste." She chuckles and starts in on her meal.

Dad's right; something is off with her. I'll have to call doc in the morning and see if I can get her in for an appointment soon.

Chapter Five

Willow

I stare into the flames, my big book of bugs perched carefully on my legs. The crickets chirp around me, keeping me company. No matter how lonely this might be, it's better than the life I'd been living with Bradley.

Once I decided to stay, I found a place to set up my camp. It's a little ways away from the farm. I don't want to get too close and risk someone finding me. I had to borrow a few things from the old woman, but I'll pay her back. The best thing was this bright blue tarp I've used to make my shelter. It was up in the loft of the barn.

I've been careful though; I don't leave any tracks behind. My eyes drop to the book in my lap. I wish I still had my brother's survival guide. It would come in handy about now. Brushing cookie crumbs from the page, my mind goes back to the man I saw today. When he first jumped out of his truck, he scared me; he looks like the type of guy you should stay away from. Then, I saw him shove a dead man right off the back of his truck into the pig pen.

Pigs will eat anything.

After he walked over to the old woman, he wasn't nearly as intimidating. He sat with her and laughed and smiled.

I grew up with all sorts of people. Living in the poorest part of the city, I learned sometimes outward appearances aren't all that they seem. Just look at Bradley. He looks like a perfect gentlemen, clean and well groomed. His face is shaved smooth, and his skin is clear of any imperfections. Those lie beneath the surface.

Monsters aren't always ugly.

Anyhow, the man seems to really love the old woman. Maybe she's his grandmother.

I put a few more logs on my fire and then make my way back to the farm. The light is on upstairs; it should go off in a few minutes. She keeps the same routine. Once it goes dark, I set to work, lighting the old lantern I found in the barn. I shine it over the chicken coup. I feel bad for eating all the man's cookies. This is the least I can do. He worked hard on it all evening.

I'm quiet as I work, smiling at the little bugs he painted along the trim on the door. Each one is different, but he made them with his fingerprint. What an odd man. One minute he's dumping a body to the hogs, the next he's painting colorful bugs on a chicken shed.

I place my finger over the top of one of his prints.

There's just something about this place that feels like home. I close my eyes and pretend the old woman who lives here is my grandmother. When I open them, I get to work, using my much smaller finger to continue his design around the windows. It takes me most of the night to get everything right, but it will all be worth it to see Grandma smile.

I wait until dawn and then she appears. She hobbles down to the coop to let the chickens out for the day. When she notices the new paint job, she stops and covers her mouth with her hand. Her gaze scans the trees before going back to the coop.

She drops her hand and smiles. "If they didn't think I was crazy before ..." She shakes her head. "You can come out. I'm not going to run you off," she says. "Come on now. I don't want to have to get the sheriff out here. That wouldn't be good for either of us."

Sighing, I step out from behind the tree.

She waves for me to come to her, but I stay where I'm at. Her old eyes take me in as we stare at each other.

"You did a real good job at finishing this." She points at the coop. "I could use someone like you to help me out around here. We can keep trading if you like."

I give her a small nod.

"I've been wanting to walk down to the cemetery to visit my husband and daughter. Would you walk with me?"

This could be a trap. I've been ensnared in one before, so I need to be careful. "How far is it?"

She wipes at her brow. "Oh, bought a half mile l would guess. My husband and I used to walk it once a week."

My gaze falls to her legs.

A smile pulls at her soft cheeks. "You're right; these old legs aren't what they used to be. You can carry my chair, so I can rest once and awhile." She turns and heads back to the house. "I'll fetch it while you gather up some flowers. Do you like cinnamon rolls?"

"Yes, ma'am," I tell her, still unsure if I should go along with this plan.

'Hurry along now. My grandson will be back this afternoon. If you don't want him seeing you, we better make quick work of it."

This spurs me to run across the brook to the field of wildflowers that runs along the tracks. After I gather two handfuls, I make my way back to the farm, hiding to make sure she didn't call someone to come get me.

I see her sitting in a folding chair in the middle of the yard with her old hound dog resting by her feet. The dog lifts his head and sniffs but doesn't move as I approach them slowly.

The old woman holds out a cinnamon roll wrapped in a napkin, so I trade her for the flowers in my hand. She grabs a bag hanging on the back of the chair and carefully places the flowers inside as I scarf down the roll.

"What's your name, honey?" she asks.

I think about lying but what's the point. My name is the one thing that hasn't been taken from me. "Willow," I say quietly, folding the napkin carefully and slipping it in my pocket.

She holds her hand out to me. "My name is Maggie. It's nice to meet you."

We shake hands and then I help her up. "You think you can carry the chair?"

I nod yes as she drapes the bag of flowers over her shoulder and then quietly we make our way down to the brook. We stop when she gets tired. I let her rest as I dip my toes in the water, filling my pockets with the pretty rocks I find.

Miss Maggie watches me as I dance around the cool water, a small smile on her face. "You remind me of my Jenny," she says.

Sitting back down beside her in the grass, I put my shoes on, assuming she's almost ready to continue on to the cemetery. "Your daughter?" I ask.

"She was a free-spirited girl, just like you."

"What happened to her?"

"Well, she ran away from home when she was fourteen. A man told her she could be a model and tricked her into meeting him in the city. Then, some bad people took her. Made her do all sorts of horrible things."

I wrap my arms around my bare legs, hugging myself. "But you found her?"

Maggie's eyes narrow. "No, honey. She eventually took her own life, but she gave me a grandson before she left this place."

"The man who was here yesterday?"

"Yep. I thank God for that boy every day," she says, then leans forward. "So, what brought you here? Are you running from something?"

My gaze rolls over the brook. "I'm not running from my family. I don't have one anymore." I pluck grass from the ground. "I was hitching a ride on the train. It stopped, so I got off to look around. I saw the mural of the dragonfly on your barn. I don't know, Miss Maggie. It just felt like a good place to stop."

Everything is true, with a few minor omissions. I don't know if I could lie to her. Maggie seems like the type of person who can read right through the bullshit anyway, so what would be the use?

Maggie stares at me for a minute or two. "I've been waiting on a sign from her for a long time now." She smiles and starts to get up, so I rise, dusting off my butt before we start walking once again.

Does she think I'm some sort of sign? I don't think it works that way. I've prayed for signs from my father and brother, but I've never gotten one. I think back to the book in my bag. The one with the dragonfly on the cover. I think it's just a coincidence.

"How old are you?" Miss Maggie wraps her arm around mine as we begin to move away from the brook.

I help her down the incline until we are standing firmly on a well-beaten path lined with trees. "Twenty."

She nods, keeping hold of my arm as we walk together. The path leads to a cemetery, and my steps begin to slow.

"You're not scared are you?" she asks, pulling me along. She weaves us through the stones, knowing exactly where she's going.

"No ma'am." And I'm not. I just haven't been to a cemetery since the day we buried my father. I swallow hard, wondering where in this world my brother was laid to rest. Did my mother finally show back up and have him buried near my dad? I guess I'll never know.

We come upon two graves. My gaze scans the stones and the items surrounding them, some flowers and cute little trinkets. A lot of them dragonflies. The breeze blows gently, the light melody of a wind chime hanging between the stones calms me.

"Why didn't you just have your grandson drive you here, Miss Maggie?"

She sits down on the chair once I have it settled properly over the uneven ground. "I just wanted to walk it one more time like I used to with my husband."

"I'll leave you to it then. You can just holler at me when you're ready." I start to walk away, but she stops me.

She points to the ground beside her. "I don't mind you visiting them with me. Sit down, honey."

Lowering myself to the ground, I take a deep breath.

Maggie closes her eyes, smiling. After several minutes she opens them again, her gaze landing on me.

"Do you talk to them here?" I ask softly.

She nods. "I do."

"I wish I could talk to my family," I tell her.

Maggie hands me the bag of wildflowers, and I begin laying them out carefully over the stones.

"I talk to them all the time. They aren't just here," she says. Then, she surprises me by reaching out and running her fingers through my long hair, raking them through the tangles. "They are everywhere. I see them in the flowers, in the clouds, sometimes even in the dark of night. They never leave me."

I think about what she says as she continues to brush my hair out. It feels nice, loving even. She puts me at ease. "My family loved the outdoors. My dad used to dream about taking us to a place just like this, with lots of trees. I love the trees on your farm."

A little ladybug crawls over a fallen leaf in front of me. I lay my hand out and let it crawl over the top of my hand, bringing it toward my face to study it. Maggie raises an eyebrow at me.

"You're not afraid of bugs?" she asks.

I feel the corners of my mouth pull up in a smile. My heart is mending a tiny bit by being here with Miss Maggie. It's nice to have a normal conversation. "I'm not. Ladybugs are my favorite."

"Why is that?" she asks, genuinely interested.

Leaning over and letting him crawl back to the grass, I answer, "I like that their wings are hidden."

"My daughter loved dragonflies … also for their wings."

"They do have pretty iridescent ones," I agree.

"A friend of hers told her dragonflies have two sets of wings so they can carry angels on their backs."

My eyes widen. "Really? I've never heard that." I let my finger trail over a glass dragonfly attached to her daughter's headstone.

"It's true," she says quietly.

Maybe it is true, because right now I feel like Maggie might be my angel. I haven't felt this at peace in a long time.

"Whelp, we better head back before Jackson shows up and has the whole club out looking for me." Her knees pop as she rises, making me wince.

I don't know what she means by club, but I don't want them looking for her. They might stumble across me in the process.

"Why don't you come back to the house after he leaves, and I'll teach you how to make those cookies you liked."

My cheeks heat to an alarming level. I hate thieving from her. "I'm sorry."

She pats my face. "No worries, honey. I know you'll pay me back in other ways. I've got a feeling Jenny brought you here for a reason."

Chapter Six

Jackson

Dad and I stand with our hands on our hips, staring at the chicken coop. I glance around, looking for Grandma.

"I'm telling you, Dad, I didn't get it finished yesterday. And I didn't paint flowers around the bottom like this, either." I lean over and point to a bright red tulip on the side of the coop.

My dad raises his brows, running his hand through his beard.

I look at the bugs painted along the windowsill that match the ones I did yesterday. I press my finger over the top of a ladybug, dwarfing the tiny red fingerprint. Just then, Grandma walks out of the forest.

My dad and I both run over to her. She bats our hands away as we fuss over her. "You boys just mind your own business. I'm fine."

We follow her into the house, a look of concern passing between the two of us.

"Grandma, where the hell have you been and who finished painting the chicken coop?" I ask as she busies herself, pulling things from the fridge.

"You boys hungry? I'll whip us up some sandwiches for lunch," she says, ignoring my question.

"Maggie," my dad tries to work his charm.

She pats his cheek as she passes him, setting the condiments on the table. "I baked some fresh bread last night."

My dad and I both sit down, waiting for her to join us. Once she sits, we both start in with the questions.

She holds up her hand. "First of all, I'm a grown woman. But if you must know, I walked to the cemetery."

"Grandma," I groan, slouching back in my chair. "You know one of us will give you a ride anytime you want."

"I didn't want a ride. I wanted to walk. And as for the chicken coop, it was the woodland fairies. They worked all night and I, for one, think it looks beautiful." She expertly runs a butter knife over a piece of her homemade bread before slapping a piece of thick ham on it.

My dad kicks me under the table. I know. I know.

"I made you an appointment with doc. It's been a long time since you've had a checkup," I say cautiously, hoping she doesn't grab the flyswatter off the hook behind her to whoop my ass. She's had to do that a time or two. Grandma doesn't like curse words, and sometimes my mouth runs away from me.

"That's fine, dear. Just write it down." She waves her hand over to the calendar hanging on the wall. A pencil hangs beside it from a piece of bright orange yarn.

Well, that was entirely too easy.

My dad reaches over and places his hand over hers. "Have you been feeling alright, Maggie?"

She blushes. My dad has that effect on women. I guess that's where I get it. I sure don't get it from my biological father, the senator, who is currently rotting in prison.

"I've been a little tired, but nothing to worry about. But while you're both here, I do have something I would like to discuss."

I take a bite of my sandwich, still thinking about the tiny fingerprints on the chicken coop outside that aren't mine. They sure aren't Grandma's, either. I about choke when I hear her say she's thinking about moving.

"You know a friend of mine from church lives there and she loves it. It gets lonely out here now that Harold has passed."

Instantly, I feel guilty for not being here more. "Grandma, I can start coming around more often. You don't have to move. I'll take care of the place. No worries; you're not moving."

My dad arches an eyebrow, studying her closely.

She reaches over and pinches my cheek hard.

"Owe," I grumble, rubbing my hand over it.

She brushes crumbs from the table into her hand, not looking at either of us. "I've been praying on this for a long time now. And today the Lord answered those prayers. He gave me the sign I've been looking for. And besides, if I move to Gladstone, I'll always have someone to play cards with. Best of all, I'll be closer to the warehouse."

"But what about the farm?" I whine.

She looks me dead in the eye. "Well, that's where you come in. I'm giving it to you."

My dad whistles and settles back in his chair. He knows I love it here, but I can't settle down in one place. I'm a bit of a wanderer. I like to go where the wind takes me. I don't get bored that way. I've moved five times just this year.

"I'm not taking no for an answer, boy. Someone's got to watch over Fred. That dog's going to outlive us all, I swear. And I sure can't take him with me."

"Grandma," I try to reason with her. "You love it here. I'll take you into town whenever you want. It's only a fifteen-minute drive. You act like it's clear across the state."

"I'll make you a deal. You live here till my time on this earth is done. Then you can go wherever the wind blows you."

Not cool. I narrow my eyes at her.

"What are you so afraid of?" she asks as she picks up her sandwich.

I flip my hair out of my eyes, focusing on my own food. "I'm not afraid of anything," I grumble.

She gets up out of her chair and opens the fridge, pulling out a container of fresh strawberries. They're my favorite. Grandma Maggie places them on the table in front of me before sitting back down. "You know, your mama was a wanderer just like you. I think you both got that from me."

"I've never known you to wander," I say with a mouthful of food.

"There's a lot about me you don't know. I've lived a lot of years, young man. My mind flitted from one thing to the next, just like yours. But then

I met your grandfather, and that man grounded me like none other. He was a Libra, you know. The scales who kept me balanced."

Maggie runs her fingers over her brow before continuing. "I think there's something here on this farm that will do the same for you. Why don't you just try it?"

My dad doesn't comment but I feel his eyes on me, waiting for my response. "Fine, but I'm only doing this for you." I lean over and give her a quick peck on the cheek, making her chuckle. "I was thinking about setting up a shop in the barn so I could help you out around here anyway. I don't need to be in town to work on my projects."

"That sounds like a wonderful idea," she says.

"So, about the chicken coop …" I begin to ask but she interrupts me.

"Woodland fairies," she says adamantly with a smile on her face.

Okay, she's not budging on this, but I guess, other than thinking she has fairies, she seems pretty coherent. I'll leave it up to the doc.

She looks at my dad. "Raffe, maybe you could run me over to Gladstone today. I think we should get started on this as soon as possible."

He nods, wiping crumbs from his beard. "You got it, Maggie. I'm yours for the day."

I roll my eyes. Great. How did I get roped into taking over this place? I'm going to be so bored out here by myself. This little arrangement won't last long.

"Oh, shit, I forgot to grab my cookies when I left yesterday. I left them in the barn." I get up to go get them, but Grandma thumps me over the back of my head lightly.

"Watch that mouth," she scolds as I fall back into my chair. Then, she tries to convince me she ate them all.

Grandma doesn't even like chocolate chip cookies.

Chapter Seven

Willow

The closer we got to the farm, I heard masculine voices. I dropped the chair and ran. Miss Maggie didn't call after me. Back at my camp, I kicked dirt over the fire I left burning, grabbed my bag, and hid over by the barn so I could see if anyone was going to start looking for me.

I thought painting the coop was a good idea, but I didn't think about how her grandson might wonder how it got finished. All I could think about was paying him back for those darn cookies I ate.

After a few minutes, my heartrate slows. Thank goodness they didn't come looking for me. Maybe I can really trust her.

Lying back on the ground, I shove my backpack under my head for a pillow and stare at the dragonfly on the barn. Miss Maggie said her daughter thought they carried angels on their backs. I've never heard that saying before, but I do know a lot of facts about them.

Did you know females will play dead to avoid unwanted male suitors? It's true; they will drop right to the ground mid-flight. I guess it works for them … I've tried it for myself. It didn't work so well for me.

It's been a week since I woke up in the back of his van. Each day of driving takes me farther away from the city. But he's been kind to me. I'm beginning to wonder if my fear of him is valid. He's fed me, clothed me, and he even buys me books to read. He's slowly making me forget my anger and despair.

This is as far away from home as I've ever been. He tells me he doesn't stay in one place for long because he's a nature photographer and always chasing the next great photo. He takes pictures of me, too. Sometimes he says I outshine the scenery. I doubt that's true, but it does make me feel pretty when he says it.

He says he can't trust me yet, so he always handcuffs me to the cabinets inside the van when he leaves. It doesn't do any good to scream when he's gone because he only leaves me alone when we are in remote areas.

We've visited a few national parks. We went to the Petrified Forest yesterday. Did you know that it's not a real forest? The trees that used to be there have turned into rocks. Bradley knew a lot about the place. He's really smart, and I like that he takes time to explain new things to me. He says he's going to take care of me; that I'm too young to be on my own.

Maybe he's right.

It has been nice not worrying about where my next meal will come from. And I haven't had to hide in the attic from the strange men my mom would bring home.

"How's your book?" Bradley asks, pulling me from my thoughts.

"It's good," I say quietly, placing my feather bookmark between the pages. I set it against the wall of the van, beside my other books, and then bury myself beneath the blankets. The air is a bit chilly here in the mountains. I like to look at the books my father gave Ash and me as I fall asleep. It makes me feel like they're both still here with me. I'm so glad they were in my bag, or they might have been left behind.

He closes his laptop and locks the van doors for the evening.

I slide to the edge of the mattress. We've slept together every night, and he always pulls me close to him. He says it's to keep us warm, but I don't like it. Every night I start out on the edge, hoping he will leave me there.

He climbs in and as I expect, he wraps his arm around my waist and tugs me against his chest. His breath is hot on the back of my neck as he waits until I stop shivering. But tonight, he does something different. His hand leaves my stomach, his fingers gently running along the waistband of my shorts.

His hand continues to explore.

I don't know what to do. What can I do?

I stare at the dragonfly on the cover of my bug book. Maybe I can play dead like the female dragonfly does when she doesn't want attention from a male. I squeeze my eyes shut and hold my breath, going limp in his arms.

He doesn't seem to care. In fact, I think it does the opposite of what it should have. His hand dips lower, and I let out a small whoosh of air, unable to pretend any longer.

"Shh," he whispers against my hair.

My eyes go back to the dragonfly on my book. It didn't work! It didn't work! *I want to scream at the insect.*

The back door bangs shut, bringing me back to the present. I sit up and watch as Miss Maggie's grandson goes out to the chicken coop. He presses his finger over one of my fingerprints, his gaze roaming along the line of trees at the back of the property.

Please don't look for me. Please don't. I like it here. I want to stay.

His shoulders drop, then he turns to go back to the house as Maggie and the other man come out. They visit awhile longer before they all leave. Maggie included. I stand and walk over to the barn, staring straight up at the giant dragonfly.

Maybe dragonflies aren't so bad after all. Even if their tactics didn't work for me, I can't blame them for that.

I smile as I take in its double set of wings. Maybe Maggie's daughter and her friend knew what they were talking about.

Because Maggie looks just like an angel with her snow-white hair and kind smile.

Chapter Eight

Jackson

When I get to my sister's house, I find the twins swinging on the front porch with Kelsie squeezed between them. She doesn't seem to mind, and she gives me a tiny wave.

"What are you guys up to today?" I ask them.

Collin shrugs his shoulder. "Just enjoying our first day of summer vacation."

I sit down on the steps, pulling my cigarettes from my pocket. "I might be needing some muscle soon. Grandma Maggie is thinking about moving to town."

"Wow, yeah. Sure, man. Just let us know when you need us," Carson says. "I'm going to miss going out to the farm. I love that place."

"Well, you won't have to say goodbye. She's giving it to me."

Collin sits forward, stopping the swing. "Hell yeah. You need a place to settle down. Maybe start a little family." He wags his eyebrows up and down, making Kelsie giggle.

I stretch my legs out in front of me. "No sir-ee. I can't even take care of my own dumb ass. If you want more babies around here, you better look to Billie Rose for that. Maybe she'll pop out another one soon."

My sister opens the door, then sets her hands on her hips. "Can't even come in and say hello?"

Hopping up, I grab Lily and place a loud kiss on her forehead. "I was just talking to the kids for bit. Don't get your panties in a wad."

She smacks me on the shoulder playfully.

When she turns to go back into the house, I follow. "Hey. Did you know Grandma Maggie is thinking about moving to town?"

This halts Lily in her tracks. "No, she hasn't said anything to me."

"Well, she just laid it on me when dad and I were out there. I think she's losing it."

"Oh, Jackson. Don't say that. Maybe she's lonely. I think moving to town is a wonderful idea."

My sister busies herself cleaning off the counter and putting things back in their proper place. I take a seat and watch her, drumming my fingers nervously over the countertop.

She stops what she's doing and places her hand over the top of mine. "Why are you so worked up over this? Do you really want her living out there all alone?" She brushes hair out of my eyes and grabs my chin. "Talk to me, little brother."

"She wants me to live there and take care of the place."

Lily's eyes soften. "Jackson, you are capable of taking care of the farm."

Avenging Skulls

Kelsie comes running inside. "Mom, Grandma Maggie's here with Raffe."

My sister and I hold each other's gaze for a moment. "Did you know they were stopping by?" she asks.

"Dad took her to Gladstone today. She probably wanted to stop by and say hi." I get up and head toward the door. I need to meet up with Brody and collect rents for the club. I look over my shoulder. "Don't be surprised if she fills your head with tales of woodland fairies."

Kelsie is already pouring our grandmother a glass of lemonade. Even though Maggie is really only *my* grandmother, everyone who meets her considers her *their* grandma.

"You don't believe in fairies?" she giggles.

"No," I say gruffly.

Chapter Nine

Willow

I borrowed a few more of Miss Maggie's eggs, even though I'm kind of getting tired of them. I never thought I'd say that because I love them. Sunny side up just like Dad used to make Ash and me on Sunday mornings before church.

The other day, I heard her shooing birds away from her strawberries. She said she wanted to trade with me, so I used some of the paint her grandson had in the barn and painted the rocks I picked up on our walk. I read that if birds are eating your strawberries, you should paint rocks to resemble the berry and then place them in the garden. When the birds peck at a few stones by mistake, they will leave the crop alone. I've never tried it because I've never had a garden, but it couldn't hurt to try now. Hopefully, it works. I left her a little note under one of the rocks, explaining why they were there.

"Willow!" I hear Miss Maggie yell through the trees.

I stand up quietly, listening for signs of others. Cautiously, I weave my way through the trees, pausing behind one to scope out her yard. She's standing in the middle of it by herself.

Avenging Skulls

Slowly, I emerge from my hiding spot. We stare at each other for a long moment, the wind blowing wisps of her white hair around her plump, wrinkled cheeks. She's the first to speak.

"I found the stones on my porch. I think it's a smart idea."

I blush at her compliment, taking a few steps closer, automatically drawn to her.

"I've got some things for you. Jackson's sister is about your size, so she helped me pick out a few things you might be able to use. I thought we could do another trade, if you're interested."

The old woman turns away from me and hobbles up the stairs. I follow her to the bottom step and pause.

She holds the door open for me. I stare up at the farmhouse. Some of the windows are open, the curtains billowing inside from the breeze. I haven't been in a home since Bradley took me from mine.

What if it's a trap? I like being outside where I can run. Where I'm free.

"I thought we could make those cookies. My grandson is coming back tomorrow." She patiently waits while I try to make up my mind. "We'll leave the door open, and this screen door doesn't lock."

Miss Maggie shows me that the door is set to close by a spring, and there is indeed no way to lock it.

Can I be so easily persuaded with the promise of a sweet treat?

"Would you like to go to breakfast this morning? I saw you eyeing that old Route 66 diner."

I squint my eyes in the bright morning sun as I lift them from the page. "Yes," I say quietly. It reminded me of a story I once read.

53

"It's a date then," Bradley says, crouching down in front of the small boulder I'm sitting on.

It takes everything in me to school my face, to not let it reflect the way I inwardly cringe at his nearness. He takes his camera out of his bag and points it at me. I don't like being the center of his attention, but I often am.

"Pull your shirt off your shoulder a bit," he instructs. When I don't, he stands and does it for me.

When he steps back, he whispers "beautiful" under his breath. "Just pretend I'm not here and then I'll take you to that diner."

I really do want to go there. All I have to do is sit and read ... and pretend he's not here.

Easy, right? But it's not because he is here. He decides the food I eat, the clothes I wear, what I read, and where I sleep. He is the air that I breathe. Forgetting him would be like my heart forgetting to beat.

"That's it, baby, just like that," he praises.

A tear plops onto my page. I watch as the paper absorbs it. Another joins it and then another and another. I don't try to stop them; I let them fall freely. Bradley doesn't seem to mind.

"Look at me, Willow," he says.

"Look at me, Willow," Miss Maggie says, pulling me from my thoughts. "We don't have to bake cookies today. I'll go get the things I have for you. I'll be right back."

The door slams behind her. I watch through the screen as she makes her way through the kitchen, disappearing for a moment before returning. She stands on the top step and hands me a couple of bags. I take them from her hands, opening one and peering inside. It's full of toiletries. The other much larger bag is full of clothes.

"What do you want for these, Miss Maggie?" I ask, my arms falling to my side, a bag in each hand.

"I'm going to be moving soon."

The bags fall, landing on the ground with a soft thud. I knew angels were too good to be true.

"Don't worry. You can stay here," she adds quickly, sensing I'm about to run. "My grandson is going to be moving in. I want to trade you those things for your promise to watch over him."

I think back to the man I watched feed a dead man to the hogs. A shiver runs up my spine. Miss Maggie notices.

She points to the chairs. "Have a seat, dear. I'll grab us a glass of tea."

I pick up the bags after she goes back inside and then sit down. On top of one is a bright blue sundress. I let my fingers sift through the soft material, pulling it out of the sack to hold against me. It's so pretty. Bradley liked me in neutral colors. Bright colors bothered him. As did loud noises, large groups, and an assortment of other things.

I've often wondered if he picked me because I was quiet. He used to tell me that I was the perfect girl for him. So quiet, so innocent, so perfect he would say each night as he brushed my hair. I feel a pang of guilt for leaving him. I hope he isn't lonely without me. I shake my head to clear my thoughts when Miss Maggie returns.

I quickly shove the dress back in the bag and place it between my feet, still uncertain if I will make the deal with her.

"You saw him the other day," she says, acknowledging what I saw him do. She hands me a glass filled with ice and a pink colored tea and smiles before continuing. "He's a good boy, but he thinks he has to pay for the sins of others. He's trying to rid the world of scum, one bad man at a time."

I glance over at the hog pen. I walked over there the night he dumped the man. There wasn't a trace of the body left. "The man he got rid of was bad?" I ask.

She nods. "The worst. I'm not saying Jackson hasn't made mistakes. All men do," she says with the wave of a hand. "But he needs to slow down and learn to live for himself. He's running from that, always has been." Miss Maggie narrows her eyes my way. "You've been running, too. Maybe this is the place you both decide to stop."

Is she trying to set me up with her grandson? Surely not. She knows I'm a basket case. I wouldn't even accept an invitation into her home.

"You are a kind girl. That I can see."

Miss Maggie's old basset hound licks my leg before lying down by my feet.

"And old Fred here, he knows a good soul when he sees one."

I scratch his ears, making his eyes drop closed. He is so trusting. I think I've forgotten how to trust. The last person I trusted let me down.

Clearing my throat, I tell her I cannot accept her offer. "Miss Maggie, I would love to help your grandson, but I don't think I can. I'm sorry."

She seems to accept that I'm unable to help her. We continue to sit quietly, listening to the birds as the sun drops low in the sky. Two souls who don't know each other but who are so easily taking up space together. I close my eyes, focusing on the wind on my face and the dog's warm body against my feet. When I open them, she stands from her chair.

"You think you're incapable of saving someone because you failed at saving yourself, but you're wrong," she says, hobbling away from me.

I stand up, grabbing the bags. "Miss Maggie, don't forget these."

"Keep 'em," she quips.

"But …"

"Think about it. If you decide to answer this old woman's prayers, leave me a sign. As for the trade, we will settle on a different one. You gave me your time tonight; that is good enough for me. You sat with an old woman drinking tea. I don't think you realize how much that's worth." She whistles for the dog, and Fred gets up and stretches before joining her inside.

The door closes behind them and soon the lights click off in the house, one at a time as she makes her way up to her room. I grab the bags, waiting until the last one blinks off, then I make my way across the lawn.

I'm so sad Miss Maggie is moving. I thought she was my angel.

I should leave and find a new place to camp.

Miss Maggie was safe.

Her grandson … I glance back at the hog pen one last time before entering the forest. Well, I don't know about him, and I can't risk making the same mistake twice.

Chapter Ten

Jackson

"Grandma, you're not taking enough. I don't need all this stuff."

She pats my cheek as she scoots by me. "I don't need it, either. Sorry, it's the curse of inheritance. You'll have to sift through it yourself to discover the treasures."

I roll my eyes. Grandma has been speaking in cryptic terms all day. She's taking very little to Gladstone.

"Jackson, the rooms there are furnished. Do you really think I could fit all this into that tiny apartment? Besides, most of this belongs to your grandfather. You can curse him out for it once I've left."

Billie Rose walks in with Aurelia. "Let's go show Grandma Maggie what we found."

I stop what I'm doing to see what Billie Rose is carrying. "What is it?" I ask.

"It's a rock painted like a ladybug. It was on the back step."

Avenging Skulls

She hands it to me. I roll it in my palm, wondering where it came from. My grandmother plucks it out of my hand and drops it in her purse.

"I think I'm ready now. Everything is in order."

I laugh. "Grandma, what's that rock all about?"

Lily comes out of the bedroom, lugging my grandma's bright orange suitcase behind her.

"I've been trading with the woodland fairies, and that was their final trade," Grandma says, not missing a beat. She brushes her hands together, a satisfied smile pulling at the corners of her wrinkled face.

My sister and cousin both look at me. I shrug my shoulders. I told them she was losing her mind.

Woodland fairies ... humph.

Later that night, Brody and I sit out back, drinking a twelve pack of fine, cheap beer. He shoves another hot dog on a stick and holds it in the fire.

"This place is the shit, brother ... I don't know why you're so bummed about it."

I glance around, the light of the fire throwing shadows everywhere. "Yeah, I guess."

He chuckles. "You guess? This place is heaven, dude."

My friend offers me the hot dog on his stick. "No, thank you. Those fucking things aren't good unless they are burned to a crisp."

I flinch, expecting my grandmother to thump me over the head for cursing. When it doesn't come, I sigh. It's weird being here without her.

"Listen, man, maybe take this time to get right with yourself. Quit dwelling on all the shit that happened with my niece. You didn't do anything to make her fall for you like she did. She was a lost soul long before she came here."

I slowly peel back the label on my beer, thinking of all the times I turned Lanie down. I'm known as the town heartthrob but in truth, I'm really the town heartbreaker. I wasn't about to do that to my cousin's best friend. But I made the mistake of making her a dresser. I remember the day Brody and I carried it into her apartment. She was so fucking happy.

I knew then I'd made a terrible mistake; it was only supposed to be a simple act of kindness. But it gave her hope for something more. I fucked up. And when I continued to turn her down, she got angry and took matters into her own hands. She took advantage of me when I was down.

It's all so stupid. One night, she invited me over for a drink. I was sad and shit because my cousin, my best friend, was slowly pulling away from me. Billie Rose didn't need me, she had Elijah, her now husband, to share all her secrets with. Lanie pretended to care about me that night. I thought we were both just venting about life. She let me get shit-faced drunk. Only I wasn't drunk.

She drugged me.

I should have told someone what happened. My silence is what got Billie Rose hurt. I knew firsthand the lengths Lanie would go to get what she wanted, but I kept quiet. I was so lost in my own shame that I let a woman take advantage of me.

She … she was evil.

I'm glad she killed herself.

If she hadn't … well, I would have fed her to the hogs. I only wish one of us would have come to the conclusion that she needed to die sooner, before Billie Rose got hurt.

Avenging Skulls

I toss the label from my beer into the fire, watching the ends shrivel up until it becomes one with the flames. To this day, no one knows what Lanie did to me.

I'm a Skull ... no one can know. If they find out I couldn't protect myself, how the fuck would the club trust me to protect anyone else?

No, this is one secret I'll be taking with me to the grave.

Brody stands up. "I have to get home, man. We have church in the morning. Get some sleep." He grabs my shoulder harshly and squeezes.

"Yeah, see you tomorrow, brother."

After he leaves, I grab the hose and turn it on the fire, watching the smoke billow over the backyard. When I'm sure it's out, I walk over to the chicken coop and place my finger over one of the small fingerprints. Woodland fairies my ass.

My eyes scan the dark trees.

I shake my head before going inside, falling into a drunken sleep on the couch.

Chapter Eleven

Willow

After a few beers, the two men seem to relax, so I creep as close to them as I can. I can't believe Maggie left today. She wasted no time moving. I didn't see them haul out much of anything. I spied on them from the hay loft, peeking out between the cracks around the hay door.

The light from the flames dances over their faces, making them look really scary. But the sound of their voices makes me stay. They laugh and joke together, an easy camaraderie between them. I wonder if they're brothers. Miss Maggie only mentioned one grandson.

Jackson looks sad as he stares into the flames.

When the other man stands to leave, I pull back into the safety of the trees. Once Maggie's grandson goes inside for the night, I creep back into the yard, sitting down on the chair he was in. It's still warm. I pick up the bottle he left in the cup holder on his chair. Cautiously, I take a sip.

I've never had alcohol before. It's good. It's fizzy, like a soda. I finish off the bottle and then stand up and spin in a circle, making my new blue sundress billow around my legs. I giggle a full out giggle.

Avenging Skulls

I'm so happy to be here, not having to worry about the games. There are no games here.

I stare at the backdoor, wondering if Jackson is a man who likes to play games. I hope not.

Before I go back to my camp, I gather some wildflowers. I have to make a trade for the beer. It was almost a full bottle, after all.

After that, I go back to my camp and lie down on the soft blanket Miss Maggie left for me. I curl up in it and read the last book Bradley gave me. I was only allowed to have one book at a time. His reason was logical, I guess. We didn't have room in the van to store them all. So, I would read a book over and over again until we would get somewhere to get another one. Then, he would make me throw the old one away.

I think it's a mortal sin to throw a book away.

"Just throw it away, Willow," Bradley says, looking up from his computer. "You have a new one. You know the deal."

I run my fingers down the cover of the novel. It really was a great story. How can I throw someone's words and imagination in the trash? I can't do it. I think back to the day my dad and I were driving by my old school, and they were throwing hundreds of books away. We went back later that night. All four of us, and we dug them out.

When we got home, Ash and I lined them up proudly against the wall in the attic. I spent hours reading them. My dad came up one evening and sat beside me, our legs curled under us as I showed him my favorites.

Bradley interrupts my thoughts. "It's getting dark, Willow. I mean it, there's a bin out there by the showers." He points out the window to the little brown building that houses the park's bathrooms.

"Maybe I could leave it here." He looks up at me with a look on his face that lets me know I need to speak fast because he's just about done dealing with me. "I could place it in a bag and hide it. Then if we ever come back here, I can read it again."

He leans back, snapping his gum between his teeth. "I guess we could do that," he says, his eyes lighting up. He gets up and digs in the cupboard under the sink before pulling out a box of plastic bags. He slides one out and hands it to me.

I'm so happy I don't have to throw the book away that I quickly drop it into the bag and then press the air out of it before zipping it closed. I hop up to go out and hide it somewhere when he stops me.

"Grab the shower basket," he tells me as he pulls two clean towels off the shelf above our bed.

There isn't a soul around for miles as we step out of the van, the crickets are beginning to sing their evening song. The sun has already left, leaving behind a trail of pinks and purples across the sky. It's beautiful here.

I hide the book under a big rock as he watches me. When I turn around, he smiles. "That's a very good hiding spot, sweetheart," he tells me, and my chest warms from his praise.

But that proud feeling is snuffed out as quickly as it's lit when I realize he wants to shower with me.

I stand in the cement stall, staring at a spider making a web in the corner. He leans over my shoulder. "You're such a good girl, wanting to save that book," he says quietly as he reaches around me to turn the water on.

That's when I learn that nothing is free in my new world. Everything comes at a cost. I close my eyes as tight as I can. He doesn't seem to mind. He never cares that I play dead. It doesn't matter to him.

Not at this point anyway.

The roar of a motorcycle pulls me from thoughts. Quickly, I run through the trees back to the farmhouse. The man from last night is here again. He's beating on the back door, his eyes on the bottle I left last night. When Jackson opens the door, I smile at his ruffled appearance. His long fingers run through the top of his hair, pulling it out of his eyes.

Avenging Skulls

"Prez is pissed, man. You're late. Jesus Christ, dude. Get your shit and let's go." He holds the door open as Jackson goes back inside. I hear a thump and then a loud curse. The man looks inside and shakes his head, laughing.

Soon enough, Jackson reappears. He stops dead in his tracks when he sees my trade.

"What the fuck is this? Are you bringing me flowers, Brody?" Jackson asks the other man, earning him a punch in the arm.

"No, fuck face. Maybe they're from Grandma Maggie's woodland fairies," he teases.

I blush. Does Grandma Maggie think I'm a fairy? The thought excites me. I love fantasy stories.

Jackson picks up the beer bottle full of wildflowers. He scowls, his face searching the trees. I hold my breath and make myself invisible. He doesn't look happy. Maybe he doesn't like flowers. Or maybe he doesn't like woodland fairies.

Chapter Twelve

Jackson

I scowl, setting the bottle down on the step before making my way out into the yard. "I've got to feed the animals before I go. Go on, I'll catch up. Tell Prez I'm sorry. I'll be there as soon as I can."

Brody follows me. "I'll help. If you take too long, he'll have your nuts."

I glance around. The chickens are already out. Shit, they've been fed too.

"Didn't I lock these little fuckers up last night?" I ask Brody, scratching my head as we head over to the hogs. Fuck, they've also been fed. I look up, watching as birds dart across the yard, going from full feeder to full feeder. What the hell?

"Yeah, man, you locked them up. Grandma Maggie must have a farm hand who comes out and helps her," he suggests, shrugging his shoulders.

Jesus Christ, I don't have time for this. I'm just thankful it's done so I can get to church. I bet Dirk is fuming at the table, waiting for us.

"Let's go." I head over to my bike and swing my leg over the seat. I give the farm one last glance before pulling away with Brody right behind me.

When we get to the warehouse and take our seats, my dad gives me a swift kick under the table. I keep my eyes downcast. "Sorry, Prez. It was a long day of moving Grandma Maggie yesterday. I overslept. Won't happen again."

Dirk runs his eyes over me. He doesn't say anything, just gives me a nod, letting me know I've been forgiven.

"Someone's been getting to our marks before us. We had Kelsie's abuser within our sights, and Petey was about to nab him when the fucker disappeared. This isn't the first one, either. We need to keep our eyes and ears open. Someone's getting word to these guys that we've found them, and they're helping them disappear."

I keep my face schooled as I think about the asshole I fed to the hogs a few days ago. Disappear he did, right the fuck on out of this world.

The Skulls turned the club legit long before I was born, but this is one activity that still remains under the table. It's only discussed here in this room. We protect what's ours, and sometimes that means we have to get our hands dirty. But Dirk is pissed that someone's getting to the scum before us.

My brother-in-law, also the VP, scans the room. When he gets to me, I turn the corner of my mouth up and salute him. He rolls his eyes and moves on to the next man.

Dirk gives orders to a few of the guys, sending them out on the road to California. "Go down to the SoCal chapter and see if they've heard anything. That douche bag just didn't up and disappear."

As a matter of fact, he did. I keep myself from smirking by thinking about the look on Kelsie's face when she saw him. That's the difference between me and the others. They might have told her he was gone once they caught him, but I *showed* her he was gone. I think that's the only way to get the victim to truly wrap their mind around it. You can tell them a million times, but they still have that one percent of doubt, thinking maybe you got the wrong guy.

Billie Rose told me once that she sometimes thought Draven, her abuser, might still be alive. He's not. The guys and I buried him ourselves. So, one night, her and I went to the spot we buried the piece of shit, and I dug him up for her. His rings were still on his bony fingers. She was able to move forward after that. These women can handle it. Seeing their abuser dead isn't the worst thing they've been through.

She was thankful. It made me feel good; it was the least I could do. Shortly after that, I started working for *Her*. She contacted me first, asking if I could help her give the victims closure. I have no idea where she gets her information from, and honestly I don't want to know. She finds and eliminates the targets and then they are delivered to me. I meet up with the victims, let them see that their nightmare is well and truly dead and then ... well, you know what happens after that. Grandma's babies get fed and everyone moves on.

Jesse, the Prez's wife, has breakfast spread out for us after our meeting. ' Come and get it while it's hot, boys," she says, kissing her son-in-law, Elijah, on the cheek as he picks her up and spins her around.

She laughs, her silver hair falling softly down her back. He sets her down when Dirk gives him a look.

"Thank you, Mom," he says, batting his eyelashes at her.

As we're filling our plates, Brody shares with the group that I received flowers this morning. My dad stops, a spoon full of scrambled eggs paused over his plate.

"It was probably the neighbors," I grumble, taking my meal outside and plopping down at the table. He follows and sits down beside me.

Avenging Skulls

"I think we better go out and take a look," he says, stabbing a sausage on the end of his fork and taking a bite.

I shake my head. "Don't worry about it. I'll do some investigating when I get home."

Brody sits down across from us, his plate piled high, stuff rolling off the edge. He shoves an entire piece of bacon in his mouth. "If I was you, I'd let them be. Fairies who do chores doesn't seem like a problem to me."

My dad runs his fingers through his beard. "The chores were done?"

"Yep," I say, hurrying to eat, anxious to get home and see what the fuck I'll find next.

"Maybe I should stop by before heading home."

I stand up, grabbing my plate after shoving the last bite in my mouth. "I got it, Dad. No worries," I say and then rush out before he can argue.

Two can play this game. Whoever is hiding out in the trees, they won't be there for long.

When I get back, I grab the old traps from the barn and strategically set them up around the property. There, that should do it.

I spend the rest of the day hauling tools back and forth from my shop in town out to the barn. Later that night, my parent's stop by. My mom spots the flowers still in the beer bottle. I've set them in the middle of the table. She sits down and pulls them toward her, taking a big sniff.

"I bet whoever it was, they left them for Grandma Maggie," she says.

"Yeah, I'm sure you're right." I hand dad a beer from the fridge and sit down with them. I don't tell her about the traps I've set. She wouldn't like it.

We dig into the pizza they brought with them. "So, what's new?" I ask.

My mom wipes her mouth with her napkin. "I'm heading down to Texas for a few weeks. There's a conference I'm attending. I'm excited to learn some new massage techniques that might help your dad's back."

My mom doesn't practice physical therapy anymore, but she's still active in the community. She's always looking for ways to help my dad. He was shot before I was born and has struggled off and on over the years with severe back pain.

"Cool, cool. Does that mean you'll be batching it, Dad?"

My dad stretches his legs out in front of him. "Yeah, it's going to suck. I'm going to starve."

He winks at my mom. We both know damn well that won't happen because I'm sure she has already frozen enough meals to last him the entire time she's gone.

She gets up from the table. "Why don't you plan on eating with your dad while I'm away. I've prepared enough food for the both of you. Keep him out of trouble for me," she suggests.

I shake my head. "No can do, Mom. I've got too much work here on the farm on top of my normal responsibilities. He's going to have to survive on his own," I laugh. "I'm sure Billie Rose and Jesse will keep an eye on him for you."

My dad looks offended, but my mom shoots me a look, letting me know she indeed has someone on the line to watch over him. It's no secret that the women of the club are the ones who are really in control.

She gives me a quick hug and kiss goodbye before my dad stands and follows her to the door. They start bickering like they normally do, but it's all in fun. He slaps her ass as they step out.

"See you later, Son," he hollers as an afterthought before the door closes behind them.

I head back outside to round up the chickens, locking them safely in their coop. Then, I head over and take care of the hogs, moving them to the pen that Grandma puts them in overnight. I sniff the air ... catching a faint hint of smoke. Quietly, I make my way through the trees, finding someone's campsite. The fire was recently snuffed out; small puffs of smoke still billow out between the logs. Whoever was here is long gone. Good. Maybe they found one of my traps and decided to move along before they found one snapped down on their fucking foot.

When I lie down on the couch for the night, I feel accomplished. I got a lot of shit done today.

~~~~~

Again, I sleep well past the time I should. Jesus, I sleep like a damn baby out here. Probably because I'm so wore out at the end of the day I can barely keep my eyes open.

I take a piss after starting the coffee maker, and by the time I head out to do the chores, it's late into the morning. I swing the back door open, my coffee mug in one hand. The fucking chickens are out in the yard again. I look down and jump back at what I find on the step. It's a basket full of eggs, a bundle of wildflowers, and one very dead rabbit. Not only dead but skinned as well.

Crouching down beside it, I see the marks on its body. It looks like it was caught in one of my traps.

Fucking hell.

Upon further inspection, I find all the farm animals to be fed and watered. Again, I head out in the trees, finding the campsite still abandoned. What the fuck?

I check all the traps. All of them are still set. All of them. But one has blood and fur on it, so I assume it's the one that caught the rabbit. I stand there, completely dumbfounded.

Whomever this is, they have some survival skills.

I spend the rest of the day working in the barn on my next project. It's a frame for a full-length mirror. I've been taking pieces off of some old Victorian furniture that was irreparable to try and give the viable wood a new life.

I'm in a groove, cutting and sanding the day away. I like working here in the barn. It's quiet. That's the only reason I jump a foot when I hear a soft knock on the barn door.

Jesus, I'm going to kill Brody. That fucker. I swing the door open wide, my mouth falling open when all I find is a plate filled with eggs and a smoked meat, assumingly rabbit. I squat down and press my fingers against it. It's still warm. My eyes roam over the dark landscape. Fuck, I've been in here all day. It looks like the animals have all been tucked away for the night, too.

I look back down at the plate and smile. Whoever made this for me must know how I like my eggs. Sunny side up. But they forgot one thing – ketchup. Well, whoever they are, I don't think they have any ill intent. Maybe I should go and pull the traps. I don't want to hurt them.

But first, I take the plate and sit on a nearby tree stump, eating the meal they made for me. I raise my eyebrows. Not half bad. I can tell it was cooked over an open fire. Again, my gaze scans the tree line. I chuckle as I scoop another bite. I think I've been going about this all wrong.

I need to draw them out.

Unfortunately, I don't come up with a plan. But I do know someone who can help me.

Chapter Thirteen

Willow

Last night I watched as Jackson ate the meal I made for him. I'm so glad Miss Maggie gave me everything I needed to cook for the two of us. She even gave me these cute little bottles of seasoning. He ate everything and left the plate and fork behind on the stump.

But then he went around and picked up all the traps. Did he not like the rabbit? Did I not do it correctly? My dad taught Ash and me; I'm sure I did it right. I was so excited when I found the furry critter. It was way better than only having eggs for supper; I thought it tasted wonderful.

I was careful to only eat a small piece, giving my stomach time to adjust to my new diet. I gave the rest to Jackson, but then he left his portion of the skinned rabbit on the step. So, when he went into the barn, I grabbed it. I wasn't about to let it go to waste. I remembered what I promised Miss Maggie; I told her I would look after him, and he hadn't eaten all day. That's when I decided to make him dinner.

She also told me some flats of vegetable plants would be delivered soon. She showed me where she and her husband planted a garden every year. I'm excited for them to arrive. I told her that when I was little, my dad used to grow tomato plants in big buckets each year. Every summer he would tell us how someday we would have a real garden once we saved enough to move out of the city.

I wonder if they'll come today.

When I get to the house, I find that the chores are already done, and Jackson is gone. My shoulders fall; I'm a little sad he didn't leave anything for me to do. Miss Maggie traded me all kinds of amazing things for my promise to watch over her grandson. I have to do something to help him today, or I won't be keeping my end of the bargain.

Slowly, I walk around the farm searching for a chore. Opening the barn door, I pull on the light string hanging beside it. Once it's on, I find tools and wood randomly set everywhere. Smiling wide, I rush to the corner and grab a broom and begin sweeping up sawdust. I'm so happy I found a way to take care of him today.

Whatever he was working on, it's hidden behind a large green army blanket. I stop to run my palm over the coarse material. My fingers slowly dig into the blanket, pulling it away. When it falls to the ground, I freeze. I spin on my heel, gulping in a few deep mouthfuls of air as I grab my knees for support.

It's a mirror.

I haven't been able to look at myself in a very long time, and I'm not sure I'm ready to now.

Quickly, I finish cleaning his workspace, organizing all his tools and hanging them over the work bench he brought in. But my reflection continues to call to me.

When I pick up the blanket to cover what I found, my eyes can't help themselves. The blanket falls from my hands as I run my fingers through my tangled blonde hair. Miss Maggie gave me a small mirror and a brush—

perhaps it was a gentle suggestion to use them. I lean forward, bringing my face close to the glass.

Who am I?

Not really sure, I toss the blanket over the mirror and rush back to my camp.

When I get there, my heart falls a little more. I stare at the object on the ground outside my makeshift tent as my heart clammers to break free of my ribcage.

He found me. I should run.

Chapter Fourteen

Jackson

Grandma Maggie smirks the minute she sees me enter the building. She points to the door of her room, indicating I should wait for her there.

As I walk over, she sits forward, throwing her cards on the table. The old men sitting around her all groan in unison. I stand quietly, watching as she scoops her winnings into her bag. She pats one of the old men on the shoulder.

"See you boys at supper." She winks at them and stands. Then I swear ... I swear to God, she swings her hips as she walks away.

I follow her into her room after she opens the door. She settles into her recliner, handing me the bag. "Here you go. You've got enough snacks in there to last a few weeks." Grandma Maggie looks me up and down. "You've been eating, haven't you?"

I sit down in the opposite recliner. "That wasn't quite what I had in mind when you said you'd have someone to play cards with."

"I'm old, not dead."

Laughing, I peek in the sack. Shit, there's some good stuff in here. These old boys don't play around. I shake my head. "And yes, I've been eating. In fact, a little woodland fairy left me a wonderful meal of eggs and rabbit."

She blinks at me, not surprised in the slightest.

"Do you want to tell me who this fairy is?" I ask.

She shrugs.

"Grandma," I warn. She's an ornery one for sure, but this is getting out of hand. I'm slowly realizing that she isn't crazy ... she's calculating.

"I've never actually seen a woodland fairy," she says, feigning innocence. "If you see one, you'll have to let me know."

"Okay, I see you're going to be no help. But mark my words, Grandma, I'll draw that little bugger out." I stand up. "Thanks for the snacks, old woman. I'll be back soon." I give her a stern look.

Before I walk out she stops me. "Try ladybugs. I heard once that woodland fairies love them."

I walk back over to her and lean down, placing a kiss on her soft powdered cheek. "I love you, Grandma Maggie."

She pats my cheek in return and then shoos me away. "My gameshow is going to be on soon. Go on; get to work."

I head straight to my parent's house. My mom and dad come out to the garage when they hear me banging around.

"What are you looking for?" Mom asks, already looking with me even though she has no idea what I'm looking for.

"My bug catcher," I tell them, not taking my eyes off the box I'm searching through.

Dad laughs. He walks over to a shelf, reaches around some things, and pulls it out.

I sigh in relief. "Oh good. I'm glad you still have it."

I take it from him, warmth spreading through my chest as I remember the day my sister helped me build it. It was the day we met. We hit it off right away. I've loved her from the moment I laid eyes on her.

My parents both laugh at me. "Is being at the farm making you miss your great bug expeditions?"

I rush around to the back of the house with my mom's question in the back of my mind.

When I get to Mom's flower garden, I stop abruptly, her question finally registering. Shit, I didn't think about how this would look. I'm sure they are wondering why their twenty-six-year-old son is looking for a bug catcher. Lucky for all of us, I'm quick on my toes.

"Oh, I was going to drop this off for Aurelia. Billie Rose says she's digging ladybugs."

"Aw, that's sweet, baby," my mom says.

Trying to keep my eyes from rolling into my head at her sickening *aw* and use of the word *baby*, I scour their yard and manage to find two of the little black and red treasures.

I head back to my truck, waving to them as I go. "Sorry, I can't stay. I've got to get back to the zoo and feed the animals," I joke.

They shake their heads; they know how I am. Always on the move.

Parking my truck a ways down the road, I make my way to the brook, following it all the way past the farm. I'm going to find this fucking fairy if it takes me all night.

And that's when I find a campsite.

A blue tarp is tied tightly between two trees. I glance around until my eyes land on a sagging clothesline. Dresses and women's underclothes blow gently in the breeze, drying on the line. I recognize a few of the sundresses; they look like ones my sister used to wear.

A woman, then.

Well, now I'm really curious. This is not what I was expecting. I peek under the tarp, spying a blanket and a bag covered in bright butterflies. It almost looks like a child's backpack.

I'm not about to snoop any further. I leave the bug catcher in front of the tent and hide.

It's not long before she arrives. When she walks by me, I only get a glimpse of her blonde hair. She's tiny. Much smaller than I expected. She freezes when she sees the bug catcher I left for her.

Something primal washes over me when I sense her fear. If she runs, I'm going to chase. I know it's wrong, but she's on my property. That makes her mine.

What? Where the fuck did that come from? This girl is trouble. I need to get rid of her, not keep her.

But the scent of her fear lingers in the air, and suddenly all those feelings morph into something different. I feel bad. I didn't mean to scare her. That wasn't my intention at all.

Her fear is greater than it should be.

She surprises me when she finally moves forward and lowers herself to the forest floor, peering into the catcher. The fear I saw moments ago instantly evaporates, her shoulders relax, and I can almost feel her smile.

It's there. I know it is. Slowly, she scans her surroundings. She's looking for me.

When her green eyes slide my way, my heart stops. Jesus. I almost choke on air at their intensity. She's the most beautiful thing I've ever seen. She looks wild. Wild and free.

I should step out and reveal myself, but I don't. I continue to watch as she climbs on a nearby rock, sitting down on it. She holds the catcher in front of her face, studying the little ladybugs inside. She is tan, and there's a smattering of freckles dusting her cheeks, which are beautifully defined by the way. And ugh, she has the cutest nose.

"Hi, little ones," she says to the bugs.

I almost groan out loud at the sound of her voice. It's raspy and soft.

Suddenly, she sets the catcher down and rushes into her tent, coming back out with the butterfly bag. She reaches inside and pulls out a book. *The Big Book of Bugs* ... I know it well. It was my favorite when I was a kid.

I know the exact page she's going to, and we both smile in unison when she reaches it. Her lips are a pale pink, like the color of cotton candy. God, she's the sweetest thing I've ever seen. Maybe she is a goddamn fairy.

She sets the bug catcher on the book and turns it, studying the designs I made when I was a child. She presses her finger against my six-year-old one, making my chest clench tightly. Her smile is so pretty, and when she does it, it reveals a dimple. Just one on the left side of her face. I want to kiss her there.

No. No. I'm staying away from women.

I don't need to be thinking about her in any way whatsoever, other than as someone I want to help. I have a feeling she's hiding.

Avenging Skulls

When she goes back into her tent, I make my getaway, leaving her to enjoy my gift.

I head to my truck and when I get back to the house, I decide to put in a few hours of work before it gets dark. When I turn the light on, I don't find my workshop the way I left it. Normally I would be angry at someone coming in and touching my things, but for some reason I don't mind that she did. In fact, it's nice to come into a clean shop. I'm a bit of a scatterbrain and not the tidiest of people. My mom tried her best. Really, she did.

I pull the blanket off my latest project. It's finally ready to be painted, which is my favorite part. I grab some paper to place over the glass so I won't get paint on it. I bite a piece of tape off with my teeth, catching my reflection. But it's not my reflection I'm focused on.

Left against the glass are handprints. I press my palms against them and then notice her lips. Her fucking lips were on my mirror. My finger traces them, and my cock instantly hardens. Fuck.

Fuck!

I leave the blanket on the ground and storm out of the barn. This can't be happening. I can't do this again. I'm a heartbreaker, and I can't stand the thought of breaking that girl's heart. Look what happened last time. I made a girl so crazy she tossed her morals out the window and decided to take what she wanted from me.

When I get inside the house, I proceed to down an entire twelve pack, trying to stifle the memories of that night. Of waking up and finding Lanie on top of me.

Sometimes I wish she would have killed me instead of herself.

Chapter Fifteen

Jackson

I wake up to someone who truly does want to kill me. Bang, bang, bang!

Jesus fuck, this better not be the cops because I can't deal with their shit right now.

Bang, bang, bang!

I crawl off the couch and all the way to the door, pulling myself up slowly, meeting Petey's ugly mug through the window. I swing the door open. "Are you trying to kill me?" I ask him.

Petey transferred to our club from the NorCal chapter a few years ago. He's in his forties, and all of the old ladies love him. He's a fucking brown noser. At least to the women, not so much to the guys.

"No, but I can sure do that for you if you want. I'll make it real quick," he says calmly.

I can't tell if the fucker is joking.

"What the fuck do you want?" I ask instead. I'm too hung over to deal with Petey.

His fucking crazy black eyes swing to his flatbed truck. "I've got a load for you. I'll back around if you don't mind me driving through the yard. Grandma Maggie said to drop it off out by the barn."

I follow him down to the truck and he pulls back a tarp, revealing a shit load of small plants. My fingers scratch over my bare chest. "What the fuck are they for?" I ask him.

He shakes his head and snorts. "You're something else, kid. They're fucking vegetables; you put them in the ground." He lays the tarp back over them and hops in his truck.

"Shit. Let me go around and make sure you don't run over any chickens." Assuming my little fairy has let them out already.

As I'm rushing around the house, I hold my breath. The thought of her leaving and running away sends me into a panic. As I round the corner, I see that she has indeed done the morning chores. I let out a long sigh of relief, but I really shouldn't be relying on her to do all the work around here. I need to pull my head out of my ass.

After I help Petey get backed up to the garden spot, I head back toward the house.

"Aren't you going to help me unload this shit?"

I stop and spin around. "Grandma Maggie is paying you, not me."

He laughs. "Can't fault me for trying."

I turn back around.

"Oh, Grandma Maggie told me to make sure you started tilling while I was here. She told me not to leave until it was done."

Jesus Christ that old woman is killing me. I stomp over to the garden shed and drag the damn tiller out. Petey does exactly what my grandmother paid him to do: deliver the plants and then sit on his ass and watch me do the real work.

When I'm finished, Petey rakes his beady black eyes over me, gives me a one finger salute, and leaves. I wipe the sweat from my brow after I drag the tiller back to the shed and notice the barn door is open a crack.

I flip the light on. Everything is perfectly in place, but then my eyes snag on the bug catcher sitting on the work bench. My stomach drops. She gave my gift back. Did she leave?

Not even taking time to close the barn door, I rush to her campsite. When I get close, I slow my steps, not wanting to spook her. A stick snaps under my foot, sending her scrambling behind a tree.

I stop where I'm at. "I didn't mean to scare you," I tell her. "I ... well, I only wanted to talk."

No response.

"I'm going to go back to the barn. There's a lock on the outside of the door ... um, you can lock me in and then maybe we could visit. That is, if you want to." I take a step back. "I'll leave now."

When I get to the barn, I shut the door and wait and wait and wait.

Several minutes later, I hear the wood slip down and lock into place. My shoulders fall, instantly relieved. But now that she's here, what do I say?

I plop down against the barn door, placing my mouth to the seam. "I thought if we're going to be neighbors, maybe we should get to know each other," I begin.

She's so quiet on the other side. Maybe she locked me in just to give her a chance to run away.

"You don't want me to leave?" she asks softly.

Her voice brushes across my heart, waking up an urge within me I haven't felt in a long time. I mean, sure, I pretend to be interested in the women who hang around the club. I have to keep up my reputation, or at least I think I do. But I haven't felt anything other than a sick feeling in the pit of my stomach when women hit on me.

"No, I don't want you to leave," I tell her. "I was wondering why you returned my welcome-to-the-neighborhood gift."

A soft thud shakes the door, and I picture her dropping her head back against it. "I ... I already traded with Miss Maggie," she answers.

Traded? I'm so confused.

"She gave me some very nice things, and she let me stay here, and I promised her I would ..." Her breathy voice stops.

I place my hand against the door. Her pain bleeds through the cracks, mingling with my own. The hesitation of her words, the fear of saying the wrong thing. It's the same for me. I hesitate every time I talk to a woman now, not wanting her to wrongfully interpret what I'm really saying. I didn't do that with Lanie. I unknowingly made her fall crazy in love with me.

"What did you promise?" I ask.

She shifts, and I can see her shadow reaching out to me from underneath the door. "I promised Miss Maggie I would watch over you," she whispers.

I press my ear to the wood, desperate to hear everything she has to say.

"I ... I don't want to trade with you," she continues hesitantly, and that is when I know. It's like a punch to my gut.

Someone hurt her.

And whoever did is going to be in the belly of my hogs very soon.

"It wasn't a trade," I assure her. "It was a gift. No strings attached."

Again, she sighs loudly. She doesn't believe me, and why would she? She doesn't know me.

"It's okay if you don't trust me right now. I understand. I have a hard time trusting, too." I light up a cigarette, blowing smoke rings over my head.

"How is Miss Maggie?" she asks.

"Ornery as ever," I chuckle, pulling my knees to my chest. "She's the one who told me you might like the ladybugs."

We're both quiet for several minutes.

"Jackson?"

My name sailing on her breathy voice tweaks at my heart again. "Yeah?"

"I like it here. And ... if we're going to be neighbors, then maybe we can trade."

I feel something nudge against my butt. I scoot forward and see she's sliding *The Big Book of Bugs* under the door. I pick it up and run my fingers over it. On the cover is a dragonfly with its iridescent wings proudly on display.

"I liked the bug catcher very much," her sweet words tug at every fiber of my being. Then, the wood lock is lifted from its place, and I know she's gone.

Shit. I didn't even ask her name.

Chapter Sixteen

Willow

Jackson left soon after I unlocked the barn door. He waited several minutes before coming out, giving me time to hide.

When I heard his motorcycle roar down the road, I went back to the house. I found the bug catcher sitting on his workbench where I left it, and I hugged it to my chest. A gift, he had said.

My stomach churned at the thought he might be deceiving me. Bradley gave me gifts too, and he expected something in return. Every time. Shaking off any thoughts of him, I went back outside.

Now, as I sit beside the plants Miss Maggie had delivered, I set my new bug catcher beside me. My mind runs through all the things my father taught me about gardening. I lay out each row, making sure the plants that need the most sun won't get shadowed by any taller growing plants. Then, I set to work. It feels good to get my hands dirty. Bradley would never have let me get my hands dirty like this. He liked me clean.

Stop. Quit thinking about him. He's not here.

But he's still living rent free in my mind, I guess.

Avenging Skulls

"You're going to grow so big and strong," I talk to the vegetables as I place each one in the ground, giving them encouragement. I laugh, remembering how my dad talked to our tomato plants. He would tell them how proud he was of them for producing such juicy tomatoes. My mom would make fun of him, but he didn't care. He told her it was the secret to getting the best produce.

The sun slides across the sky as I allow my memories of them to come back to the forefront of my mind. I'd kept them so far out of reach from Bradley that I'd begun to worry I might never be able to find them again. Shortly after he took me, I realized I had to protect everything I could.

The Willow I was before turned into a ghost, living inside myself, going from room to room, avoiding the living at all costs. Sometimes at night I might visit her, and she would give me a peek at what I left behind. I didn't do it often because it hurt too much. It was better for the new Willow to remain numb.

A rumble and the cloud of dust that follows tells me it's time to go. But I pause just inside the trees, standing on the threshold of my world and his. I watch as he gets off his bike, his friend doing the same. It's the man he drank with the other night.

"You're becoming quite the little farmer, brother," I hear him say.

Brother? This surprises me. They look nothing alike. But they do act like siblings.

Jackson has rich brown hair and eyes. He's tall with a broad chest and strong arms. The other guy has hair that's almost the color of mine. He's shorter than Jackson, but big and bulky. He would be intimidating but for his eyes. He has kind eyes. I'm not sure what color they are from here, though.

Jackson lights up a cigarette, shaking his head. But he doesn't tell his brother it wasn't him who planted the garden.

"Yep, Grandma Maggie insisted." He crouches down and pinches a tomato leaf between his fingers. "I'll be right back," he tells his brother and then goes into the shop, coming out with a big smile on his face.

I think he's happy I took the bug catcher back. I didn't mean to seem ungrateful. I … I just … I compared him to Bradley, and I can't allow myself to do that.

They sit in the chairs, each cracking open a beer. I move in as close as I dare, suddenly not wanting to go back to my campsite alone.

They laugh and tease each other, and I come to the conclusion that they are indeed brothers. My fingers rub over the ache in my chest. The pain of Ash's death is as fresh as the day I found out he left the world behind.

"Hey, I talked to the twins today. They said some dude showed up at Junkyard Treasures looking for a runaway. They're going to send a picture to the club so we can keep our eyes open for her."

The men's phones ding at the same time, both of them immediately pulling them from their pockets.

"Speak of the devil," Jackson laughs.

Both are quiet for a moment before Jackson suddenly sits up straight, his gaze scanning the tree line.

His brother whistles. "Damn. Ain't she pretty?"

"You have to go," Jackson rushes out.

His brother's head spins his way. "What?"

Jackson takes a deep breath. "I mean, I forgot I promised Billie Rose I would stop by. I need to get cleaned up before I go over there."

His brother nods. "Sure thing. I'll see you tomorrow at the barbecue."

Avenging Skulls

Jackson walks him to his bike and then waves to him from the porch. The minute he's gone, he jumps down and rushes toward me. Something is wrong. I'm about to dart away when he calls for me.

"Hey! I need to talk to you," he yells.

I glance over my shoulder, peering through the trees. He's pacing back and forth like a caged animal, running his fingers through his hair.

He calls for me several more times but doesn't leave the yard. After a few minutes he gives up and goes inside, the door slamming shut behind him.

I slowly walk back to my tent, wondering why he was acting with such urgency. Just as I return to camp, a hauntingly beautiful sound tugs at me, enticing me back toward the farm. I try to resist it, but each note reverberates through my chest, awakening something new inside of me.

Rushing back through the trees, I pause on the precipice between my world and his. Jackson is sitting on the back step with a large wooden instrument between his legs. His hand draws a bow across the strings. It's a cello.

Bradley didn't like music ... he liked silence. The only music I've heard is what came from the overhead speakers at the restaurants or truck stops we visited.

Before I know what is happening, I'm standing a few feet from him. The only thing separating us is Miss Maggie's dog, Fred.

Jackson's eyes remain closed, giving me time to study the ink on his fingers as they play the most beautiful music I've ever heard. It slowly filters through my body, finding my soul and waking her.

When he finishes the song, he doesn't move. His eyes remain closed. "Please don't run away," he says softly.

My gaze roams over his skin, so dark with ink it's almost frightening. He's messy and chaotic, and I find I want to know everything about him.

After a few more seconds, he slowly opens his eyes, revealing the warmest brown orbs I've ever seen.

"I didn't mean to make you cry," he says, tipping his head.

My hands fly up to my cheeks. *Am I crying?*

I am.

He gently lays his instrument aside but remains seated. His big brown eyes roam over me as he gets his first real look at me. My head falls back, and I let him take me in as I am. Dirty, wild ... free.

"Someone is looking for you," he tells me. When his words begin to sink in, I start to back away.

He rises from the step, making me jump back. "I can help you."

He offers me his hand, but I don't take it. I accepted an offer of help once. Nice words mean nothing to me now. The moment I see his muscles flinch, I run.

His boots thud behind me as my mind races for a place to hide, but he seems to know the forest better than I do. He's gaining on me. I need my bag ... and my book, the one I gave to him. I should never have trusted him. How many times am I going to make the same mistake?

I stumble over a tree branch, giving Jackson just enough time to tackle me to the ground. Air rushes out of my lungs as we land with a thud. A stick slides across my thigh, making me cry out. But Jackson doesn't budge, his breath coming out in hard pants against the back of my head.

Avenging Skulls

I try the only tactic I know. It didn't work against Bradley, but maybe it will work with this male. Starting at the top of my head, I purposefully relax each and every muscle in my body.

He rests his forehead against my hair. "I'm not going to hurt you."

When he doesn't get a response from me, he leans up and rolls me over, laying his body back down on mine to keep me pinned to the earth.

I remain playing dead.

"Goddammit, woman. What is it about you that makes me want to ditch my morals and kiss you?" he rasps, his chest bumping into mine with each breath he takes.

Now this makes me pause. Kiss me. He wants to kiss me. Like on the mouth? I've never been kissed there before. That is one thing Bradley never asked of me.

When he shifts and his breath whispers over my lips, my eyes fly open. My gaze pins his brown one, turning the tables and holding him hostage. His eyes aren't only brown; they are speckled with green. The same green as the moss that grows on the side of a tree.

He shifts, taking some of his weight off of me, his hair falling into his eyes. "I don't want you to run away. Please," he begs with longing in his voice. He's desperate for me to stay.

"Are you going to kiss me?" I whisper quietly. I'm not really sure I want him to, but I think I do. His music brought my soul to life and now it wants more. It's been dormant for so long. It yearns to feel a connection to something ... to him.

His fingers tremble as they brush lightly over my collarbone, coming to stop firmly against the side of my neck. "Do you want me to?"

I think about it as he patiently waits for my response. "What if I say no?"

He blinks a few times, his eyes never leaving mine. "I will never take anything from you that you don't freely give. That is a promise."

I don't know this man. This could all be part of his plan to lure me inside the house. To keep me.

"We could start with a butterfly kiss," he suggests.

"I don't know what that is," I tell him. But I want to know.

He leans close to me as I hold my breath. His eyelashes gently brush against my cheek, and just like that I know why it's called a butterfly kiss.

When he pulls away, he smiles.

My chest bubbles with something unfamiliar, and a giggle erupts from between my lips, not only surprising me but him as well.

"Do you want me to do it again?" he asks, and I nod my head like an idiot.

And when he does, I focus on his warmth, the way his hard body presses against my soft one. He smells like leather and the outdoors. It's so nice and natural.

But then the world stops as I hear someone calling my name. Jackson stills, placing his finger over my mouth.

"Willow!" Bradley calls from downstream.

Jackson stares at me; the look of terror on my face must tell him everything he needs to know. He sits up, grabs my hand, and then we run through the trees to my camp. We both frantically grab my belongings, leaving the tarp behind.

Avenging Skulls

"Willow!" the sound of Bradley's voice trickles like a cold winter rain down my spine.

Jackson rushes us to the house, but when he tugs on my arm to enter, I dig in my heels.

"You have to hide. I'll keep you safe inside, I promise."

"I can't ..." I say, pulling away from him and rushing around to the front of the house. I dive through the tiny opening that leads under the porch. I spotted this hiding place a few days ago, knowing that eventually Bradley would come looking for me.

Jackson curses but shoves my bag in behind me, leaning a wheelbarrow over the opening. Then I hear his boots stomp above me and the wooden screen door slam shut behind him.

The last of the daylight peeks through the crisscross slats that surround me. I watch as a spider spins her web in the corner. Light thumps sound above me, and I close my eyes, slowing my breath.

Knock. Knock. Knock.

No answer.

Knock. Knock. Knock.

The screen door creaks open. "Can I help you?" Jackson asks.

"Sorry to bother you. I was following the brook out back and found a campsite. I was wondering if you might have seen this girl?"

The screen door slams shut, and Jackson's boots thud onto the porch. He pauses, and I'm assuming he's looking at one of the many photos Bradley took of me. "Oh shit, yeah."

My heart drops into the churning pit of acid in my stomach.

"The club sent me a picture. Sorry, man, but I haven't seen her."

I slowly release the breath I was holding. He didn't betray me.

"Oh, you're a member of the Rebel Skulls," Bradley says. "I met the twins and Kelsie in town at Junkyard Treasures."

"Yeah, they're good kids. I really wish I could help you out," Jackson tells him. "The club will keep their eyes open for her, though."

"I saw the tarp just down the way and was hoping …"

Jackson cuts him off. "We get a lot of drifters around here. With the train and all," he adds.

"Yeah, I'm sure."

"Hey, I was getting ready to head into town to get a bite to eat. Have you eaten?" he asks Bradley.

Bradley sighs loudly. "No, but if it's okay, I think I'll look around some more before I decide to call it a day."

"Sure thing, man," Jackson says without hesitation. "I'll help you. I know these woods like the back of my hand."

"That would be great, thanks. I'm really worried about her."

"Yeah, no problem, dude. Then I'll take you back into town and we can grab a bite."

"Thanks. Your club might have a bad rap, but you guys are okay."

Jackson laughs at this. "That's because you're a good guy. If you weren't … well, then that'd be a different story."

"Duly noted," Bradley says, their voices fading as they walk away.

Avenging Skulls

I begin to tear up, frozen in fear. He was right here. Above me.

I'm never going to be able to escape him. Why did I think I could? And now I may have put Jackson in danger. I groan quietly to myself.

Angrily, I shove my backpack under my head, thinking about the first time I realized my actions might put someone in harm's way.

"I saw you looking at him," Bradley says, taking his reading glasses off and setting them beside him on the picnic table.

I keep my eyes on the page of my book. "At who?"

When he doesn't say anything, I glance up at him.

"Don't play games with me, Willow. I don't like games."

He does. He loves games but only ones where he can make the rules.

"I wasn't looking at anyone."

But I was. There's a boy about my age here at the campground. I watched him while he fished with his dad. He had the cutest smile.

Bradley reaches across the table and takes my book away from me. My chin falls to my chest, knowing that it will take a whole lot of time and ass kissing to get it back.

"Do you want to be with him?" he asks, accusation in his tone.

"What? No," I say, shaking my head.

"I can make that happen, you know."

My stomach does this weird flip the way his eyes dilate. I've seen this look before. My heartbeat picks up, wondering where he's going with this. "I don't want him, Bradley."

He shrugs his shoulders and picks up his glasses, placing them back on his face. "If you say so."

He goes back to reading his book, leaving me empty handed. When the boy and his father walk past us on their way back to their camper, I keep my eyes focused on an ant dragging a potato chip across the table.

The chip must be three times as big as the little ant. If only I could drag that much weight. I feel Bradley's eyes on me, but I don't dare look at him. Would he be able to detect the murderous glint in my eye as easily as I can his?

I'll never look at another boy again.

Chapter Seventeen

Jackson

As I'm sitting down to eat with Ash, I remember I still don't know his sister's name. He hasn't offered it up yet.

"So, what's your sister's name?" I ask, smiling up at the waitress as she hands us each a menu.

She grins back prettily at the both of us. I guess we're both handsome men, but we couldn't be more different. He is a clean cut All-American boy, and I'm a dirty biker. He has virgin skin, and mine is blackened by dark ink. Light versus the dark … or so it seems.

"Willow," he answers as the waitress walks away.

"Your dad must have liked trees, yeah?" I joke but Ash looks at me with a blank, confused stare.

"Sorry. I'm kidding, man. You know you're both named after trees, right?"

Ash leans forward, resting his arms on the table. "I guess I've never thought about it. So, how long have you been with the Skulls?" he asks, deflecting the conversation away from himself.

I lay my arm across the back of the booth, relaxing into our conversation. "My entire motherfucking life."

His bright blue eyes widen in surprise.

Laughing, I wink at the waitress as she brings us our drinks. "I was born into the club. Just like the twins. We all started out as club brats."

"So, your father is in the club?" he asks.

"Yep, he's the Sargent at Arms. He's been with the Skulls a long time." We each give the waitress our order and then I decide to dig a little deeper.

"What's your sister running from?" I ask.

He raps his knuckles over the table. "She's running from herself." He runs his fingers through his hair, tugging on the ends. "Our mother is a drug addict. The last time I was home, Willow was pretty much raising herself. So, I decided to bring her along with me. I travel around in my van as a nature photographer. She seemed happy and was really enjoying exploring new places, but then I realized she had stopped taking her meds. Her personality changed almost overnight. She became depressed and then manic. One day, I stopped at a truck stop outside of Reno to get us a few drinks. When I came out, she was gone. I searched everywhere and then I saw her running alongside a train. I ran to catch up, but she jumped on a grain car. I didn't get to her in time."

"Did you check with your mom? Maybe she went back home. Did she have friends or a boyfriend she might have been missing?"

He shakes his head. "She's not there. She didn't have any friends, let alone a boyfriend. Our mother is so pissed at me for losing her." He leans his head back against the seat, staring up the ceiling. "She told me she was doing better raising Willow than I was. Told me that at least Willow hadn't run from her."

If this dude is lying, he's good.

He continues, "I don't know. Maybe my mom's right. Maybe I should have left her there. I ... I didn't want her to worry about keeping up the house. And I especially didn't want her having to hide in the attic anymore."

I lean forward at that. "The attic?"

He sighs loudly and runs his hand down his face. "Yeah. My mom used to bring strange men home all the time. Willow would hide in the attic ..." He lets his words trail off as he turns away from me to stare out the window. "I wanted to give her a better life."

Jesus. Maybe I should tell him where she is. I know she's still at the farm; I didn't give her the option of running. My dad is making sure of that.

But ...

I need to give her a chance to explain. Sometimes things aren't what they seem.

Bad guys aren't always recognizable.

I know this for a fact. Look at Lanie. She was beautiful. None of us knew she was capable of all the horrible things she did to Billie Rose ... and to me.

I watch as Ash wipes tears away from his icy blue eyes. Is he the hero in Willow's story or the villain?

Chapter Eighteen

Willow

A couple of motorcycles roar into the driveway soon after Jackson and Bradley leave for town. *Shoot.* I should have run the moment they left, but I wanted to make sure they were far away before I crawled out.

I stay hidden, but whoever it is walks over to the side of the porch and moves the wheelbarrow. I suck in a breath, scooting to the far end of the porch.

"Come on out now. We're not going to hurt you. Jackson sent us," a man says.

No. No way. If they want me, they're going to have to drag me out.

One of the men comes into view. It's the older man who was with Jackson and Miss Maggie the other day. A whimper escapes me as I crawl farther away from him.

"Hey, listen. I'm Jackson's dad. I promise you, you're safe with us."

Avenging Skulls

I shake my head, hug my knees, and tuck my face between them and my chest.

"Why don't you call Rachel?" the other man asks.

Jackson's dad shifts to look back at him. "She left for Texas this morning. What about Jesse?"

The other man laughs. "If she's scared of you, she's damn sure going to be hesitant around Jess. I'll give Billie Rose a call."

Both of the men linger around the porch, giving me no chance to escape. I begin to panic. They're going to tell Bradley I'm here. He's looking for me, and they all know it. He's going to twist this and make me look like I'm the crazy one. I have to get out of here.

I turn myself around and begin kicking at the lattice board that's keeping me locked inside. It must be old and brittle because one good kick with both my feet and it breaks. Unfortunately, as the wood splinters apart, it cuts into the sides of my calves.

Ignoring the pain, I push the boards aside and scurry out the hole I made. Scrambling to my feet, I take off, running right into a solid wall of muscle.

Slowly my eyes raise to meet the most frightening man I've ever seen. He smirks as he wraps his arms around me.

"She's a feisty one," he says.

Jackson's dad curses, coming around to the side of the porch. "Jesus, girl. Look at what you did to your legs. Dirk, let her go," he tells the big guy holding me hostage.

When he does, I try to run but Jackson's dad snags my wrist. "Sorry, honey, but we can't let you go."

"You don't understand," I rush out, trying to pry his fingers away from my arm. Oh my god. They are going to call Bradley. I can't go back. I just can't go back.

"Shh, hey, we aren't going to hurt you. We aren't going to tell anyone you're here until we figure out what's going on. Okay?"

My chest is heaving, and I'm pretty sure I'm going to throw up.

Just as I'm about to start fighting them again, another bike pulls in, this time with two riders. A young woman gets off, shaking her long dark hair around her shoulders after she removes her helmet. Another guy in a leather jacket gets off after her. I let out another whimper because too many people have seen me. This is bad … so bad.

"What in the world is going on?" the woman asks.

Jackson's dad tugs me close to him, keeping my wrist locked in his hand. His other arm wraps around my waist, holding me securely to his side.

"Don't know. Jackson asked me to come out here and make sure she didn't run. She was hiding under the porch."

Everyone turns to look at the damage I did. Then the younger guy with the girl squints his eyes at me. "Oh shit. This is the girl that guy is looking for."

This gets the woman's attention. She holds her hand out to me as she studies my face. "My name is Billie Rose," she says kindly, taking my free hand in hers.

I remember her now; she was here the day Miss Maggie moved out. She was playing with a little girl in the backyard.

I wish Miss Maggie was here.

Billie Rose points to the guy behind her. "This is my husband, Elijah. That asshole …" She pauses to point at the scary guy. "Is my dad. His name is Dirk. And this guy …" She waves a hand toward Jackson's dad. "This is my Uncle Raffe. He's Jackson's father."

I'm trying not to freak out. This is Jackson's family, and he asked them to come here. I want to trust them so bad, but I just don't know how.

"What's your name?" she asks, rubbing her hand over my arm.

I try to calm my breathing. "Willow," I answer quietly.

"Willow. That's such a pretty name," she says, soothing me with her soft voice.

She looks back at her husband before gently nudging Raffe to let go of me. He reluctantly does.

Billie Rose wraps her arm around my shoulder. "Are you running from the man who is looking for you?" she asks.

I glance at all of them before nodding slightly. I'm not sure if I can trust them, but they are giving me no choice. It's them or Bradley, so right now I'm willing to risk it. The thought of being stuck in that van one more day makes me want to claw my way out of my own body.

"Okay," she says. "We're not going to let him near you." She glances down at my injuries. "Why don't we go inside and get your legs cleaned up?"

I start shaking my head and pulling away from her.

She gets a worried look on her face but remains calm. "We don't have to go inside. We'll sit out back, and I'll go in and grab the first aid kit. No worries."

I can handle that. I nod my head.

We walk past the big scary guy, and he smiles proudly at his daughter. I let out a shaky breath. *It's going to be okay* I tell myself. They are family.

My heart squeezes painfully.

She ushers me to a chair near the fire pit. "I'll be right back," she says, giving my hand a gentle squeeze.

"I'll get it," her husband offers.

At the back step, he notices the cello Jackson left behind. "Why is this outside?" he asks the other men.

Raffe's brow furrows. "I don't know. It was Harold's."

"Jackson played it for me," I explain, remembering how his music made me feel. How it drew me to him. If it hadn't ... Bradley would have found me.

Dirk laughs. "Jackson played it?"

I nod my head, lifting my face to the sky and closing my eyes. "It was the most beautiful thing I've ever heard."

When my eyes open again, they're all staring at me like I have two heads.

Sucking my bottom lip between my teeth, I drop my gaze. They don't know. Oh, I hope Jackson doesn't get angry at me for telling them.

Elijah picks it up and takes it into the house with him. I study the sky as dark clouds move in to replace the sun. I don't like sitting out here in the open like this, knowing Bradley is close.

Billie Rose pulls up a chair across from me, tugging my leg over her knees. "Ouch. You've got some splinters, girl."

My cheeks heat at the dirty state of my legs and feet. But her hands feel good on my skin … different. It pulls up a good memory of my mom. One where I'm sitting on the toilet seat and she's kneeling in front of me, cleaning my scraped knee. A knot lodges itself in my throat. That seems like an entire lifetime ago.

Dirk walks away, perusing the perimeter of the property while Raffe pulls up a chair next to me.

Elijah brings the first aid kit out and hands it to his wife. She grabs the tweezers and begins to meticulously dig splinters out of my legs.

"I'm sorry about the porch. I … I just got scared."

Raffe sets his hand on my shoulder. "Hey, honey, don't you worry about it. Dirk and I get that reaction quite a bit, actually," he laughs.

I offer him a small smile, and he returns it tenfold.

Just as Billie Rose is finishing with my legs, the motor of a car gets louder and louder. I have to hide.

I jump up, but Billie Rose pushes me gently back down in the chair. Raffe once again wraps his arm around my shoulders, pinning me in place.

"It's only Jackson," he says calmly.

A car door slams, and Jackson runs around the house, pausing for a moment as he takes us in. Then, he's in front of me, dropping to his knees, his hands cradling my face.

"Are you okay?" he asks.

I stare at him, mesmerized by the way his long lashes brush against his cheeks. A flutter low in my belly makes me blush. "I'm okay," I whisper, staring into the warmth of his eyes.

A slow rumble of thunder rolls in the distance.

"What's going on, Son?" his dad asks, reminding us we're not alone.

Jackson reluctantly pulls his gaze away to look at his father. "I don't know, Dad. I don't know." Then his focus returns to me. "Are you afraid of Ash?" he asks.

My head snaps back and my heart stops. "Ash?"

He nods. "If you are, just say the word and you'll never have to see him again."

My heart slows to a standstill as I realize what's happening. A second later it lets go with a loud rush, making my ears ring.

"Willow, talk to me," Jackson pleads, lifting his hand to my cheek, forcing me to look at him.

"Ash is my brother," I stutter.

He nods. "I know. Are you scared of him? Is that why you ran away?"

"I'm not scared of my brother ... I didn't run away from him. He's dead. He left me," I say, choking on the words.

Jackson slowly stands, running his fingers through his messy brown hair. His father rises with him.

They don't believe me.

The blood in my veins turns to molten lava as I realize what Bradley has done. What lies he must have told Jackson. I'm so tired of games. So tired. I rise from my chair and take a few steps away from them.

Jackson holds out his hand to me, like I'm a horse he's trying to tame.

"Did he tell you his name was Ash? That he was my brother?" I don't know why I'm suddenly so angry. But I'm furious he's pretending to be Ash.

With his hand still held out, he slowly approaches me. "He did."

I chuckle, glancing over at the hog pen. Jackson's gaze follows mine, and his face falls.

"He's not your brother, then?" he asks, confusion pulling at his brow. He takes another step toward me.

My shoulders drop. "No. He's not my brother. My brother was a good man."

Jackson looks back at his family before turning his eyes my way. "I have a question for you," he says.

I bite my lip and shake my head. He doesn't believe me. I'm so done with Bradley and his fucking games. I'm never going to win.

"How did you get your name?" he asks.

My gaze immediately goes to the trees, and I smile sadly.

"Tell me," he coaxes softly.

Wrapping my arms around my stomach, I decide to tell him. Because my brother was good, and I don't want anyone believing Bradley is Ash. I have to try ... for my brother.

"My father," I begin as the wind changes direction, bringing with it a cool breeze and the scent of rain. I inhale deeply. "He loved the outdoors." I wave my hand around the farm. "We were going to move to a place like this, with trees. We were going to plant a garden and ..."

That stupid knot lodges in my throat. It wasn't supposed to be like this.

Everyone is staring at me, so I finish, "He named us after his favorite trees." Then, I turn away from them to face the incoming storm. It doesn't matter. Bradley is better at the game than me. He can make anyone believe his lies. I can't even get someone to believe the truth.

Warm arms wrap around me. "I believe you," Jackson whispers in my ear.

Time stops. Wait a minute. He believes me? Does he really?

A raindrop falls on my cheek. And then another. I swipe at them angrily, struggling to stop myself from losing it.

"It's okay. I've got you." Jackson's arms tighten. "You don't have to be scared anymore. You're right where you belong."

I want to believe him.

Billie Rose walks over and stands in front of me. Watching me blink rapidly, she wraps her arms around me, too. "Jackson's right. Let us be your sanctuary in the storm."

The catch in her voice tells me she's not talking about the storm that is quickly approaching. She's talking about the one I'm about to go through as I try to separate myself from Bradley.

And for the first time since Ash left for the Army, I have hope.

I rest my chin on her shoulder, letting my tears mix with the rain. The dragonfly on the barn stares back at me.

Maybe this is why Miss Maggie left. She knew if she stayed, I would learn to only rely on her.

Maybe she is the gatekeeper of angels.

Chapter Nineteen

Jackson

She lets me and Billie Rose hold her. I remember when we were kids, and we would play in the woods behind the warehouse. We were always finding wounded critters out there. Our parents would help us load them up and take them to the vet.

But this ... this is different. I found a girl.

She is broken and dirty, like the animals we found, but I don't want to take her to someone else who can help her. Our parents never let us keep any of the stray animals we rescued.

I have a feeling I'm going to have to fight all of them to keep Willow.

The rain is starting to come down harder, and the lightning is getting close. Reluctantly, I pull away. Billie Rose does the same.

Spinning Willow around to face me, I tell her, "I need to get the animals into their shelters." I glance back at the house. I really need to convince her to go inside. She wouldn't come in earlier. "Go inside with Billie Rose. I'll be there in a few."

I step away, but she grabs my arm.

"No, I'll help you."

So, together, with the help of the others, we quickly get the animals put away for the night. When we're finished, we all head toward the house just as a bolt of lightning strikes nearby. Everyone rushes inside, but Willow stops outside the door.

I press myself against her back, reaching around and opening the screen door. She stares inside as cold water runs off the roof and over my shoulders.

"Miss Maggie's house is safe. I promise," I tell her. She might not trust me yet, but I know she trusts my grandmother.

She shivers against me. She's so cold. I don't know how long she's been living outdoors or what her phobia of the house is, but I need to coax her inside.

"We can bake our favorite cookies. I noticed grandma left the recipe taped to the fridge."

Willow glances at me over her shoulder, our faces inches apart. Big drops of water cling to her wet lashes, highlighting her brilliant green eyes. I lean in close. She doesn't back away, so I brush my nose along hers and whisper, "I will never deceive you, Willow."

"I have a question for you," she says, her breath mingling with mine.

I rub my thumb over her cheek. "Go ahead."

"What's your favorite game?" she asks.

Without hesitation and with a straight face, I tell her, "Candyland."

An instant smile pulls at her cheeks, that lone dimple making an appearance.

Avenging Skulls

"I think Grandma has one. Do you want to play it?"

She bites her bottom lip in the most adorable way and nods her head, then turns and steps inside.

Well, that was easy and embarrassing all at the same time.

Billie Rose is waiting for us with towels. The guys are all in the living room drying off. "Do you want to take a shower? It will help you warm up," she tells Willow, rubbing her hands up and down her arms.

Willow takes in my grandmother's home with wide eyes. "Oh, I don't know," she says, her teeth chattering as her lips turn blue.

"Come on, I'll help you. Jackson will make us some hot cocoa while we're at it." Billie Rose wraps her fingers around Willow's wrist and gently tugs her away from me.

I release the breath I'd been holding when she complies and allows my cousin to pull her farther into the house. Their soft footsteps thump lightly up the stairs, and soon the pipes groan quietly as the water turns on.

The guys come into the kitchen and sit down as I start the hot cocoa. When I turn it to simmer, I fill my arms with beer and join them, sliding amber bottles across the table.

"Should we contact the authorities?" my dad asks after a few minutes of silence.

Dirk shakes his head, tapping his cap on the table. "I think we need to wait and find out more. We don't know what we're dealing with here."

"What do you think?" Elijah directs his question toward me.

Leaning back, I stretch out my legs. "Her brother ... shit, not her brother. Whoever the fuck that guy is, he portrayed her as an unstable person who went off their meds, but I don't believe him."

"Don't believe him or don't *want* to believe him?" my dad asks.

'I don't believe him." I state firmly.

His gaze goes to the ceiling before dropping back to me. "I agree with you. I don't think she's lied about anything she's said. But Jackson, she's a broken girl. There is something very wrong here."

I huff, blowing hair out of my eyes. "I see that, Dad."

"Do you?" He leans forward, resting his arms on the table. "If we aren't calling the authorities, then I think she needs to stay with either Lily or Jesse. They will know how to care for her."

"She can stay with us," Elijah chimes in. "She seems to be comfortable with Billie Rose."

Why the fuck do these assholes think they get to decide where she stays? There is only one motherfucking place she's staying, and that is right here with me. When I say this out loud, every set of eyes turn my way.

"What?" my dad asks, his mouth falling open.

I cross my arms over my chest and stand my ground. "I said she's staying here."

Everyone starts talking over each other until Dirk whistles, silencing us. I turn my head to see Willow standing in the doorway wearing one of my t-shirts and a pair of sweats tied tightly around her waist. How long has she been standing there?

She runs her toe over the threshold, staring at it. "I would like to stay here," she says softly.

Billie Rose appears behind her. "Shoo, get out of here. I'm going to make us something to eat." She dismisses us men and waves Willow into the room.

Dirk snaps his fingers, pointing toward the front door. I nod to him as the men leave. As I follow, my fingers brush lightly over Willow's shoulder as I lean down and whisper in her ear, "I'll be right back."

She shivers, but this time it's not from the cold.

Chapter Twenty

Willow

My fingers trail over the white and blue checkered tablecloth as I sip on my hot cocoa. Tiny teacups are randomly trapped within the squares. It's cute and homey. It's so Miss Maggie. I feel her here. Her small, sharp handwriting is scribbled on a tablet laying in the middle of the table. I pull it to me, smiling when I see what it says:

"I took a walk in the woods and came out taller than the trees."

It's my favorite Henry David Thoreau quote. My father used to recite it often.

"Are you sure you don't want to stay with me? My daughter would be thrilled to have a new person in the house to read to her." Billie Rose rinses the pasta she boiled. "It's all she wants anymore. And she has quite the library started. Every member of the club gave her their favorite childhood book for her first birthday."

While that sounds lovely, I know where I'm supposed to be. And I can't risk Bradley finding me there. I don't want him going anywhere near Billie Rose's daughter.

Avenging Skulls

"I would love to read to her sometime. I'm a bit of a bookworm myself, but I would like to stay here."

She stares at me as she goes back to the stove to stir the sauce. "You feel safe here?"

I wrap my arms around my waist. "As safe as I've felt in a very long time."

"Okay, then." She taps the spoon on the edge of the pan before coming to sit down beside me. "Who is the man looking for you if he's not your brother?" she asks.

Sighing, I lay my palms flat on the table. "He was someone I made a terrible mistake of trusting."

"He's not related to you at all?"

I shake my head. "No, he's not related to me."

A loud crack of thunder makes me jump. Billie Rose reaches out and places her hand over mine. Her long hair falls over her shoulder as she leans across the table, curling her legs beneath her.

"Do you have family somewhere we could call?"

My head shakes back and forth slowly, my chin falling to my chest. "I don't have anyone but him."

The sauce starts to boil over, and she jumps to her feet. "Shit, shit, shit," she says, pulling the pan from the burner. "I'm no cook. It's too bad I didn't inherit my mother's abilities in the kitchen." She smiles at me over her shoulder.

The front door bangs open, and the men all rush in. "Come with me, baby," Jackson says as he wraps his hand around mine.

I let him pull me from my chair, but the urgency in his movements makes me freeze.

He's back.

My gaze snaps to the windows.

The other men have their phones out and are either typing vigorously or speaking into them in hushed, urgent tones. This can't be happening. Then, I see red and blue lights flashing through the sheer curtains. Another crack of thunder makes me jump against the wall.

Jackson takes my face in his hands, demanding my full attention. "Listen to me. I'm going to hide you in the attic. Just stay there. It will be fine. I'll get rid of them. He must not have believed me that you weren't here. I'm sorry," he says, sincerity laced in his apology.

I let him pull me out of the room and up the stairs, pausing under the attic. He jumps to grab the string hanging from the ceiling. When someone knocks at the front door, I scramble up the steps.

"Stay up there," he orders.

I nod to him as I pull the door closed, suddenly enveloped in darkness.

Voices filter in through a large grate a few feet away from me. I lie face down, pressing my ear to the cool metal.

"Dirk, I don't want no trouble with the club. You boys haven't given me any problems for several years, but I'm going to need you to hand over the girl."

"She's not here," Jackson says.

I hear Dirk reply, "Sorry, Jim. None of us have seen the girl he's looking for."

"I know she's here. I appreciate you guys wanting to protect her, but the only danger my sister is in is what she's inflicting on herself by not taking her meds," Bradley says.

My stomach turns at the sound of his voice.

I'm about to find a better hiding spot when I detect a commotion. There's a lot of yelling, and when it finally settles down, I hear someone say, "Jackson, I'm going to have to take you in for assault. We could have done this the easy way, Son."

No! I can't let Jackson go to jail for me. I quickly lower the steps and rush downstairs.

When I step into the room, all eyes snap my way. Jackson starts to fight against the two deputies holding his arms behind his back. Bradley is wiping blood away from his lip.

"Willow," Bradley and Jackson both say in unison.

Bradley rushes toward me, but Raffe reaches out and grabs him by the throat. "I wouldn't do that if I were you." His voice low and deadly calm.

The sheriff steps forward. "Raffe, let him go."

When he does, a deputy tells Bradley to wait by the door.

Bradley plays his part well, his eyes remaining on me as he steps back. His chest rises and falls fast. "I'm sorry; it's just I'm so happy to have found my sister. I've been so worried about her."

Sister ...

Darkness pulls at the edge of my vision as the sheriff comes to stand in front of me.

"Willow, you don't have to do this," Jackson pleads.

But I do. Oh, how I do.

And then I fall, fall, fall … going limp, just like the female dragonfly.

A sharp pain radiates down the back of my head, and then a blissful nothingness begins to swallow me whole.

"Willow, Willow," someone calls, shaking my arms.

The last thing I hear is the broken white noise of the sheriff's radio as he talks into it, calling for an ambulance.

~~~~~

When I wake up, I'm in a sterile smelling room. I slowly sit upright, raising my arm, confused as to what is strapped to it.

"It's just an IV, hun. Nothing to be scared of." A woman dressed in navy blue scrubs pushes a tray my way. "Are you thirsty? I've got some water here, if you want to give it a try."

I blink at her and raise my hand to rub the ache at the back of my head. A wave of nausea rolls over me.

She adjusts my blankets, helping me to lie down against the soft pillows. "Just rest, sweetie. I'll go get the doctor."

I open my mouth, but it's so dry I can't get any words out. She hands me a Styrofoam cup before she opens the door and waves someone toward her. A man in a white coat steps in. He sits down on the edge of my bed.

"How are you feeling?" he asks.

I don't say anything.

"You passed out and hit your head. You have a slight concussion, but you'll be okay," he reassures me.

Oh, that's right. I remember falling.

"We're going to keep you overnight for observation."

I continue to stare at him, emotionless, giving nothing away.

"If you're feeling up to it, the sheriff is outside. He has a few questions for you. I'll send him in."

Tearing my gaze away from him, I stare out the dark window. Lights twinkle over the streets below.

The doctor pats my hand before leaving the room. He nods for the nurse to follow him. I turn my head as the door closes, watching them through a pane of glass that runs lengthwise along the door. I see the doctor and nurse speaking to the sheriff who was at Miss Maggie's.

I hope he didn't arrest Jackson. This is all my fault. What a mess I've made. I should've just stayed in the van with Bradley.

When the door opens, he pauses, holding it open for a female deputy. They both smile at me as they approach. I pull the blanket up to my chin, shielding myself from the questions that are coming.

"I'm glad to see you're awake," he says. "I'm Sheriff Anderson, and this is Deputy Johansen."

He takes a seat beside my bed and Deputy Johansen circles the room, resting her butt against the windowsill and blocking my view of the town's lights.

"Can you tell us your name?" she asks.

I screw my eyes shut tight and ignore them. My mind wanders back to Jackson and the way he brushed his nose along mine as we stood in the rain. I imagine his strong arms wrapped around me, keeping me from falling apart. If only he were here now.

I must fall asleep because when I wake up they're gone and I'm alone. Nurses and doctors continue to come and go, along with a few deputies. But I remain in my own world. Following along with their requests to eat and drink but refusing to speak.

No one else visits me. I don't know why that bothers me. It's not like I had a family to come and sit by my side. Only Bradley. I wonder why he hasn't convinced them to let him see me.

He was so angry. The warning in his icy blue eyes was as clear to me as a full moon in the fall. I run my sweaty palms down my legs, nervous about what's to come. How long will they allow me to hide here?

A few nights ago, I thought I heard Jackson yelling, but I must have been dreaming because he never came to see me. Probably because I got him in trouble. Miss Maggie will be so disappointed in me. I told her I would look after him. What a failure I am. I can't do anything right.

~~~~~

I guess it's been about a week since I hit my head. Every day the sheriff comes to ask his questions, and each time I retreat into the few memories I have of Jackson.

A soft knock on my door pulls me from my thoughts. I'm expecting a nurse, but instead it's a young blonde woman with short hair and bright blue eyes. Her gaze scans the hall before quickly shutting the door behind her.

"I'm Kelsie," she says as she rushes to the window, cranking it open. "I don't have much time. I'm supposed to be on the fifth floor with my therapist. The hospital won't let any of us in to see you."

Us? Who's us?

After the window is open, she turns to face me. "I'm Jackson's niece."

"Is he in jail?" I ask quickly, sitting up in bed, praying no one catches her. I don't want her to get in trouble for me.

"No." She sits down on my bed. "Listen, they can't find him."

"Who?" I'm confused. They can't find Jackson? Did he run from the police?

She brushes a wild strand of hair behind my ear, her eyes bouncing over my face. "The man who was looking for you. Jackson told me he's not your brother. I knew he was bad news when he came into Junkyard Treasures. I knew it," she whispers harshly. "Anyhow, Jackson wants you to know he's here. He hasn't left the hospital since they brought you in. He's down there." She points out the window.

A cart rolls loudly down the hallway. "I have to go," she says, rising from the bed. She hesitates at the door. "I want you to know it's okay to talk to them. The club will have your back. I know because they've always had mine." She smiles at me and then darts out of the room.

Several minutes later my nurse comes in. "Who left your window open?" she says more to herself than to me, not expecting an answer.

"Leave it," I tell her.

She stops abruptly, her eyes catching on mine.

"I would like some fresh air," I tell her.

"Of course," she says before hurrying back out of the room, no doubt to report that the mute has finally spoken.

When the door shuts, I slide off the bed, no longer held hostage by the IV; they took it out a few days ago. My gaze drops to the figure sitting in Miss Maggie's metal folding chair with a cello perched between his legs. I can't hide the smile that breaks out over my face. His shoulders drop, and he returns one that literally makes me suck in a deep breath. I climb up on the sill and hug my legs, resting my chin on my knees.

My eyes fall closed when the music climbs the walls of the hospital, reaching my ears. It's like a balm to my soul. I can't explain it. I wish I was down there with him where I could really feel the notes reverberating from the wooden instrument.

I hear someone come in behind me and sit down, but I don't turn around. I stay where I'm at, letting Jackson's melody gently pull me back to reality. I don't know whether I should be happy or not; he's tugging me out of my head and back into the real world.

When the song ends, he stands, his eyes never leaving mine. I place my hand over my heart, letting him know how much I love it. He nods and taps the hand still holding the bow over his own.

"Willow, Jackson's family hired me to see if I could help you," a man says from behind me. "My name is Owen. I'm an attorney."

Jackson keeps his gaze locked on mine. This is his way of letting me know he trusts this man. I don't understand why the hospital won't let me see Jackson in person.

"Is your name Willow Taylor?" the man asks quietly.

Jackson sits down and begins to play again.

I haven't heard my last name in such a long time. A tear runs down my cheek as the soulful music plays the soundtrack to my life. He's sad for me. I place my hand against the screen, unsure of whether I should answer Owen's question or throw myself out the window. Will it all be worth it?

There is no going back from this. If I tell him who I am, Bradley will find me and he will kill me. I know too much about him for him to let me live.

The tempo changes; Jackson's hand runs the bow across the strings in short bursts. He's telling me it's going to be okay. I hope he's right.

Then, a dragonfly lands on the screen in front of my face, sealing my fate. Whatever that may be.

"Yes, my name is Willow Taylor," I answer quietly, turning away from the window.

The world needs to know who Bradley really is.

Chapter Twenty-One

Jackson

After the ambulance left, the asshole Willow's been hiding from told the deputies he was going to follow behind, still sticking to his story that Willow was his sister. That was the last time anyone saw him. He vanished, giving us and the bastard cops the answer to what kind of man he is.

The sheriff said he told them he had her birth certificate and his, or I should say, Ash's. But the dumbfuck sheriff never confirmed any of this. He didn't even get a last name. He just jumped at the chance to bust our balls. Did they really think we would be holding a girl against her will? That's never been our thing, and he knows it.

The hospital appointed a shrink to her case, but between the psychiatrist and the sheriff's department, they've gotten nowhere. She shut down, not speaking to anyone. And the fuckers won't let me in. Not that I haven't tried. Eventually they kicked me out of the hospital altogether, so I've been camped out across the street.

No one could even answer me the simple question: who is Willow?

That's when I took matters into my own hands and went out to the farm, retrieving a copy of one of the fingerprints she left behind in the paint on the chicken shed. It took the club's computer geek, Nate, less than five minutes to get a hit.

The entire table sat in silence as he read the report. She went missing at fifteen; she's twenty now. When he turned his computer around to show us, a young Willow with bright green eyes stared back at me. It was like a punch to the gut.

She's a missing child.

We haven't told the sheriff yet. We're still not sure who or what she is really hiding from. Who was the man who said he was her brother? Are there others she's running from? Is there someone at home waiting for a call to let them know whether she's been found dead or alive?

Dirk and Jesse hired the club's attorney to help her, and hopefully she will feel safe enough to talk to him. But I had to give her a sign that it was okay. That I was still here, fighting with her. After I finished playing the cello, I knew she understood. She placed her hand over her heart. I had to come up with a way to let her know she could trust him.

But now she's left the window, and I'm going insane waiting for Owen to let us know how she is.

My dad approaches me. Shit, when did he get here?

He crouches down in front of me. "Did your grandfather teach you to play?" he asks, his eyes bouncing over my face like he's seeing me for the first time.

I nod and my face gets hot as I put the cello back in the case.

He stands up, grabbing my arm. "Jackson, why have you never told anyone?"

Shrugging, I keep my eyes on my task. "I don't know. It's not a very manly thing, you know?"

"No, I don't know. You have an incredible talent, Son."

I pick up the cello and the chair, heading for my truck. He follows me.

"What else don't I know about you?"

Shaking my head, I place the cello behind the seat of the cab and toss the chair in the bed. "Dad, come on. It's just a stupid instrument. It's nothing. Grandpa used to teach me whenever I stayed out at the farm. No biggie. I'm sorry I didn't tell you. I didn't think it mattered."

"Does it help?" he asks.

I sigh loudly and look up at the white puffy clouds floating overhead. "It slows my brain down, yes. But it's something I like to keep private. Okay?"

He leans against the truck, facing me. "You were just playing across the street from the hospital. I don't think that's too private."

Here we go. Another lecture about Willow is coming; I can feel it. Especially now that he knows her history. Which is total BS because there are a lot of people in the club who have experienced trauma in their lives.

"It was private. A private concert for her, and I don't give two fucks if you like it or not, old man."

He pushes me against the truck roughly. "But I do give two fucks about you." He shoves away from me. "She's a missing kid, Jackson. Do you know what that means?"

I rub my hand over the side of my neck. I've never seen my dad so riled up. But I guess I've also never talked back to him like that.

"You don't have any idea what she's been through," he continues.

My dad and I have never fought. Never. And it's not in me to start now, but I have to get through to him. I don't know why I have this overwhelming urge to help her, but I do. So, I take my tone down a notch and try a calmer way of handling this.

"No, I don't, but you do."

His hands fall to his sides.

"And my mom did. No one was there to help her. We can help this girl, Dad. I know this is what my angel mom would want me to do," I say, shoving my hands in my pockets. I haven't called her that since I was a child, and my mention of it makes him spin around, digging his thumb and finger into his eyes.

My biological mom and adopted dad were friends. Friends who found themselves in a very bad situation. My dad made it out, but my mother never did.

"Jackson, the club has been through so much …" he sighs loudly, raising his head to look at the building in front of us.

"You're right. We have. But who better than the Skulls to help this girl?"

Willow is standing at the window watching us, her hands pressed against the screen. Her eyes are locked on my father's. He must smile at her because she returns a shy one of her own.

And then our phones ding at the same time. It's Owen texting to the club's group message.

She's agreed to talk to the sheriff but only if Jackson is there with her.

Owen is standing at the window beside her now.

My dad speaks to me over his shoulder. "This isn't something you can start and not finish, Son. That's all I'm trying to say. She has a long road ahead of her."

"And I have an empty space on the back of my bike to take her down that road."

He looks back up at them. "What do you feel when you look at her?" he asks.

I stare at the beautiful girl with green eyes and freckles. "Safe," I answer without thought.

This makes him turn back to me, concern creasing the corner of his eyes.

I didn't mean to say that. Why the fuck did I say that?

His shoulders fall as he replies back to the group. My phone dings.

Call the sheriff. Make it so.

He stares at me as I read his message.

Owen instantly walks away from the window, his phone going to his ear.

Willow climbs up on the sill, hugging herself.

"She shouldn't have to comfort herself," I say out loud.

My dad closes the distance between us, wrapping his arms around me and patting my back. "No one should. Your angel mom would be real proud of you."

Chapter Twenty-Two

Willow

I've thought about this day since I woke up in the back of Bradley's van. Owen gave the hospital my name and what I guess is the club's contact information and demanded they release me. I guess that's okay. I'm not sure I felt safe here. Bradley could easily convince a nurse to let him in. He has that way about him.

Owen says we are meeting with the sheriff and then we will go from there. That is the part I'm worried about. *Go from there.* That sounds terrifying.

He also brought me something to wear. I feel somewhat human now that I'm dressed. The attorney the club hired is nice; he's taken care of everything. As we wait for the elevator to open to the main floor, he puts his hand on my shoulder.

"Jackson is waiting for us outside."

As soon as the elevator doors open, I run. The nurse hollers at me, but I don't stop. As soon as the door to the outside world slides open, I'm jump into his arms.

' Hey, it's okay, baby. I got you," Jackson says into my hair as I tuck my face into his neck.

And just like that, I don't feel so alone.

I don't think I've realized how lonely I've been. And not only during this hospital stay. I've been lonely the past eight years of my life.

It doesn't make any sense. I don't even know this man. The only thing I do know is that I want to. He doesn't set me on my feet, he just starts walking. Then, he gently sets me in the seat of his pickup truck.

He cradles my face in his hands, standing between my legs. "God, it's so good to see you. I've been so worried."

I stare into his warm, inviting eyes. "I was worried about you, too."

He pulls his head back. "Why?"

"I didn't want you to go to jail for me," I say quietly.

Jackson's father is standing a few feet away, talking with Owen but his eyes are trained on the two of us.

Jackson runs his thumbs over my cheeks. "Don't worry about me."

Owen approaches us. "We should get going."

I scoot back in the truck, pulling my legs in front of me. Everything is getting real. What if my mom really did let Bradley take me? Then I've made a fuss for nothing. It's not kidnapping if your mom gives you away. But she wouldn't do that. How would Bradley even have found her that night?

Owen pushes Jackson aside so he can speak directly to me. "Hey, I know this sounds scary, but you are safe. I can promise you that. You did nothing wrong. Just tell the truth about what happened. Okay?"

Avenging Skulls

I nod, keeping my eyes focused out the windshield.

"We'll meet you there." He gently closes the door.

Jackson slides behind the wheel as I tuck my hands under my legs, biting my bottom lip. Am I making a terrible mistake? Bradley is a dangerous man. Am I putting Jackson and his family at risk by doing this?

For years I've waited for someone to notice me. Every time I saw a missing person's poster, I hoped that one day I would see one for me and someone might recognize me. No one ever gave me a second glance, though. Bradley's smile and charm outshined me. I was just the plain, quiet girl at his side.

"How did you find out who I was?" I ask once we pull out of the parking lot.

"Your fingerprints," he answers.

My brows pull together and then I remember. *The chicken coop.*

He reaches over and wraps his tattooed hand around my much smaller one. "Your family will be happy to know you're safe," he tells me.

I don't have a family, but I don't say this. He will find out soon enough. I'm so nervous; I think I'm going to be sick. How much am I going to tell them?

We pull to a stop in front of a tall brick building. I press my hand to my stomach. I can't do this.

Jackson shuts off the engine and turns to me. "I'll be by your side the entire time." He keeps his eyes on me as he exits the truck, comes around to open my door, and takes my hand, squeezing it tightly.

Jackson's dad pats him on the back as we walk past. Owen and the sheriff are waiting for us inside the sheriff's office.

Everything after that is a blur. The next thing I know, I'm sitting across the table from several deputies, Jackson on one side of me and Owen on the other. I glance down the table and stare at the camera set up on a tripod.

"Just start with your full name, Willow. Then tell us your story in your own words. If there is anything that isn't clear, we'll save our questions till the end."

Jackson takes my hand in his again, and I take a deep breath and pause. Jackson thinks I wanted him here for support, but that's not it at all. I *want* to tell him my story.

So, I turn myself fully and speak directly to him with my hand still cradled in his strong grip. "My name is Willow Taylor."

The sheriff begins to grumble that I'm not facing them, but the female deputy stops him. "Continue, Miss Taylor."

I keep my eyes trained on Jackson, and I tell him how I met the man who took me. He listens to every word, never once turning away.

"And when I woke up ..."

I stretch awake, not opening my eyes, happy to wake up on a soft mattress instead of the hard attic floor. But an unfamiliar scent stirs a sense of unease in my belly. Slowly, I blink my eyes open. I bolt upright, my pulse spiking. Our eyes meet in the rearview mirror. He glances over his shoulder for traffic, then slows to a stop as he clicks the lock button on the doors, trapping me inside the van with him.

He climbs out of the driver's side and crouches down between the two front seats, leveling me with his icy blue stare. "I found your mom. She said she didn't want you to be alone anymore. She said I could bring you with me."

"No," I whisper, scooting farther back on the bed.

Avenging Skulls

He points to a tiny fridge. "There's snacks and water in there. Help yourself." He turns to climb back in his seat when I stop him.

"She wouldn't do that. I want to go back. Take me back," I say in panic, the air stuck in my lungs.

He moves toward me and sits on the edge of the bed. He taps my knee with one finger and smiles. It sends a thousand insects scurrying up my spine.

"I know this is hard for you right now, but you'll see how good it can be with me. Look, she even packed a bag for you."

He hands me my butterfly bag, and I hug it to my chest.

When I begin to cry, he reaches for me, dragging me across the bed and onto his lap. He begins to pet my hair. "Shh, this what your mom wanted. It's for the best. I'd never lie to you."

I watch out the window as cars go by. All unaware of the terror I'm experiencing inside the van parked along the side of the interstate.

"I'm going to take care of you, Willow."

"Willow. Willow," Jackson says, gently shaking my shoulders.

Blinking wildly, I pull away from him.

"I think that's enough for today," Owen says. "You have her name and the city she was living in at the time of her abduction. In the meantime, she'll be staying at Maggie Reynolds home."

The deputies sitting across from us look like they want to argue, but they don't.

"You have my number if there is something urgent that comes up," he says, helping me from my chair.

Raffe rises from where he was waiting outside the door. I stand by Jackson's side numbly as they visit with Owen. The sheriff pauses beside us. "I'll send some of my guys out to the farm to keep an eye on things."

"I think I'll go sit in the truck," I say, feeling like I've upended all of these people's lives.

Raffe grabs my hand. "I'll go with her. Stay and take care of things. She'll be okay," he tells Jackson.

As soon as the door opens, I suck in a large breath and double over. Raffe waits for me to get my bearings and then he helps me in the truck.

"I rode with Owen, but I need a ride back to the hospital to get my bike," he tells me while gently nudging me over to the middle of the seat.

I slide my hands under my legs and focus on the scar on my knee. My mom took good care of my knee when I fell off my bike, but it left a scar nonetheless. My mind always goes to the same thing when I think of her. *Your mom said I could take you … I'd never lie to you.*

"I was taken, too," Jackson's dad says, breaking the silence.

When I don't respond, he continues. "It's not your fault."

"I was stupid. It *was* my fault," I tell him.

His arm slides behind me, resting on the back of the seat. "He preyed on you, Willow. He knew you were alone."

Jackson comes out and hops in the truck, sandwiching me between the two of them. He drapes his arms over the steering wheel and sighs. "They recommended we stay at the warehouse."

I blink at him. What is the warehouse? No, I don't want to stay there. I want to go back to the trees. I begin to shake my head.

"That might be a good idea. The girls will be there …"

I sit up straight. "No, I want to go back to Miss Maggie's farm," I say, crossing my arms over my chest.

Jackson pulls my arms down, taking my hands in his. "Willow, there is better security at the warehouse. Don't worry; it's not as cold as it sounds, and there are trees there and a lake."

No. No, I don't want to go anywhere else.

"Billie Rose lives on the other side of the lake," he continues to try and coax me.

"I promised Miss Maggie I would take care of Fred and the chickens and the pigs and ..." My face drops. "And you," I finish quietly.

Raffe pulls out his phone and makes a call. "Hey, can you see who would be up to providing some security out at Maggie's?" He pauses. "She doesn't want to stay at the warehouse, Dirk. Yeah, I know. No, she doesn't need to go up to the damn cabin. Just see who you can round up."

"If we stay at the farm, you have to sleep inside the house. No more hanging out by yourself in the woods," Jackson announces, laying out the rules.

Relief washes over me. "Okay," I say eagerly, lifting my face toward him.

He tucks a strand of hair behind my ear, his gaze bouncing over my face. "Would you like to stop and visit her?"

"Miss Maggie?" I ask, bouncing on the seat in excitement.

He nods, chuckling lightly.

"Yes, please. I would very much like to see her."

Jackson leans over, looking at his dad. "Do you want me to drop you off before we head over there?"

Raffe runs his hand through his greying hair and sighs. "As much as I love seeing that old woman, I think I'll pass. I'm going to see about getting some better security set up at the farm."

"Sounds good, old man." Jackson fires up his truck and spins out of the parking lot.

I grab the dashboard, trying to steady myself.

"Not necessary, Son," Raffe scolds, but I catch the hint of a smile on his face.

"I hate those fucking pricks. They would have kept her there all day if Owen hadn't stepped in."

Raffe runs his fingers down his beard. "They were only trying to get as much information as possible. Hopefully, they find that fucker and soon."

I listen to their banter back and forth. The way they speak to each other is so natural and easy.

Jackson shakes his head, lighting up a cigarette. "We should have just found him ourselves. Save all this bullshit hassle they're going to make her go through. The system sucks."

Biting my lip, I stare out the windshield. What kind of hassle is it going to be? Won't they just find him and put him in jail?

"Sometimes we have to do things the right way," Raffe says.

Jackson snorts. "Yeah, the right way. Dad, you know he isn't going to get what he deserves if we go this route."

My head continues to bounce back and forth between the two of them, a headache slowly creeping up on me. I don't understand any of this.

Avenging Skulls

"She has a family, Jackson, they need to be notified. She doesn't belong to us," he says as the truck pulls into the hospital parking lot.

I'm about to tell them I don't have a family when we stop beside his bike.

"You're wrong about that, old man. She does belong to us, and you know it. You think she found herself at the farm by chance?"

The two men stare at each other over the top of my head.

In a quiet voice, I speak up. "It ... it was by chance. I took the train," I try to explain. I don't want them to fight over me. "I'm sorry I've made so much trouble for the both of you."

Raffe gets out, waiting to close the door until I slide over to the seat he vacated. He stands beside me, placing his hand on the back of my head. "I'm glad you found us, sweetheart. Jackson is right; you're right where you belong. Please don't think I'm upset with you. I'm only angry at the situation. You were fifteen," he chokes and then he turns away and gently shuts my door.

As we wait for him to get on his bike, Jackson's phone dings. He pulls it out of his pocket, flicking his cigarette out the open window. He laughs. "Looks like we don't have to go to Grandma Maggie. She came to us. She asked someone from the club to take her out to the farm."

I give him a small smile and then turn back to watch as Raffe pulls away. He said someone took him, too. The ink on his skin makes sense now. I run my hand over my leg. Bradley always liked that my skin was unmarred. My eyes roam over Jackson's arms as he turns the wheel, guiding us out of the parking lot. I like their skin. It's interesting; it makes them stand out. I've never stood out.

No one ever notices me.

Miss Maggie comes out of the farmhouse as soon as we pull in. She waves for me to go to her as she waits on the front porch. All of my stuff is still underneath it.

Jackson must notice where my attention is. "I'll crawl under there and get it. Go on. She needs to pinch someone's cheeks, and I'm offering you up as the sacrifice."

I tip my head shyly and make my way over to her. And yes, she pinches my cheeks just like he said.

"Oh, honey, I've been so worried about you. I'm glad you're home." She doesn't hesitate this time, pulling me right over the threshold with her.

The big guy who was with Jackson stands from his chair as we walk into the kitchen. He wipes his hands down the front of his jeans, swallowing the bite of food he just put in his mouth. "Hey, I'm Brody, Jackson's best friend," he says, holding his hand out to me.

I take it but then I hear Billie Rose call out from upstairs. "I'm his best friend!" she yells.

Miss Maggie pushes me down in a chair, shoving a glass of tea in front of me. Elijah walks around the corner, holding the little girl I saw the other day.

"Billie Rose is just finishing up, Maggie. I think we are going to head out." The little girl takes a sucker out of her mouth and sticks it in his.

He wiggles his eyebrows at her, making her giggle.

"You two just sit down. I've made enough to feed an army. We aren't wasting it."

Brody is already back to his plate. Elijah rolls his eyes but plops down beside me, dropping the tiny child into my lap as he does.

Avenging Skulls

Oh, oh. I don't know what to do with one of these. The little girl giggles again, putting her sticky hands on my face. She leans over and rubs her button nose over mine.

Billie Rose comes out. "Elijah, she's all sticky." She tries to take the child out of my arms, but the little girl buries her face in my chest, her tiny fingers latching on tightly to the material of my dress.

"She's okay," I say hesitantly, bringing my hand up to run over the child's dark brown curls.

Jackson walks in, shoving Billie Rose out of the way. "Grandma, are you throwing parties without me?" he teases, giving her a quick peck on the cheek.

"Sit, sit. You all need to get some food in your bellies." She shoos him and everyone else to fill their plates.

He fills one for me before loading up his own. The little girl in my lap instantly dive bombs him as he sits down.

"Hey, Squirrel, what are you doing?" He laughs, hugging her to his chest. She squeals and then turns around on his lap and starts plucking food from his plate. "Okay, yeah sure, go ahead." He looks at Billie Rose. "Do you guys feed her?"

She reaches over me to smack him on the arm. "Yes, we feed her," she mocks with wide open eyes.

Everyone laughs and jokes at the table. No one treats me any differently than they did when they first found me. I watch as Miss Maggie hustles around with a big smile on her face. I can tell she loves these people very much.

It's such a contrast to the life I've been living that it overwhelms me … in a good way, I think. I jump up and rush to Miss Maggie, wrapping my arms around her and burying my face in the old woman's hefty bosom.

"There, there, child. It's okay. It's okay," she shushes. The room quiets down around us.

"You're the angel, Miss Maggie. It's you," I whisper.

"Oh, honey." She pushes me back so she can see my face. My heart melts even more when she wipes my tears with her apron. "No need for tears. You're safe now." She pulls me back into her chest, and she hugs me so tight and with so much warmth that I feel some of the tiny cracks in my heart meld together.

"Can I call you Grandma Maggie too?" I ask on a hiccup.

She pats my back. "Of course, of course. I'm everyone's grandma around here. You know, I didn't think I would be a grandma after my daughter disappeared, but look at me now."

I cry a little more but then she grabs me by my shoulders and guides me to the sink to wash my face with a warm washcloth. Her eyes lock on mine. "Life has a way of taking you right where you belong. Sometimes that road is narrow and scary but eventually it widens out and you find yourself –"

I cut her off. "You find yourself in a beautiful place with trees, and chickens, and a wonderful grandmother."

She chuckles, the soft skin around her eyes wrinkling. "Yes, you understand."

I nod, trying to make the tears stop.

"This family is going to take care of you, and you're going to let us." She points a bony finger in my face. "And don't you worry over how much you think it's putting us out because it's not. We've all had troubles. All of us. You're no different."

Straightening my shoulders, I give her a small smile. "Yes, ma'am," I tell her. I'm happy she isn't giving me any other options. I don't want another option. I want her *and* them.

I glance over my shoulder, and everyone quickly looks away, going back to their food. Everyone except Jackson. He blatantly stares at me. His gaze softens when I smile at him, embarrassingly hiccupping again.

She scoots me back to my chair. "Now, who's ready for dessert?"

Brody raises his hand while still shoveling food in his mouth.

Everyone laughs and goes back to their easy banter. Jackson reaches under the table and wraps his hand around my thigh, giving it a gentle squeeze. "You better eat up. Grandma makes the best apple pie in the entire state."

After everyone gets their fill, Billie Rose and her family head out with Grandma Maggie. She tells Jackson that she and Billie Rose set me up in the master bedroom.

"If she needs anything else, you tell one of the girls." She pinches his cheek before turning to me one last time.

She brushes my hair out of my face and stares at me. "My Harold would have loved you."

Jackson, Brody, and I wave to them as the gravel crunches under their tires and they pull away.

"You guys head inside and get some shut eye. I'm taking the first shift along with Petey. He's already out here somewhere. He's keeping an eye on the back, and I'll hang out here on the porch."

"Thanks, brother," Jackson says, patting him on the back.

"So, you two are brothers?" I ask quietly.

They both laugh. "Brothers as any of us can be. In our club, we all consider each other brothers. Not by blood but by choice."

My eyes widen. "That's wonderful. Everyone should have a brother."

"We're all family here," Brody says, placing his hand over Jackson's chest. "Go on, get your girl inside."

His girl?

I like the sound of that.

When I pass by Brody, he places his hand on my shoulder. "We'll keep you safe, little fairy."

I stare up into his scruffy face. "You seem like a very good brother, Brody."

He leans down and places a kiss on the very top of my head. Ash used to kiss me like this …

I miss him so much.

Chapter Twenty-Three

Jackson

She walks around the room Billie Rose set up for her. It's my grandparent's old room. She runs her hand over the handmade quilt on the bed and smiles at it before making her way to the window. The breeze makes the sheer curtains billow into the room.

"Your club has men out there?" she asks, her hands leaning on the windowsill.

I remain in the doorway. "Yes, you don't have to worry. If Bradley is out there, he won't be getting past them."

She turns around to face me, perching her butt on the sill. "The hospital bed was the first real bed I'd slept in in such a long time."

"Well, I hope this one feels like you're sleeping on a cloud. Hospital beds aren't notoriously known for being comfortable."

Her next question is asked while her eyes are still focused on the bed. "Where will you sleep?" she asks.

point to the room across the hall. "I'll be right in there. It's my room. I've always slept there when visiting my grandparents."

She wrings her hands together, biting her bottom lip. She's nervous.

"Do you want to play a game of Candyland before we hit the hay?" It's been a long day, but I think she needs something to help her unwind and take the focus off everything that has happened.

Willow hops up, a bright smile pulling at the corners of her mouth. "Yes!" she says, excited.

We head back downstairs, and she watches as I go to the closet. The top shelf is packed high with all sorts of board games.

"Miss Maggie has so many wonderful things in her house," she says as Fred leaves his dog bed and settles himself beside her on the floor. She leans over and places a kiss on the top of his head. The dog always has sad eyes, he's a basset hound after all, but I swear he looks happy tonight.

She continues to scratch his ears as I set up the game.

We play quietly, the only sound coming from the tick of the clock in the kitchen. I can't explain it, but when I'm with her my mind slows down and I can think clearly. I don't have to worry that she's with me because of the way I look or because I'm part of the club. I can be myself and that makes it easy.

When she wins, she stares at me with an expression I can't translate. "You *let* me win," she accuses quietly, her voice catching.

"No. No way. You won fair and square," I tell her, picking up the pieces and placing them back in the box.

Her gaze bounces over the room, her eyes blinking rapidly.

"Hey." I stop what I'm doing and brush my hand down her arm.

Avenging Skulls

She swipes tears away from her cheeks. "He never let me win."

I'm not sure what she means by that, so I question her gently. "You played games?"

Fred scoots closer to her, resting his head in her lap. She laughs lightly, smiling at him. "We played his games."

Taking a deep breath, I rise to put the game away. I don't know what to say to that. When I turn around, I find her right behind me.

"I'm sorry," I tell her. "I ... I don't know what you've been through, and I don't want to upset you by saying the wrong thing."

"Please don't worry about it. I want you to be yourself around me. Nothing you say will be wrong if it comes from here," she says, placing her hand over my heart. "Why did you let me win?" she asks.

"I wanted to see you smile," I tell her without hesitation, and it earns me just that ... a beautiful smile, one that reaches her stunning green eyes.

"That was very kind of you." Her face turns pink. "But next time, I'm going to beat you for real," she teases.

I detect her nervousness at joking with me. Her body tenses as she waits for my response.

"Oh, it's on," I tell her, gesturing to all the games. "I'm a master at all of these."

A million emotions play over the soft features of her face, and before I know what is happening, her lips are on mine. She kisses me with such passion it takes my breath away. When she ends the kiss, she takes a step back.

"Just be you, Jackson. That's all I need."

I give her a small nod, my hair falling over my eyes. In the second it takes me to brush it away, she's gone. The echo of her soft footsteps floats down the stairwell.

My breath is caught in my throat until the soft click of her bedroom door closing releases it. It comes out in a loud rasp. I grab my knees, praying they keep me upright. I let her kiss me. I haven't let that happen since …

She surprised me with it, and I didn't hate it. I didn't feel like shoving her away from me. A huge weight lifts off my shoulders. I didn't realize how much I've missed this feeling – the excitement, that warm feeling that tugs low in your belly. Lanie stole all that from me.

But Willow unknowingly gave it back. She doesn't realize the gift she's handed me.

I feel like a man again.

Chapter Twenty-Four

Willow

I slip the nightgown Billie Rose left for me over my head, watching it caress my naked skin as it falls over my body. When it drops into place, I stare at my reflection in the mirror that Jackson had been working on in the barn. It's sweet that he's placed it in here for me.

It's still so strange to see myself. A woman stares back at me. I don't really know her. I've kept her hidden, and I'm so glad I did because tonight she was finally able to come out.

I'm a woman, I tell myself, spinning around in a circle, the bottom of the pale blue nightgown billowing around my thighs. When I hear Jackson's boots thudding up the stairs, I rush to the door, pressing my ear against it.

He pauses outside. I inhale a quick breath, waiting to see what he does next. My heart kicks up but then he steps away. The door across the hall opens and closes with a soft click. I release the air in my lungs as the quiet settles around me.

He didn't lie about where he would be sleeping.

I turn back to the mirror. "I think we can trust him," I whisper.

Maybe Bradley's right, and I am crazy.

If I am, he made me that way.

I climb into bed, reaching over to shut off the bedside lamp. Sitting there, I wait to lie down until my eyes adjust to the dark. The moon shines in through the curtains, so it doesn't take long. I slide my legs and arms over the sheet, stretching out as far as I can.

Smiling at the ceiling, I let myself enjoy the moment. The bed is so soft, and the sheets are cool across my skin. I take a deep breath and then another, letting go of the tension I've been holding in my muscles for way too long.

But as I relax, something begins to happen. It rushes my system, and the only warning is the ringing in my ears. The earthquake started when I decided to run. The ripple effect has been slowly gaining on me, and now that I've let my guard down, the tsunami is here.

Bolting upright, I cry out, my hands flying to my mouth as I try to stuff it all back in. I shouldn't have let myself relax.

Jackson knocks on the door. "Willow, are you okay?"

This is what I was afraid of. The storm is finally here.

The door opens, and he takes a step toward the bed.

My eyes must look wild because he slows. *Oh no, he's going to think Bradley was right and I'm crazy.* Another sound breaks free from my soul as I open my mouth to tell him I'm fine.

But he already knows I'm not.

Avenging Skulls

The bed dips as he presses his knee into the mattress, climbing up beside me. He wraps his arms around my shoulders as I hug my knees to my chest, rocking myself back and forth on the bed.

"You're safe," his gravelly voice whispers against my ear. "You're safe. You're safe. You're safe," he repeats.

He decides to crawl behind me, placing me between his legs. His arms wrap around me again. "Let it out, baby. Let it out."

My body aches as it purges years of confusion, fear, sadness, and loneliness. The pain is so real; I think it might kill me. But it's okay because I got to live amongst the trees, if only for a short time. And I got to meet Jackson, the man trying his best to be my port in the storm. But even he's afraid my tether is slipping.

"You're safe, Willow. You're safe, baby. Just hold on; I'm not letting you go," he chants louder and louder.

And he doesn't. He sits with me through the night, letting me cry. When I quiet, he shoves the covers back and then slides under them, pulling me with him. My body is pliable, rung out and dry. Jackson presses his body against mine, but I don't even flinch. My exhaustion won't allow it.

"I'm sorry," I say quietly, embarrassed now that the storm is dissipating.

"Don't be. I'm glad you got that shit all out." He presses a soft kiss to the back of my head. "Now I get the chance to fill you back up with happiness."

My eyes fall closed. "Happiness?" I mumble.

"Yes, happiness. Trust me, your smile is going to be the rainbow at the end of this storm."

I smile weakly.

He must sense it. "Isn't it beautiful?" he says as sleep steals me away from him.

~~~~~

When I wake, Jackson's still here. He's turned toward me, his arm resting over the covers, his hand laying lightly over my hip.

Bradley was always up before me. I never really had the chance to study him as he slept. He would never have allowed me to see him in such a vulnerable position.

Jackson is incredibly handsome, in a messy, dark sort of way. My eyes roam over the ink on his skin. It tells me a story, and I like that. I'm sure there so much more to him, though. He looks like the other men in his club, but he's different. He's special.

The light peeks in through the curtains. The animals need tending. Careful not to wake him, I slide out of the bed, his hand falling off me with a soft thud.

Quietly, I gather my clothes and tiptoe out of the room.

Once I'm dressed, I head outside. Brody is sitting in a chair in the backyard with another man – the scariest looking man I've ever seen.

I pause on the top step, and Brody laughs. "This is Petey. Don't let his looks scare you, darlin. The ladies in the club all love him, so he can't be that bad."

But there's something I recognize in the black pit of his eyes. This man is a killer.

Petey nods his head toward me in greeting.

Avenging Skulls

Brody continues. "It was a quiet night. My guess is that asshole you're running from is long gone."

Highly doubtful, but I'm glad it was an uneventful evening, nonetheless.

"Are you guys going to be here for breakfast?" I ask as I turn the outdoor faucet on to fill Fred's water bowl.

"Yes ma'am," Petey answers.

I straighten, shielding my eyes from the sun to look at him. "Good. Give me thirty minutes, and I'll get it started."

Brody hops up. "I'll help you with the critters," he says, falling in step with me.

We work quietly together. Brody is older than Jackson, but I can see why they are such good friends. He's easy to be around, and he takes up space with you without any expectations. I think Jackson has a hard time showing people who he really is. I'm not sure why. His family clearly loves him.

We're gathering eggs when Jackson barrels in, still shirtless, his jeans unzipped and his black boxers showing. I swallow hard as we stare at each other. He's breathing heavy.

"I thought you ..."

"Jesus, man, settle the fuck down. Your girl is good," Brody says, stepping out of the shed to give us some privacy.

There it is again. *Your girl.*

My shirt is full of eggs, and I hold it open to show him. "I'm going to make us breakfast."

He glances down at my t-shirt before rushing toward me, stopping just short of crushing the eggs between us. He lets out a frustrated groan, running his fingers through his hair. "I thought you ran away," he says, his voice cracking.

I have an overwhelming urge to hug him, but I can't let go of my shirt. Shrugging my shoulders, I stare into his warm brown eyes. "I won't run away, Jackson. I promise."

He runs his hand over the dusting of hair on his chest. "Are you feeling okay?"

I nod, warmth rushing to my cheeks. "I'm fine. I'm so embarrassed about last night." I drop my gaze, spying a basket in the corner. I walk over to it and gently lay each egg inside.

"You have nothing to be embarrassed about." He holds the door open for me as we step outside. Reaching over, he takes the basket from my hand and then sets it on the ground.

The minute it hits the grass, he turns and pushes me against the side of the shed. A little woosh of air rushes out of me. His bare skin presses against my chest, and a strange feeling tugs at my gut. He scares me but ... it's exciting. I'm excited.

His brown eyes pierce mine. "I want to take the pain from you. I want to pull it from your body slowly and wear it like a badge of honor. Last night," he pauses, his breath sending stray hairs to flutter around my face, "I hate that someone caused you so much pain."

The chickens are clucking around our feet, but we are caught in the moment, neither of us able to look away. "How did I find you?" I rasp, my heart thumping against the hardness of his chest.

He cradles my face in his hands and presses his lips to my forehead, whispering against it, "I don't know, but I never want to be away from you. That must sound scary after what you've been through."

My fingers trace one of the black designs on his skin before I look up at him. "You do scare me but in a good way, Jackson. You're nothing like him. I know this."

He breathes out a sigh of relief. "You'll tell me if I ever make you uncomfortable, yeah?"

I give him a small smile. "Yeah."

The back door slams, and a woman starts yelling. "Where is she?"

My eyes widen, but Jackson chuckles to himself. "It's my sister. I'm sure she's dying to meet you."

When we step around the back of the shed, a delicate looking woman pulls away from a mountain of a man and rushes toward us. She stops in front of me, covering her mouth as tears pool in the corners of her eyes.

"Grandma Maggie has told me so much about you," she says, her gaze darting over my face.

Suddenly, she has me wrapped up in her arms, hugging me to her. I keep my arms at my side as she squeezes the life out of me.

Jackson locks eyes with me and mouths an *I'm sorry*.

She releases me long enough to give me another look and then I'm pressed to her once again.

These are the huggiest people I've ever met.

It's nice.

Chapter Twenty-Five

Jackson

I watch my sister squeeze the life out of my girl.

Brody's right. She's mine.

When did that happen?

I'm pretty sure it began with the creation of time. It's the only explanation I can come up with. Our souls had to have known each other before. Does it scare me? It should, but it doesn't. The only thing that worries me is that I'm going to scare her away.

This feeling is so intense; I can't reign it in. It's like a thousand galloping horses pulling me toward my destiny with her. My fingers tap over my jeans, the notes of a new song tugging at the tips of my fingers. I wish everyone would leave so I could transfer all this energy to my cello.

Lily barrels into me next. "Oh, Jackson. Jenny would be so happy you're helping this girl," she whispers into my ear.

I set my sister back on her feet, gently prying her away from me. My sister wears her heart on her sleeve. She doesn't hide how she feels.

"Willow, this is my sister, Lily. Lily, meet Willow." I motion between the two of them.

Lily wipes at her eyes. "I'm sorry. I ... like I said, Grandma Maggie told me how sweet you were and well, I couldn't wait to meet you. I made Dan drive me straight here from her apartment."

Willow drops her gaze and leans into me. I wrap my arm around her.

"It's nice to meet you," she says quietly.

My sister's face falls when she recognizes Willow's pain. "I brought you some more clothes and things," she tells her.

Willow brushes her face over my arm, a sign that she is uncomfortable under all the scrutiny. "We were getting ready to whip up some breakfast. Do you guys want to join us?"

Big Dan rubs his belly. "That's a stupid question, kid."

We all laugh, and Willow relaxes against me, happy the focus is no longer on her. When we get inside, she sets right to work, looking through all the cupboards to acclimate herself to the kitchen. The guys stay outside, cracking beers by the fire pit without a care in the world that it isn't even noon yet.

"We had a late night," I explain to Lily as I pull the milk and butter for pancakes and eggs from the fridge.

Willow turns away from me at the mention of her distress.

"It's supposed to storm again tonight. The weather's been crazy," my sister says.

I give her a small smile in thanks. It didn't storm last night, but it deflects from the real reason we were up.

Willow isn't the first girl we've been around who's been hurt, and I'm sure she won't be the last. That's what we do. We help people. What's the point of life if you don't live to help others?

"How do you all like your eggs?" Willow asks, her voice soft and sweet, such a contrast from the demons that were being wrenched from her a few hours ago.

I bump my hip to hers as I take the space beside her at the stove. "There's only one way to eat eggs, and that is sunny-side-up," I tell her.

Her green eyes narrow on mine when I add, "with ketchup." I shake the bottle in front of her face for effect.

She starts to laugh but then stops, pretending to gag.

I place my hand over my heart. "Please don't tell me you don't agree. I don't think we can be friends if you don't eat ketchup on your eggs."

She waves the spatula toward the bottle. "You keep that stuff away from my eggs. Yuck."

She sticks out her tongue, and my cock jumps in my pants.

Wow, fuck. That hasn't happened in a while.

The distraction my dick caused gives her the opportunity she was waiting for. She snatches the ketchup out of my hands and holds it behind her back.

I wrap my arms around her playfully, pretending to try and get it from her. I have her bent over backward, my face inches from hers, when my sister clears her throat to remind us we're not alone.

Lily's gaze bounces between the two of us. Her brows pull together. "How long have you two known each other?"

Avenging Skulls

I straighten, pulling Willow with me. "Oh, I don't know." I shrug. "A couple of weeks."

Willow nods in agreement.

Lily laughs lightly. "Okay."

Can she see it, too? That our souls have known each other considerably longer?

My phone vibrates in my pocket, so I pull it out. It's the sheriff. "I'll be right back," I tell the girls.

I step out front and answer the call. We're scheduled to continue Willow's statement at three today. I wonder why he's calling. Maybe something came up, and they have to cancel. Or maybe they found Bradley.

That would suck.

I'm hoping *she* finds Bradley before the cops do. I want him gone from this earth, not just locked in a cell.

"Hello."

"Hey there, Jackson. Callin' to give you a heads up that Miss Taylor's family has been notified. They took the first flight out and should be here within the hour. I sent a deputy to meet them at the airport."

I glance back in the house, spotting my sister and Willow with their heads bowed looking at something on my sister's phone. "Oh, okay. Yeah, yeah. I'm sure they were happy to get the good news."

"I guess her mother fainted when they told her. But anyway, you'll prepare her?"

"Sure. Yeah, thanks for calling. We'll see you later."

When I get inside, Willow's green eyes catch mine and she pauses, the spatula in her hand floating mid-air. "Something's happened," she rasps.

I nod. "Your family's been notified. They'll be there today."

Her eyes crinkle at the corners. "My family?"

I step toward her, taking the spatula out of her hand and passing it off to my sister, who picks up where Willow left off. I guide Willow to a chair and sit her down.

"The sheriff said your mom was really happy. She hopped on the first plane she could find."

Willow's breathing picks up, and she begins to tug at the bottom of her t-shirt.

"Hey, slow down." I rub my thumb over her cheek. "It's okay."

She shakes her head. "He told me she let him take me." Her breath starts to come out in short bursts.

Lily joins us, running her hand over the back of Willow's head. "Take a deep breath, sweetie."

Willow continues to shake her head. "I'm so stupid. I believed him." Tears begin to leak out the corners of her bright green eyes. "She's really coming?" she asks, pleading with me for reassurance.

"She is," I tell her, my heart breaking. I'm getting a glimpse of the little girl who sat in the back of that asshole's creepy van, thinking her mother had given her away.

My sister and I exchange a glance. She pulls up a chair beside us. "Willow, men like the one who took you, they're liars. I'm sure your mother never would have let him take you. But it wasn't your fault if you believed him. You were a child."

Willow balls up her fists and rubs at her eyes. "I don't think I can eat now."

Lily goes back to the stove to tend the eggs. "How about you try to eat a little. You need to keep something in your stomach."

I scoot her chair to the table and take the seat beside her. She reaches out and pulls my grandmother's little notebook toward her. I saw what Grandma Maggie had scribbled on it about walking into the trees and coming out taller. I wasn't sure what it meant, but maybe grandma left it here for her.

Willow glances at me nervously before focusing back on the notebook. "There is more to the story than I shared yesterday," she says with a slight tremble in her voice.

"It will be okay. Just tell the truth," I reassure her.

The smell of bacon wafts out the backdoor, luring the men inside. "Smells good, babe," Dan says, swatting Lily on her butt as he walks past her.

He parks his large frame right beside Willow. She swipes at her eyes, embarrassed they came in to see her crying.

"So, I hear you've been keeping this one in line." He nods his head toward me.

She giggles, her tears quickly dissipating. "I'm trying, but it's a lot of work," she jokes back with him.

"You know, its fine you've been hiding out here, but you really need to come to the warehouse. The club is dying to meet the girl who's keeping Jackson's feet firmly on the ground."

Willow runs her finger over the notebook. "I don't want to put anyone else in danger," she says quietly.

"The only person in danger is that asshole. He isn't getting to you here or there," Dan states matter of fact. He places his finger under her chin. "You're safe with this club. You understand?"

She nods, more tears pooling in her eyes.

"My daughter, Kelsie, the girl you met at the hospital, she really wants you to come to the barbeque tomorrow night. You two are about the same age. I think you should join us."

Willow looks to me.

"It's up to you," I tell her. I don't want to pressure her, but my days revolve around the club. I want to share that part of my life with her.

She gives him a tiny nod.

"Good," he says, leaning back while his wife sets a plate of food in front of him. He looks up at my sister like she is the sole reason the sun shines. Then, he directs his focus back to Willow.

"And if you're ever in need of some ink, you come see me. Don't let Jesse talk you into going to her. I've got a perfect design in mind for you."

Willow's green eyes turn huge. "You're a tattoo artist?" she asks.

He nods while pouring syrup on his pancakes. Lily pushes a plate in front of Willow, then Big Dan leans over, adding syrup to Willow's as well. They're already taking care of her as if she were one of their own.

When he's finished, he picks up her fork, hands it to her, and answers, "Sure am."

Willow takes a bite, her mind busy with thoughts outside of herself. My sister raises her eyebrows as if to say *ha, I knew I could get her to eat.* I shake my head.

"I would love to get one, but right now I have so much …" Willow drops her head, not finishing her sentence.

He pours a glass of orange juice, handing it to her. "No hurry, sweetheart. You're not going anywhere. The club has already claimed you."

Jesus. Why did he say that?

But her shoulders drop, and a hint of a smile ghosts her face.

Dan winks at me.

My club has her.

Chapter Twenty-Six

Willow

The closer we get to the sheriff's department, the more I'm sure the pancakes I ate are going to retaliate.

"Tell me about your mom," Jackson says, pulling me from my manic thoughts.

"I don't know what to say. She was gone a lot the last few years I lived with her."

Lily helped me pick out a sundress to wear and helped me pin my hair away from my eyes. The clothes Grandma Maggie had given me were Lily's. We are both tiny and wear the same size. Anyway, Lily told me this dress always made her feel confident. I know she was trying to help, but I don't think anything could make me feel reassured in this moment. My mind is racing with a thousand scenarios of how seeing my mom for the first time might go.

"Did you two have a good relationship?" Jackson tries again to pull me out of my worries.

Avenging Skulls

I shake my head no, turning to look at a group of kids sitting on the curb with ice cream cones in their hands. They look like they don't have a care in the world. I bet this is an amazing place to grow up.

The streets here aren't lined with tents and drug addicts.

"We can stop at the ice cream shop on the way home," he tells me, noticing what has my attention. "They have the best chocolate shakes. It's really cool inside. You'll think you've stepped back in time."

"It looks like we've stepped back in time," Bradley says as he slides into the booth across from me, his eyes scanning the room.

The minute his gaze finds her, I know. She is his next mark.

My heart falls into the pit of acid in my gut, and I wonder what type of man requested her.

And I can't even warn her. The last time I tried, I made it worse. But maybe death isn't the worst thing that can happen to someone.

He nods for the waitress and catches not only her attention but the young girls as well. She smiles at him, and he gives her his most charming one back.

When his gaze finally slides back to me, he kicks my foot under the table. "Smile," he tells me, raising his brow in warning.

The waitress pauses by the table. "You ready, sweetie?" she asks him, totally ignoring me.

While he's ordering for the both of us, I risk a glance at the girl. She's pretending to eat a piece of toast her baby brother is shoving in her face. He's giggling so much his entire body is shaking in his highchair.

Another kick comes from under the table.

"We're here," Jackson says, pulling me from my thoughts. The young girl's smile fades from my mind.

I notice all the bikes parked around us, men with black jackets exactly like Jackson's are leaning against the building.

"Everyone wants to show you their support and make sure there's no trouble today," he tells me.

He goes to reach for his door, but I stop him, grabbing his arm. "Jackson. There is something I need to tell you."

But then something pulls my attention away from him. My mother is standing outside the door of the building, her hand covering her heart. All I can think about is how much her hair has greyed.

Jackson squeezes my hand and then hops out to open my door. She rushes toward us the minute I'm out of the truck, but I put my hand up, stopping her.

"Willow," she cries, her eyes darting around the bikers who have surrounded me.

I keep my hand extended. My heart pumping loudly in my ears as Jackson places his hand at the small of my back.

"Willow, baby, I'm so glad they found you," she continues.

No one *found* me.

An awkward silence hangs in the air. She hasn't moved, and a nervousness settles low in my belly.

And then someone walks up behind her.

My brain is confused.

It's not possible.

"Willow …" my brother says, stepping around my mother and barreling toward me.

He pushes his way through the crowd to get to me, but Jackson holds him back. "Slow down, man. Give her a minute. She's a little overwhelmed."

A little overwhelmed? Is that what I am?

"Why don't we all go inside?" the sheriff suggests, his arms out, trying to control the group that is slowly building around us.

"I think that's a good idea," my brother says, turning to escort my mother inside the building.

Jackson tugs at my arm, but my feet are firmly planted to the ground.

"I … I just need a minute," I say, stepping around to the back of the truck. Jackson follows me, but as soon as I'm out of arm's reach, I run.

"Willow!" he yells.

But I don't stop.

My brother wasn't really there, was he?

My last shred of sanity evaporates. I don't want to do this anymore.

I dart behind a building, then run alongside it and cut across someone's lawn, startling their poor cat. I'm losing my mind. I keep running, even though I hear many voices yelling for me to stop. I scramble down a steep ditch and crawl inside the drain tube that runs under the road above me.

Sucking in deep breaths, I try to slow my breathing. Quiet. I need to be quiet.

I cover my mouth and press my head to my knees. Ash is gone. That wasn't really him. He's gone. My mind is playing tricks on me.

A bike roars to a stop on the highway above. Boots stomp close to where I'm hiding. I scoot a little farther into the tube. Thank god it's dry in here.

"Honey, come on out. There could be spiders in there," Petey, the killer, says from outside the tube.

I angrily swipe at my tears. I'm not in the mood for this guy. "I'm not afraid of spiders, asshole."

He chuckles and then I hear Dirk. "Jesus Christ, please tell me she's not in that fucking thing."

"Yep," Petey says, popping the p.

"Well, I'm not going in after her." Dirk squats down and peers in at me. "Do you always have to hide in such tiny places?"

I ignore him.

"So, first thing," he holds up a finger, "I don't like it when anyone from my club runs. I'm getting too old for this shit."

"Good thing I'm not part of your club," I smart off. I'm not sure why I'm standing up for myself now. I guess I'm tired of being a doormat.

His eyebrow slowly raises to a very scary angle. "Oh, you're part of this club. You're Jackson's girl, so there isn't any other way."

I cross my arms across my chest because the more they say it, the more I want it to be true.

"So, do you need a minute? Because Skulls don't run and hide. We show up and kick ass." He shifts position, his fingers splaying out over the ground for balance. "You," he points to me, "are not alone. We have your back. So, whatever that was back there … we'll get you through it."

Avenging Skulls

"I ... I thought I saw a ghost, okay?" I sniff, turning away from him to stare down the long, dark tube. Only a sliver of light comes from the other end.

"Seeing things, huh? Well, that wasn't what I was expecting."

"Great. You think I'm crazy."

He shrugs. "Aren't we all?"

I wrap my arms around myself. "I thought I saw my brother, okay? He's dead. I know he's dead. Two military officers came to our house and told me so."

He gives me a funny look, but I keep going.

"I've been missing him so much that I think my brain made him up when I saw my mom. It's fine. I ... I just need a second to regroup, okay?"

He rubs his tattooed hand over the silver scruff on his face. "Take as long as you need. I'm going to have someone come back and give you a ride. I'd let Petey here give you a ride on the back of his bike, but I think Jackson would kill him."

My eyes go wide.

"Yeah, you only ride with Jackson unless it's an emergency. And this isn't one." He looks up at Petey. "Don't lose her. I'll send someone back with a truck."

He bends down one last time. "I'm going to tell you this as many times as it takes ... you're safe. Now, be good. No more running."

I give him a tiny grunt in response.

Once he's gone, Petey sits down in the ditch, facing away from me.

"You're not coming in to get me?" I taunt.

"Nope. Like I said, there are spiders in there."

"Please don't tell me someone like you is afraid of spiders. I don't buy it."

"Everyone's afraid of something, honey." He glances at me with his soulless black eyes and then turns away again.

We sit quietly for a few minutes, then I cautiously scoot out, sliding up beside him. "I'm sorry. That was rude of me. I don't know why I'm being so snarky. I'm usually well behaved."

He laughs. "Oh, I think snarky might be part of who you are. That asshole who kidnapped you just didn't let her out to play."

I bite my lip and watch the cars passing by on the highway. "Well, I don't even know you. I didn't mean any offense."

This time he looks directly at me, holding my gaze hostage. "You see it, don't you? You know what I am."

I blink a few times, trying to break the hold he has on me.

"Just so you know, I only take out the worst of the worst." He finally looks away.

I let out a long breath. "So, you're the one who gives the dead men to Jackson?" I ask.

His head snaps to mine, a questioning look on his face.

"I'm sorry." I shrink in on myself. "I saw Jackson toss one to the hogs. I wasn't snooping around." This is bad. What if he thinks I know too much?

He shakes his head and chuckles. "No worries, honey."

Avenging Skulls

We both get quiet again until Jackson's dad pulls up behind Petey's bike.

"Well, it looks like your ride is here."

I dust off my backside as we both stand. When I start to walk away, he stops me.

"The man who hurt you, I'm going to find him. He isn't going to hurt you or anyone else ever again. I promise."

And I believe him.

Both men are killers. It's just a matter of which one will prevail. The good guy has to win, right?

If Petey is indeed a *good* guy.

Chapter Twenty-Seven

Raffe

Dirk came back and explained the situation. No wonder she was freaked out; she thought her brother was dead. But he's very much alive. Jackson stayed back to talk with him privately, away from the deputies, and I'm going to go get her.

The mother wasn't too keen on them having a private conversation, but we didn't give her much choice. Jesse is with her now while they wait for Willow to return. A few minutes after Jesse sat down beside her, she gave me a look, tapped on her arm, and tipped her head toward Willow's mother. She was letting me know the woman shows signs of being an addict. Jesse is good at picking up on those things.

Willow and Petey are having a tense conversation as I step around the truck to open the door for her. She stares at him for a long time before giving him a curt nod and rushing toward me.

I pull her into my arms. "You okay, sweetie?" I ask.

She tenses in my hold but relaxes after a few seconds. I read once that you have to hug someone for twenty seconds for it to do any real good. This girl needs all the feel-good oxytocin she can get.

"I'm okay. I feel silly, really." When I finally let go, she offers me a weak smile. "Thank you for coming to get me."

"No worries." I help her into the truck, giving Petey a one fingered salute before pulling out onto the highway behind him.

"Dirk told me you thought you saw a ghost."

She nods, her cheeks turning bright pink. I see why Jackson is so enthralled by her. She's sweet; she reminds me a little bit of Lily.

I pull off the highway and into the drive-thru of a fast-food restaurant. "I need a coffee," I tell her. "You want something?"

She pauses a moment, but then nods her head. "Yeah, a coffee sounds great."

After we get our order, I park in the lot. "Why'd you hesitate? Are you not used to accepting things from others?"

She blows through the tiny hole into her cup, cooling her coffee. "No, I'm just not used to getting things without strings attached. I'm trying to remember not everyone is like him. But I was with him for so long."

Boy, do I know what she means. I was trafficked as a teenager. It took me years to learn to trust people again.

"So, your brother. Someone told you he passed?" I ask, feeling like we're doing the law's job in figuring out what happened to this poor girl. But I'm not willing to leave it up to anyone else, so here we are. This girl is special to my son, and that means she's special to me, too.

"Yes. Right before Bradley took me, two uniformed officers came to the house and told my mom and me that he'd been killed in some kind of explosion. He was only months away from coming home."

"Army, right?"

"Yeah. He joined so he could get us out of the city." She takes in the scenery around us. "He would have loved it here," she says with a deep sadness in her voice.

I don't have all the answers, but I do have the most important one. She's not afraid of her brother. She loves and misses him.

I reach over and take her hand tightly in mine. "Well, it's a good thing because I don't think he has plans on going anywhere until he sees you."

She blinks rapidly, her hand going to the door handle.

Tightening my grip, I try to calm her. "Shh, listen. Your brother is very much alive, and he misses you. There must have been a mix-up or miscommunication, but you didn't see a ghost today. He's really here for you."

The way her bottom lip trembles breaks my heart. It's bad enough she was kidnapped at fifteen, but all these years she thought her brother was dead. I can't even imagine what's going through her mind right now.

She covers her mouth, her green eyes filling with tears. I scoot closer to her and give her a hug. I've never had a daughter. Billie Rose is as close as I've come. I guess I never thought about the day Jackson would find someone to share his life with.

I try to imagine her as my daughter-in-law as she begins to cry.

"He ... he's really here?" she hiccups.

I brush her hair away from her face. "He's really here," I assure her.

She looks hopeful and happy, but it's short lived. Her face begins to fall, and she pushes off me slowly.

"He knows," she rasps. And this is something I recognize. "Oh my god. I can't face him." Her eyes plead with me.

"Willow, whatever happened to you is just that ... it happened *to* you. You have nothing to be ashamed of. And without even spending time with your brother, I can honestly say he's not going to look at you any differently than he did before."

"He must think I hate him the way I ran."

I slide back over to the driver's seat. "He doesn't hate you. But I think it's time you go and see for yourself. He's with Jackson."

A small grin tips the corner of her mouth, and she blushes. "That makes me feel a little better," she says quietly.

"You really like my son, don't you?" I ask, still unsure whether these two will be good for each other. He has always had a hard time staying focused on one thing and she ... well, we're just starting to know her story.

"The dragonfly led me to him." Her fingers dance lightly over her forehead. "I ... I can't explain it."

My heart squeezes painfully at the mention of a dragonfly. Once upon a time, I bought Jackson's real mother, Jenny, a dragonfly necklace. I had the biggest crush on her, but we were so young ... and dumb. It wasn't in the cards for us.

"What dragonfly?" I ask. This has to be a coincidence.

"The one painted on the barn."

Okay, maybe not.

Could we be coming full circle?

Chapter Twenty-Eight

Willow

I sit quietly as we drive back to the sheriff's department. Ash is alive.

Ash is alive!

How did this all happen? First I find this place, and then I find my brother …

There's this weird mix of happiness, fear, joy, and sadness in my gut.

Just a few weeks ago, I was ready to give up. I was literally thinking about throwing myself off a cliff. If Bradley had driven to a place where that could have happened, I don't know if I'd be here right now.

But now.

I read a quote once that said "Just hang on. Tomorrow is a new day, and with it brings so many possibilities."

I guess I never really believed it. Until now.

Avenging Skulls

Finding a place like this, with people like Jackson, Raffe, and Miss Maggie. They're all so wonderful. My mind never could have imagined them. And now my brother is here, too.

Raffe parks, and I notice Petey out of the corner of my eye. He's waiting with Brody. Each stand like sentinels on one side of the door. I glance over at Jackson's dad.

"I'm not used to all this." I point at the two men patiently waiting for me to get out of the truck.

"Well, you better get used to it because you're going to have a hard time shaking them," he says, smiling.

Raffe doesn't look like Jackson, but they have the same charm. It's not phony. It's real.

"It's not every day a girl magically gains so many bodyguards," I say, trying to keep the moment light.

He laughs. "Come on. Are you ready?"

I give him a confident nod. "Yes."

This time there's no crowd bombarding me the minute I step out of the truck. It's quiet; the only sound is a backup beeper from a nearby construction site.

Petey holds the door open for us, and as I walk by, I pause. Quietly, I ask him a simple question. "They aren't going to be able to help me, are they?" I point to the deputies standing inside the door.

He shrugs. "Depends on what your idea of justice is."

I rub my hand over my neck. The deputies look impatient ... and bored. A woman dressed in a black tank top is animatedly speaking to them. Her long silver-black hair swings down her back. God, she's beautiful. Then, it hits me. She has to be related to Billie Rose. They carry the same confidence.

An office door to the left of us opens and Jackson steps out, his eyes instantly finding mine. With one look, I relax. *Everything's going to be okay.*

And then my brother steps out behind him.

Ash.

I run, but this time I don't run away. It takes seconds before I'm jumping into his arms. He picks me up, burying his face in the crook of my neck.

"Willow," he whispers harshly.

"Ash."

He holds me close, his arms big and strong. He's changed so much.

"I never stopped looking for you," he says, walking us both inside the room he came from.

Jackson gives me a reassuring smile as he closes the door quietly behind us, giving my brother and me a moment alone.

Ash sets me on my feet before grabbing my cheeks and staring right into my soul. "Willow, god, I can't believe you're here." He places a kiss on my forehead, setting everything right in the world.

"They told me you were dead," I choke out.

He leans back, his eyes narrowing. "Who? Who told you that, Willow?"

"The men in uniform. They came to the house and told mom and me you were killed in an explosion," I tell him, tears flowing down my cheeks because the wound from that day still bleeds strong.

His eyes bounce frantically over my face.

"Someone from the Army?" he asks.

I nod, wiping my eyes with the palm of my hands. "One was a … a CAO, I think he said."

He pulls me close, hugging me tight. "That can't be, Willow."

"But it was. They came to the house. Mom left me in the room with them and then she left shortly after they did. She said she couldn't handle it anymore," I cry into his chest. "She never came back."

He growls. The sound comes from somewhere deep in his chest. I lean back, reigning in my sobs.

"She said you ran away," he says angrily.

The shock of what he said steals my breath. I take a step away from him, covering my mouth. "No," I whisper harshly.

I turn in a circle, taking the room in for the first time since stepping inside. "I … I didn't run away. I had nowhere to go." I brace my hands on the back of a chair. The room is starting to spin.

Ash pulls out another chair and guides me to sit down. "Willow, you don't have to explain yourself to me. I believe you."

My head swivels toward the door. "She … is she?" I ask, not sure if I want to know the answer.

"She's still using," he answers, running his fingers through his short blond hair.

We stare at each other for several long minutes. Both of us not quite believing the other is really there.

He's the first one to break the silence. "When I got home, Mom was so fucking high. It took me two days to get her cleaned up enough to answer me about where you were. She said you ran away. That you had met someone named Bradley, and you had left the state with him. She said she tried to stop you."

It's as if he doused me with an ice-cold bucket of water. All the air in my lungs expels in one giant whoosh.

"Willow, please tell me what really happened," my brother pleads.

Slowly, I stand and walk to the door. I glance over my shoulder before opening it. "I don't know anymore," I answer honestly.

Everyone stops what they're doing to stare at me when I step out.

"Where's my mother?" I ask the room.

"The sheriff is questioning her," Jackson answers.

"Where?"

He points to a door down the hall. I start toward it as my brother reaches out for me.

"It's not worth it, Willow."

I swivel around and stare at him. "She gave me to him," I grit out through my clenched teeth.

He pulls his head back, his eyebrows shooting to his hairline. "What are you saying?" he asks.

The bikers in the room all tense. I allow my gaze to travel over each of them, stopping on Petey. I raise an eyebrow in his direction, and he gives me a slight nod.

Just then my mother comes out with several deputies, her eyes red-rimmed and swollen. "I'm so sorry for the misunderstanding," she tells them before spotting me.

The sheriff walks over. "Willow, we're ready to finish your statement."

I look him dead in the eye. "No."

He starts to argue when a deputy steps forward. "Miss Taylor, please. We have a few more questions for you."

I wave my hand toward my mother. "I'm sure she's filled you in, hasn't she?"

They all look at each other.

"But yesterday you said …"

I wave him off. "Whatever she said is true. Sorry to have bothered all of you. I've been a little confused." I turn to face my mother.

She shakes her head nervously. "I'm sorry. I had to tell them the truth," she says, her voice fading.

My brother whispers in my ear, "What are you doing?"

My mother looks at me. "I think we should get Willow back to our room so she can rest," she says, walking over and placing her hand on my arm.

I shake it off. "No. I'm going home."

Everyone stares at me like I've lost my mind. And maybe I have.

"Honey, we can't go home right now. We'll get plane tickets as soon as we find an available flight."

My eyes narrow on her. "Not *your* home, Mother. *My* home. I'm twenty years old; you don't get to decide where I go anymore."

Her mouth falls open.

"I'll take mom back to the hotel and get her settled and then we can catch up," my brother says, grabbing our mother's arm and pulling her toward the door.

The sheriff lets out a sigh. "Miss Taylor, we can't let you leave without …" he starts.

The woman with the long silver hair steps in front of him. "Are you charging Willow with something?"

He shakes his head. "No, of course not. But we need to make sure of no foul play."

She sneers at him. "I think you know what's going on here." She gives my mother a disgusted once over before continuing. "But that's okay; your services are no longer required." She points to the club's attorney, who has his phone to his ear. "You have our lawyer's information if you need anything else."

He takes a step back, throwing his arm out and letting us pass. When we get outside, my mother grabs my arm.

"Aren't you even going to hug your mother?" she asks.

I glance around, making sure none of the deputies followed us out. No one but the club surrounds us. "My mother?" I laugh.

She straightens her shoulders, her fingers fidgeting over her blouse.

"How much did they pay you?" I ask.

She claws at the skin on her neck, leaving a trail of red behind. "I … I don't know what you mean," she says, working her jaw back and forth.

Raffe catches my meaning and begins to circle the woman who claims to be my mother. But my brother steps in, holding his hands out.

My mom pleads with him. "Ash, please, let's go. I told you she's changed."

His gaze bounces from me, to her, back to me. "I'm taking Mom back to the hotel. Then we need to talk."

The woman with silver hair steps in. She pulls a pen out of her pocket, biting off the cap and then scribbling an address on my brother's hand.

"Get her settled and then come to this address." She points the pen at him. "But only if you're coming with an open mind."

He stares at her for a second. "She's not only my sister; she's my best friend," he says, pointing toward me without taking his eyes off her.

The woman's face softens, and she reaches out to squeeze his hand. "Good 'cause she's my nephew's girl, and I won't let anyone fuck with her. You got that?"

A million butterflies swarm my chest as I take in the woman. She's defending me harder than my own mother ever has.

When he nods, she pats him on the arm and then bumps her shoulder into my mother rather harshly before coming to stand beside me. She wraps her arm around me.

"Come on, sweetheart. Let's get you home."

She gently turns me away from the crowd and toward a rusty old hot rod. Jackson jogs to catch up with us.

"Jesse," he says breathlessly.

She places her hand on the top of my head and gently shoves me down into the passenger seat. "I'm taking her to the farm. I just need a minute with her," she tells him.

He sighs, running his fingers through his hair. "Okay, I'll follow you," he grumbles, kicking a rock on the way back to his truck.

When she gets in beside me and fires up the engine, my eyes go wide. It's loud. She steps on the gas and spins us out of the parking lot.

The first thing she says is, "My mother was a fucking crack whore, too." She lights up a cigarette. "Mind if I smoke?"

I shake my head, holding back tears.

She cracks her window as we fly down the street, turning heads along the way. "So, Raffe has told me a little about you, but I think I learned everything I need to know from that little show you put on back there."

I cross my arms over my chest. "They weren't going to help me."

"I don't doubt that. But I saw the looks passing between you and Petey. Do you want to explain that?"

"I'm not sure what you mean?" I study the tattoos that run down her arms.

She laughs. "I've been around a long time, darlin'."

Can I trust her? Does she know who Petey is? They are all in the same club, so I guess it will be okay to tell her. "I think he can help me," I finally admit.

She flicks the ashes of her cigarette out the window. "If anyone can find him, it's Petey," she says. Her gaze drifts away from the road to me.

"Bradley told me my mom let him take me," I say quietly, turning away from her to watch the trees passing by. "I didn't want to believe him until today."

"It was probably the drugs talking."

I bite my lip. "But how could a mother do that?"

She shifts gears, throwing me back even farther in my seat. "She's forgotten she is one. She's loyal to one thing and that is her addiction. But you gotta remember that's on her, not you."

"The deputies wouldn't have believed me anyway. I thought my brother was dead, and he clearly wasn't. That alone makes me look crazy."

"I believe you."

Covering my face in my hands, I try to hold my emotions in.

"You're in for a muddy ride, girl, but we're going to see you to the other side. We don't let anyone go through it alone. We'll get dirty right along with you."

"I don't know what I'm doing," I admit. "He … he was my everything for a while. He …" I let my hands fall into my lap. "He took care of me."

"Men like that are good at the game. Don't you dare feel bad about any of your feelings. Good, bad, ugly, they are all valid."

But are they? Bradley made me so dependent on him, I don't really know how I feel about anything anymore. "I'm so tired of games."

"Let us take care of you, baby," she says, reaching over and wrapping her hand around my knee. "It will give you time to sort it all out in your head."

When we pull into the driveway, Jackson is right behind us. "Okay," I agree quietly as she shuts off the engine.

"Good. Now, you go inside and relax. Jackson will bring you out to the warehouse after a bit, and I'll feed you. Billie Rose and Kelsie will be happy to see you there."

Jackson opens my door. He bends down, his arm draped over the top of the car. "Everything good?" he asks, his eyes raking over me. He cradles the side of my face in his hand, his thumb brushing tears away.

I answer with a nod of my head.

"She'll be okay. She's a strong one," Jesse says.

He takes her in before resting his gaze back on me. "She'll make a perfect Skull."

Jesse makes a small noise of approval and then shoos me out of her car. "Go on, get inside and regroup. I expect to see you both at the warehouse by seven."

Jackson leans back and salutes her. "Yes, ma'am." He reaches in and takes my hand, gently tugging me out of the car.

When we get inside, Fred stands up and stretches, immediately coming to my feet for scratches. I sit down in the middle of the room and let him rest his chin on my leg.

Jackson leaves us alone and goes out to the kitchen. He comes back with two sodas, cracking one and handing it to me.

"Thank you," I say quietly, taking a sip.

He takes a big swallow as well. "That was some crazy shit," he says in true Jackson fashion.

I giggle, taking another sip. "It really was."

But then my mood turns somber, remembering what it felt like when I saw Ash. "How many people can say that their brother rose from the dead?"

He tips my chin with his knuckle, forcing me to look at him. "He loves you."

"I know." I close my eyes. "I'm so confused. Military men came to our house and told me he was dead. But he told me that couldn't be." I shake my head.

Jackson pulls up his knees and rests his forearms on them, the can of soda swinging loosely from his hand. "Could it be that they were all in on it?"

I think about that for a minute. It was a bit of a coincidence how everything played out. "But why?"

He shrugs. "Maybe they thought you'd be less likely to run away if you thought he was dead." Jackson sets his drink down beside him and scoots so our knees are touching. "I think you were trafficked, Willow."

He's not stupid; he's finally figuring it out. That I went along with it all. This is it. He's going to hate me.

"When you fell asleep last night, you cried for the other girls."

I blink at him as my heart picks up speed, threatening to race right out of my body. He places his hands on my knees, sensing that I'm about to jump from the floor.

"Willow, it's okay. Please don't run. I can't let you run," he says calmly.

The back door opens, and in steps Petey and Brody. They both halt in their tracks when they see my face.

"She's okay," Jackson says, waving them in.

My head snaps back to him. "But I'm not. I'm really not."

The other men sit down on the floor right beside me. Petey rests his arm around my shoulder. "Tell us the whole story, Willow. I'm going to kill that motherfucker for you and then Jackson here is going to feed him to the hogs."

Jackson's eyes widen. "What the fuck are you talking about?" he snips.

Petey pulls me close to him, cradling my head to his chest. "Your secret is safe with me," he tells Jackson.

Brody's head bounces between the two of them. "What in the ever-loving fuck did I miss?"

Jackson sighs loudly, and I give him an apologetic look. I shouldn't have said anything to Petey about the hogs. He obviously didn't know. In typical Willow fashion, I've fucked up.

Jackson notices the look on my face and dips his head. "It's okay. It was bound to come out sometime."

Brody is still shaking his head, utterly lost.

"Seems Jackson here has been feeding dead men to Grandma Maggie's hogs," Petey says calmly. He squeezes me tight. "And Willow here is going to share her story with us so that asshole can join them."

"You're all going to hate me," I say, gripping on to Petey's shirt. I'm not sure why Petey brings me comfort.

Jackson rolls his eyes. "Willow, look at the three of us. There is nothing you can say that will change anything." He then raises an eyebrow at Petey. "But this asshole better remember whose girl you are."

Petey chuckles, and it makes me smile because it shakes the both of us.

"I don't think you have anything to worry about, kid. I've seen the way she looks at you."

Jackson winks at me, but then he gets serious. "Tell us, Willow. Tell us everything."

I close my eyes and hold on tight.

"Okay," I whisper.

And then I tell them the entire story ... all of it, ending with the part that finally pushed me over the edge.

"Open your eyes, Willow," Bradley demands.

I'm a dragonfly. I'm dead. Nothing can hurt me if I'm dead.

He shoves off me roughly and climbs off the mattress. When several minutes pass, I do what he spent the last ten minutes begging me to do. I open my eyes.

He's staring at me with his computer open. He's typing something but his focus remains on me. He hits the last key with emphasis.

"It didn't have to be this way," he says, shaking his head. "I've given you everything. Where do you think you'd be if it wasn't for me?"

I sit up and wrap the blanket around me. "I'm sorry," I whisper. And I am. I don't like it when he's unhappy with me. He usually doesn't care that I don't participate. I don't know what's changed.

"You know I could have kept any of the girls, but I kept you. You, Willow."

His jaw clenches as he looks away from me, staring out the window.

He slams his laptop shut and then hops out of the van. I watch as he paces back and forth, the dust of the desert clouding around his feet.

A shiver runs up and down my spine. He's done something. Something drastic that he can't take back.

"Open your eyes, Willow," he says.

No. No. Never. I can't. I just can't!

"Willow!" someone yells.

My eyes fly open, and I gasp for breath.

"Jesus, it's okay, baby." Jackson pulls me away from Petey and sets me on his lap. "Look at me. You're safe," he says, pushing my tear-soaked hair out of my face.

I can't catch my breath. Oh god, I'm going to die.

"It's not working," he tells the other two men.

Brody stands and scoops me up into his big arms. "You're going to be okay, little one. Hold on. Just hold on for me."

When we get outside and the wind hits my face, I can finally breathe again. He gently sets me down on the grass. I let out a little whimper, and he shushes me.

"It's okay. Nothing to be embarrassed about."

Jackson and Brody are each holding one of my hands. The warmth of their fingers wrapped in mine and the cool grass beneath my feet slowly eases the tightness in my chest. I raise my face to the sun, proud that I was finally able to share my story with someone. When my head drops, I'm met with Jackson's worried stare. I never could have imagined someone looking at me like he is right now.

My journey here didn't begin with the bad things that happened to me. You can trace it clear back to the beginning of time. I've always been stumbling through the ages, lost and confused. But I've finally reached my destination.

It's him.

"Jesus, Willow. That was some fucked up shit," Brody says.

Jackson thumps him hard in the arm.

"Ouch," Brody says, letting go of my hand to rub his bicep.

It makes me giggle. Jackson's eyes slide back to me. "I'm sorry. He's a heartless bastard."

"I am not." Brody takes my hand back in his. "I've always supported your dumbass." He tosses his chin toward his friend.

"You two really do act like brothers," I tell them.

Brody rubs his thumb over my hand. "I meant no disrespect."

I lift my shoulders to my ears. "It's okay. It was fucked up," I admit.

"So, what was it that he did that he couldn't take back?" Brody asks.

"He gave me to his grandfather, and he had him ... he had him punish me. He wanted me to see how bad things could be for me. It was what gave me the motivation to finally run."

"I'm going to kill Bradley for you," Jackson says, grinding his molars.

I shake my head. "We need him."

He scowls at this.

"He knows the players, Jackson. He doesn't set up the board, he's just a token in the game. Just like I was."

"You were innocent," he reminds me.

I sigh and plop down on the ground. "I know. I'm not saying he doesn't deserve to die. But he can lead us to the man who owns the game. To his grandfather."

Both of them sit down with me. Brody starts plucking at the grass. "We should take this to Dirk. This is bigger than we initially thought."

Jackson remains quiet, but I can see the wheels turning behind his warm colored eyes. "We're not using her."

"I didn't say that, brother."

They stare at each other.

Petey comes out of the house, the screen door slamming shut behind him. "Found one!" He shakes something over his head. "Grandma Maggie has one of everything."

He approaches us as he unfolds a large piece of paper. When he drops it to the ground and lays it out between us, my eyes roam over it. It's a map of the United States. When I lift my face, his gaze holds mine.

"Show me. We have chapters all over this fucking country. We can have men at every spot you remember by morning."

"You guys don't hate me?" I ask.

Jackson's hand snaps out and grabs my arm. "Don't ask that again. We don't hate you. You know who is to blame. Almost everyone in this club has been through the same thing as you. Coincidence?" he questions. He tips his head, his eyes boring into mine. "Most of the members in our club have spent time with the devil. That's how we so easily recognize the fucking demons he's released into this world."

I blink at him.

"Fate didn't bring you here by accident. You're a Rebel. Don't ever doubt your place here."

When he releases me, I let out a shaky breath. He's right. I don't think I'm here by accident, either.

"Hang on." I hold up my finger, jumping to my feet. I rush inside, grab my bag, and then run back to them.

"Cute bag," Petey teases.

I cock an eyebrow at him. "Sorry. I haven't had much time to shop," I snip.

It doesn't faze him. "That's the spirit. You'll fit right in with the others," he tells me. "Don't ever be afraid to put one of us in our place."

I dip my head, hiding the smile on my face. It's still so new to me. Being able to speak freely without fear of consequences. None of these men have played any games with me.

I dump everything I own in the world on the ground in front of us. The guys all lean over. Jackson starts picking through my things, but Petey instantly goes for the maps of all the national parks I've visited.

His eyes spark with a hunger that both scares and excites me. I've dreamed of a million ways I could bring Bradley and the others down. I don't know if I ever really believed it would happen. I was scared to trust law enforcement for a reason. The men who work with Bradley have eyes and ears everywhere, but I think I've finally found a band of men his group hasn't infiltrated. The Rebel Skulls are so far on the other end of the spectrum, I know I can trust them.

I smooth one of the maps out, running my hands over the memories I have scribbled there. They're all silent as they take in the markings I've made.

"When he first took me, I believed him when he said he was a nature photographer. He always took his camera with him when he would leave our campsite. But as time went on, he started to feel more comfortable around me. And then one day he took me with him. We walked along the trail and came upon a girl sitting on a bench. She looked up at us, but that was her only reaction. Her gaze immediately went back to the ground."

Bradley lets go of my hand, the snap of his gum breaking the silence as he slowly walks over to her.

I'm frozen in my spot as I stare at the girl. Why is she here?

And then I hear footsteps behind me. "Did you get me two this time?" *a man asks.*

I'm so scared, I don't even turn. I just continue to focus on the girl.

Bradley straightens. "No. You said I could keep one. Well, this is the one." *He points to me.*

The man, who looks so out of place against the backdrop of the desert, walks around me. His eyes roam up and down as he makes a full circle. "Is this the one who was destined for the buyer in Seattle?"

Bradley nods, sitting down beside the girl as the older man continues to appraise me.

He reaches out, and I flinch. His fingers dig into the back of my head as he tips my face side to side. He makes a clicking sound in the back of his throat. "She's a little plain, isn't she?" *he asks.*

"That's what I like about her," *Bradley answers. The girl sitting beside him shivers when he rests his hand on her leg.*

"Hmm, to each their own. I thought my grandson and I would have similar tastes, but I see that's not the case. Although, I'm proud of you for finally allowing yourself to indulge in the goods."

This is Bradley's grandfather? What the hell is going on?

"This one must be important for you to come and get her yourself," Bradley says, ignoring his grandfather's remarks about me.

He waves his hand in the air over the girl as he takes a seat on the other side of her. He tugs on his expensive slacks as he crosses a foot over his knee, resting his arm along the back of the bench. "Not at all. I just needed to have a word with you about the next job."

Bradley whistles, rolling his eyes to the heavens. "Are you telling me I get to end one of the assholes?"

His grandfather chuckles low.

That's when I see the first sign that the girl sitting between them is indeed paying attention to what is being said. Her muscles tense. The old man runs his gaze over her leisurely. "I want you to take the buyer out on the next contract. He's compromised."

Bradley weaves a business card through his fingers. "What about the girl you have lined up for him? If we take him out, will there be a backup buyer?"

"Yes, and the new buyer will be keeping her, so no worries on what she will see."

Bradley's eyes darken with a hunger that scares every fiber of my being. And then his grandfather adds, "I've found one who is at the end of her usefulness."

The girl sitting by him twitches. She's going to run. Maybe I should run, too. Maybe one of us would have a chance of getting out of here if we do it at the same time. I glance around the landscape, my heart plummeting. Where would we even go?

When my gaze goes back to them, the grandfather is staring at me with a smirk on his face. "I see it now. What you see in her," he says, tipping his head. "She's a thinker."

This seems to irritate Bradley. "She's just quiet."

With the focus on me, the girl makes her move but she doesn't even make it off the bench before Bradley has his hands around her throat, pulling her back into him. "That was stupid."

She starts to cry. I don't know what to do. How can I help her? She should have run before we got here. She was just sitting there all alone.

This time, I'm able to pull myself out of my own memories. I level my gaze on the three men sitting with me. "These are powerful men. If they catch wind …"

"They'll change course," Petey finishes for me.

I nod.

"Can I take these with me? I'm going to talk to Prez about this. See what his take is."

My reflection stares back at me in the black pits of his eyes. He wants this. Almost more than I do. Men like Bradley hurt someone he loves.

"Who was she?" I ask.

He swallows hard as he begins to fold up the map. I don't think he's going to answer when he stands, tucks the stack of maps in his back pocket, and heads toward his bike. But he pauses a few feet away.

"My wife," he tells me, not turning around. And then he picks up his step and disappears around the corner of the house.

We all sit quietly long after the roar of his bike fades down the road.

"That dude scares the shit out of me," Brody finally says.

I suck my lips between my teeth, trying to stifle a laugh.

Jackson nudges me, and it bursts out of my mouth. "I'm sorry; there is no way you two are afraid of him."

Brody crosses his arms across his chest. "Why is that?" he asks, sounding offended.

"You *all* are scary."

They both chuckle at that, shaking their heads. Jackson stands and pulls me to my feet with him. "There is a difference between plain scary and crazy scary. That fucker is definitely crazy scary."

Brody runs his hand down my arm. "Why don't you go in and rest before we head to the warehouse? It's been a long day."

Jackson agrees with him. "We didn't get much sleep last night."

"I'll keep watch," Brody says, pulling up a lawn chair.

"You were here all night," I tell him, feeling guilty that he feels the need to guard me.

"Don't worry about me. Someone else will take over for me later tonight. I'll sleep then." He points to the house. "Get your little ass in that house and take a fucking nap."

In my past life, I would have thought he was being rude, but not now. He's being straight. And that is exactly what I need.

I salute him, which makes his face soften.

"Thank you for not treating me softly," I say quietly.

His face turns red as he waves me away.

Jackson takes my hand and leads us inside. The stairs creak as we make our way up to the bedroom. He stands in the doorway watching as I kick my shoes off. "Sweet dreams," he says, turning away.

"Please stay," I blurt out.

Slowly, he turns back to face me. "Are you sure?"

"More sure than I've ever been," I answer honestly.

He sits down on the end of the bed and unlaces his boots, tugging them off one by one. "What you said to Brody about not treating you softly ..." his voice fades.

I crawl to the end of the bed and cautiously wrap my arms around him. "I don't want you to treat me softly either, Jackson."

We stare at each other in the reflection of the mirror across the room.

I place my mouth next to his ear. "He treated me softly."

He fists his hands in his lap, his gaze penetrating mine through the glass.

In one smooth motion, he flips me onto my back and then his lips are on mine. I keep my eyes open as his fall closed. He kisses me with such heated passion, it floods my body with a new sensation. When the piercing in his tongue rakes over mine, it makes my stomach flutter. My hips lift off the bed, and I rub myself against him.

He groans, his eyes fluttering open as he pulls away. "I don't know how far to take this." His gaze roams around the room. "I don't want to scare you."

My heart beats wildly against his. "I don't know, either. But I do know that I'm not afraid of you."

His thumb brushes over my temple as he processes what I just said. He leans down and whispers in my ear, "We'll continue this tonight."

My lips part, and I release a tiny puff of air. "Okay," I rasp, a tiny bit disappointed I have to wait yet excited for the night to come. "Promise me you'll treat me like you would any other girl."

Jackson stares down at me. "No, I'm not going to treat you like any other girl."

My heart free falls out of my chest.

He rubs his nose along mine. "I'm going to treat you like *my* girl."

My heart springs firmly back into place, and I smile.

He stares down at me. "We're going to take our time in here. Go slow, yeah?"

I bite my lip and nod, feeling that all too familiar lump form in my throat.

"Does that mean you plan on sticking around this place for a little while?" he asks.

"There's no place I'd rather be," I tell him honestly.

"But what if your brother wants you to go back with him?"

When I don't answer right away, he lifts off of me and situates us against the pillows, spooning me from behind. "It's okay if you want to go with him, Willow. We just met; I understand."

"I'm never going back there," I tell him, my eyes falling closed.

"It was your home, Willow."

His fingers rub lightly over my stomach. The scent of pine wafts in through the window on the breeze. "It's not home unless you have someone there who loves you."

His fingers pause. "Your brother loves you, Willow."

"I know. That's why I'm keeping him here with me."

And with that final thought, sleep steals me away.

Chapter Twenty-Nine

Jackson

I let her sleep for several hours until the messages from the warehouse started coming in so fast I couldn't ignore them any longer. Jesus Christ the women of this club are pushy.

She stands beside my bike, shaking her hands out in front of her. "Are you sure I won't fall off?" she asks.

Brody laughs. "If you're scared, why don't you hop on with me, sweetheart?" He wags his eyebrows up and down.

"Fuck you," I say, flipping him off. "You're not going to fall off, Willow. If you're too nervous, we'll just take my truck. No worries," I tell her, pulling the truck keys out of my pocket.

She reaches out and stops me. "No, I want to do this. So, I just have to hold on? There's nothing else I have to do?"

"Just hold on. I'll take care of everything else."

I swing my leg over the seat, smiling as she copies my movements. She wiggles as she settles in behind me.

With the exception of Billie Rose, no one has ever road on the back of my bike. She wraps her arms around me tightly, and my dick instantly hardens. Fuck. Nothing like showing up for a family gathering with a boner.

"Is this good?" she asks.

"Fuck, baby, it's more than good. You ready?"

"As I'll ever be."

I take off slowly, not wanting to startle her. When we get a few miles down the road, I feel her relax against my back; her grip loosens a bit. We follow Brody into town, stopping at Gladstone to make sure someone picked up Grandma Maggie. Of course, someone already got her.

"I'm so happy Miss Maggie is going to be there tonight," Willow says before I start up the bike again.

My grandmother was the one who orchestrated this whole thing between Willow and me. She told me my grandfather used to ground her, then hinted that something on the farm might have the same effect on me.

Willow does indeed ground me. Maybe it's only because she gives me something to think about besides my own ass. But that's okay; I'll take it whatever it is. All I know is that I don't want to rush or overlook anything when it comes to her. That alone keeps my feet firmly on the ground.

I run my hand over her leg and she shivers, making the corner of my mouth tick up. When I pull in front of the warehouse with her on the back of my bike, a new feeling washes over me. I'm proud; I wish everyone would come outside and see her with me.

I hop off and hold my hand out to help her. Her gaze roams over the building towering in front of us.

Avenging Skulls

"This is the warehouse you've been talking about?"

"The one and only," Brody answers, clapping his hands together.

He's just excited for the food. Jesse always puts out an amazing spread, and I'm sure she spared no expense for our guests.

The minute we step inside, Willow's eyes widen, and she turns in a circle. "Wow," she whispers. She does a full spin before her gaze lands back on mine. "It's beautiful."

Dirk walks out, whistling sharply when he spots us. "Table now." He points toward the door he just came out of.

I pull Willow to me. "I have to go, but I'll help you find one of the girls first."

When I turn around, Dirk is right behind me. "Her too," he says.

"Dirk," I begin to argue.

He steps in front of Willow and runs an inked finger gently over her cheek. "She's strong enough. Don't doubt her. She's got bigger balls than any of us. Me included."

I shake my head in disbelief. Did Dirk just say someone had balls bigger than his? That's a first.

Willow drops her head, drawing her toe over the pattern of the wood grain on the floor.

"You went through some shit to get here. You're a fucking little warrior, so get your ass in there and let's figure out a way to get that motherfucker. We strike hard and we strike fast. I'm not beating around the bush with this one. No way in hell is he ever getting near you again."

Dirk speaks to her with such confidence and strength that I can visibly see Willow's respect for him grow. He may be an asshole, but he's a good man. A born leader.

My father is leaning against the door, his gaze meeting mine from across the room.

And it's in this moment I realize who the fuck I am.

And who I want to be.

I'm a goddamn Skull, and someday I'm going to be standing in Dirk's shoes. I need to put the shit with Lanie aside. I'm a survivor. I deserve more than I've ever let myself imagine. But right now, my dreams are soaring high. I want to be the president of this club someday.

My dad gives me a hard stare and thumps his fist over his chest. Can he see how much my perception of the world just changed? In one single moment and by the words of our reigning king, no less.

I straighten my shoulders and hold my hand out to Willow. What a perfect name for the woman who's going to be by my side through it all. Dirk is right; she is strong enough.

She peeks up at me through her long eyelashes. When she places her hand in mine, a bolt of energy courses through me. Her green eyes tell me his words affected her, too.

I offer her my signature smirk, but she surprises me by rising to her tiptoes and pressing her lips to mine for all to see.

We can do this. Together we can do anything.

Chapter Thirty

Willow

I've got this weird feeling. I'm not sure what it is, but I think it's pride.

The longer I'm away from Bradley, the lighter I feel. It's like the world is slowly transitioning from black and white to color. I love being with Jackson; he has this charisma about him. It is clear people love him, too. Yeah, I've seen his brothers tease him, but they also hold a look of respect in their eyes as they do it.

He is humble, so I doubt he even notices.

"Okay," I say, taking a deep breath in response to Dirk's request.

Jackson and I follow Dirk into a room with the longest table I've ever seen.

"You'll be great," Jackson whispers in my ear as I settle in a chair he's pulled out for me.

Petey sits in the spot next to me; he gives me a quick wink before directing his attention to the head of the table. My maps are spread out in front of Dirk. I swallow hard.

"How did you hide these maps from him?" Dirk asks, getting right to the point.

A million butterflies erupt in my stomach as I remember the day I came up with this plan.

I sit down beside the rock and spread the map out in front of me, biting the cap off a pen. It scrapes against the paper as I circle the spot where we've stopped.

"What are you doing?" Bradley asks, looking at me over the top of his camera.

"I'm marking the spot where I'm hiding my book, so when we come back I can get it and read it again," I tell him, not looking up from my task. My heart is knocking so loudly against my ribs, I'm worried he'll be able to hear it.

I tip my head to the side, giving him a better view of the slender slope of my neck. My hair falls over my shoulder, and it's then that I look at him, batting my lashes slightly. This is a dangerous new game I'm initiating. We'll see if he wants to play. I'm sure I'll have to take a few steps back from time to time, but it will be worth it if I can win in the end.

My lips part as we stare at each other.

"That's a smart idea," he says, no emotion whatsoever on his face. He snaps his gum so loud it echoes against the rocks surrounding us.

"I figure the maps are much smaller than keeping a whole book. Like you said, there's no room to keep them all."

"But what if someone else finds it before we return?" he asks.

Avenging Skulls

I beg the bead of sweat forming on my forehead to hang strong at the same time willing my heartbeat to slow. I answer smoothly, "Then I will be happy that someone else might have enjoyed it."

"Your heart is too soft, Willow," *he says, buying my bit of innocence hook, line, and sinker.*

"If I found a book that I'd never read under a stone, I would be happy." *I shrug.* "It's like finding a portal to another world."

He laughs, tipping his head back, his perfect white teeth glinting against the high noon sun. When he returns his gaze to mine, a look of hunger has replaced his mirth.

"And this is why I love you," *he says huskily.*

Love. He's been using that word freely the past few weeks.

It was my first clue that it was time to make my move. That one word gave me power.

When Ash and I were kids, my father took us camping in very remote places. He drilled into our heads that if we were ever caught in a bad situation, to remain calm. "If you lose your head, you won't be able to think clearly. Be patient, and an answer will come to you eventually," *he had said.*

And that's what I've done.

I'm not able to help the others right now, but someday, someday I'm going to save them.

Or at least that's what I tell myself. That this is why I have to endure him. For the others.

It has to be me. I'm the one he shows his dark side to. I could look at that as an unlucky thing ... or I could look at it as an opportunity. My brother went into the Army to give us a better life, but also because he wanted to protect the people of this country. This is my opportunity to continue his legacy.

And that's why I'll gladly take the bullet.

Bradley walks over, crouching down in front of me. His fingers brush over my shoulder as he pushes my hair behind me.

"Tip your head back," he orders, pressing his thumb under my chin. "That's it. Open," he demands.

When my lips part, he smiles and pulls his camera to his face. "Beautiful."

The room is quiet as Dirk stares at me.

Then, he bursts out laughing. "So, you're telling me if we go to these locations, we're going to find books?"

I give him a confident nod. My dream is coming true. I was meant to find these men. These dark angels are the ones who are going to avenge me and all of the others.

He stands and presses his knuckles into the table. "Way to yield your power." He smirks with what I think is a look of admiration. "That bastard fell for it. And now we have every one of their rendezvous points mapped out for the taking."

My gaze roams over each of the men. They're all looking at my maps with a murderous glint in their eyes, making them look scarier than ever. All but one man. Lily's husband is staring at me. I can't decipher what he's thinking. When Dirk bangs his gavel on the table, he turns his focus away from me.

"The plan Petey came up with stands. Let's get busy." He bangs the gavel again, and everyone begins to leave.

Jackson pulls his phone from his pocket and starts to take a picture of the maps. Petey's hand lands on his chest.

"What the fuck?" Jackson asks, taking a step back.

"This shit stays here. Don't be sharing any of this with your secret friend."

Jackson glances around nervously. "Fuck you. I don't share anything that comes out of this room." He jabs his finger into the table.

Petey raises his eyebrows in disbelief. "This one's mine, kid. Whomever you've been sharing information with might've been getting the jump on me, but this one's mine," he repeats. His black eyes slide my way.

"It's not me giving her the jump, man. I'm just the end game. The one who makes the assholes disappear. So don't go blaming me for your short comings. Maybe she's just better than you," Jackson taunts.

Petey's eyes go wide. "She?"

"Fuck," Jackson whispers under his breath, turning away from us. "Let's just drop it."

Jackson grabs my hand and pulls me from the room, leaving Petey standing with his mouth hanging open. Evidently he doesn't like the thought of getting beat by a girl.

When Big Dan sees us, he stops us. "Hey. Can you tell Lily I'll be back in a few? I've got to run home quick."

"Sure thing, man."

Dan rushes past us, turning to look over his shoulder at me one last time before the door shuts behind him.

Everything seems so strange to me. Like everything is not only turning to color, but also speeding up. The realization that I've just spilled all my secrets in the last twenty-four hours is finally catching up with me. And there's also the fact I told them to complete strangers.

But when we round the corner and I see my brother sitting with Miss Maggie out in the middle of the lawn, my nerves evaporate. Everything is right in the world. My brother is alive, and we are here together. And I'm safe. I'm safe.

He stands as we approach. "Willow," he rasps, still in disbelief.

Jackson releases my hand so I can go to Ash. Immediately he wraps his arms around me. This time feels even better than the last.

When he lets me go, I notice Miss Maggie swiping at her eyes. Jackson has his arm draped over her shoulders. She waves her tissue at us.

"You two are making an old woman cry," she scolds.

Ash sits down on the other side of her. "Aw, Grandma Maggie, we didn't mean to make you cry," my brother tells her.

Grandma Maggie?

Miss Maggie chuckles lightly. "I want you both to call me that." She wags a bony finger in my direction.

I give her a shy nod.

"Your brother's been filling us in on what kind of woodland fairy you are," she teases.

I plop down on the grass, looking up at her. She looks like an angel. Her white hair sparkles against the sun. "Oh, did he now?" I pretend to give my brother a stern look.

"He did. He said you like to read, so Kelsie had the twins run her home so she could bring you back some of her favorites. That girl loves books, too. I'm glad she'll have someone to share that with now."

"Hey, I like to read," Jackson grumbles.

She swats him over the back of the head. "When was the last time you picked up a book?"

He rubs his hand over his hair with a smart-ass grin on his face. "You mean those Playboys under my bed don't count?" he jokes, hopping out of her reach just before getting swatted again.

He continues to laugh, holding his stomach. I love this side of him. He looks so young right now. His brown eyes positively swim with mischief and chaos. He swipes his hair out of his face, holding it on top of his head.

"I had you with that one, huh, Grandma?" He jogs backward. "I'm going to go see if the food is done. I'm starving."

Miss ... I mean, Grandma Maggie, shakes her head. "I love that boy more than life itself, but don't ever tell him I said that."

I'm sure he already knows how much she loves him. She couldn't hide it even if she tried.

"So, how are you doing, honey?" She runs her palm over the back of my head. "I'm so proud of you for sharing your story with Petey. You can trust him; he's a good boy."

I giggle. Petey is the furthest thing from a boy there is. He's a man. A deadly one.

"I'm okay." I direct my attention to Ash. "How's Mom?"

He glances away.

"What? What is it?"

"She found a flight out. She's ..."

"Gone?" What did I expect? She lied to the cops, she lied to my brother, she lied to me ... but she's still my mother.

"I'm sorry, Willow," my brother says.

Grandma Maggie takes his hand and then she takes one of mine. "Now, you two listen to your new grandma. Take a look around."

She nods out toward all the people lounging about, talking. A group of little kids run up the hill, chasing Billie Rose's husband, Elijah. He has a treasure chest in his arms, and they're running after him with plastic swords in their hands.

"A band of misfits some would say," she continues. "But you know what I think?"

My brother and I both look back to her.

"I think they are all pieces of a perfect puzzle. Some of them have razor-sharp edges, but one thing I'm sure of is that they all have their place." She squeezes our hands in her soft ones. "And you two are now part of the puzzle."

Ash scans the area before resting his gaze on me. "Well, there are a lot of trees here," he says.

My shoulders drop in relief. I was worried he might want to leave.

"And there are chickens," I add. "Well, not here but back at the farm."

He smiles. "What about goats?"

"No goats, but I'm sure Jackson won't mind."

"Won't mind what?" Jackson asks, walking up behind me.

Grandma Maggie answers. "Goats, boy. We're getting goats." She claps her hands together like it's a done deal. "So, is the food done? I need to get back to Gladstone. I've got a hot date tonight," she adds, wagging her eyebrows.

Avenging Skulls

Jackson grumbles, pulling me to my feet. "Ugh, goats stink."

"They do not," I argue, but then he pulls me into his chest, his mouth coming to my ear.

"I'm just kidding. I'll give you whatever you want."

We continue to walk, hand in hand up to the picnic tables.

My brother watches Jackson and I closely as we sit down to eat. "How long have you been here?" he asks.

"A few weeks," I answer, covering my mouth with my hand.

"You two seem pretty chummy," he says before dropping his fork on his plate. "I'm sorry. That was uncalled for. I'm just ... I mean, Maggie filled me in on how you came to the farm. And they let me sit at the table when Petey explained what happened to you. But what is this?" He points between Jackson and me.

"We both like bugs," Jackson answers before shoving another bite of food into his mouth.

Everyone at the table is quiet and then a giggle erupts out of my mouth. But he's right I guess. "That and Miss, I mean Grandma Maggie, kind of pushed us together. But I don't know exactly what it is," I answer honestly. "All I know is that I like being with him. He makes me feel new and wonderful things."

"Yeah, Grandma told me she had woodland fairies."

"I bet you were disappointed when you found out I was just a human."

His brown eyes narrow and then bore into mine. "I wasn't disappointed. I was enchanted."

A few chuckles erupt from the men sitting around us. I'm sure none of them have ever used the word *enchanted*.

He looks embarrassed for all but a second then picks up his spoon, scoops up a large dollop of mashed potatoes, and flings it at the nearest laughing biker.

The man turns around and looks at Jackson with surprise mixed with anger.

Jackson trumps his scowl with a middle finger. "Like I said, I was *enchanted*." He smiles at me before turning serious. "And just so everyone here knows, this is my girl."

He rises from his seat slowly, spinning in a circle to look at every man there. "She's mine, and I'll gut any motherfucker who says different. I've seen all of you assholes eyeing her, so don't tell me you're not fucking *enchanted* as well."

Lily sits down beside me. "Don't worry. This is normal. All the men in the club think they have to assert their claim when they find the woman they want to spend the rest of their lives with."

She reaches into her pocket and pulls something out. "Hold out your hand."

When I hold my palm out to her, she drops a necklace in it.

Jackson sits back down, straddling the bench. He rests his chin on my shoulder. "Sorry about that," he whispers. Then, he notices the trinket in my hand. "Is that?" he asks his sister.

She nods. "I think she would want Willow to have it. Don't you?"

Jackson takes it from me and holds it in front of my face. A tiny silver dragonfly hangs daintily from the chain. He gives me a moment to look at it before resting it gently around my neck and clasping it.

"It was my biological mothers," he tells me, his fingers brushing lightly over the back of my neck.

"I can't accept this." I reach behind my head to remove it.

Jackson grabs my hands and lowers them to my stomach. "It's yours. She would want you to have it," he repeats.

Lily nods at me with tears in her big brown eyes.

"But we just met," I argue.

"No matter what happens between us, a dragonfly brought you here. This is where it belongs … for now."

Lily runs her finger over the pendant. "You'll know when it needs to travel on. I did." She smiles at me.

"My mom was trafficked, too," Jackson says sadly. "This goes way beyond you just being my girl."

"It looks beautiful on you," Lily sniffles.

Their tiny gift holds so much love, I can't deny I want it. "I'll treasure it."

And yet again, this club gives me something with no strings attached. I don't know that I'll ever be able to accept something without a nervousness in my belly, but I'm trying. And that's all that I can do.

She nods and then spots her husband. "Excuse me," she tells us.

I watch as she walks toward him. He looks my way for a brief second before he notices his wife is crying. His brows pull together in concern. As they're chatting, his gaze bounces between her and me. I hope he isn't angry about the necklace.

"Do you want to go watch the sunset?" my brother asks, pulling my attention away from them.

Jackson stands and helps me up. "Go on. You two need some time to yourselves."

Ash takes my hand and walks toward the trees. We sit down on the incline of the lawn. It's the perfect spot to watch the day fade to night.

"I should never have left you," he says as soon as we lower ourselves to the ground.

I sigh. "Ash, it was the only way you had to get us out of there. What happened to me isn't your fault."

He grips his hair, resting his elbows on his knees. "It wasn't the only way. I could have gotten a construction job like Dad. There're a million things I could have done differently," he chokes.

My heart slowly breaks. My brother has been beating himself up over this for a long time. He's been held hostage just as much as I have.

I place my hand on his arm. "They needed me. Don't be sorry for it. I'm not."

He lifts his face, tears streaming down his unshaven cheeks. He looks so much like my dad right now.

"Who?" he asks.

"The other girls. It had to be me. I'm the only one he would've let in. I'm going to stop them, Ash." I turn back to the trees. "Don't take that away from me. It's how I survived."

He sighs, turning to watch the sunset with me. "I did some things ... you know, in the Army. I told myself the same thing. That it had to be me, that it was my duty. I understand, Willow, I do. I won't take that away."

Avenging Skulls

"Do you think Mom knew what she was doing? Or maybe they tricked her …" I trail off, knowing he understands my mother's addiction no better than I.

"I don't know what to think."

"Maybe we'll never know," I say quietly. The sun kisses the tops of the trees. "I always missed you most at sunset," I admit.

He laughs lightly. "Every night I've watched it and wondered where you were. I always tried to imagine you were happy. What a fool I've been."

"I was," I whisper.

He turns his head, his stare heavy upon my face.

"He wasn't always mean to me. He taught me a lot about the world and myself. It was … is … confusing. But I was always happy when I got to watch the sun set, because that's when I let myself think about you and Dad. Those few seconds every day brought me peace. It felt like you were both there with me. I always imagined it was a greeting card from Heaven."

When the last diamond of light ducks behind the trees, I finally turn to meet his gaze.

"I've missed you terribly," he rasps.

"I've missed you, too."

The noise from the party behind us is slowly getting louder.

"So, you really like it here with them?" He nods over his shoulder.

"Yeah, I do. I really do."

Chapter Thirty-One

Willow

My brother and I continue to talk for hours, and by the time we go back to the party, most of the guests have left and the food has been cleared. The members who remain are lounging on patio chairs with beer bottles in hand.

Jackson pulls me down onto his lap at the picnic table as my brother sits to our right. Kelsie bounces up and down across from us. She's been impatiently waiting for us to join them.

"Your brother told me you like to read. I brought some of my favorites from home, if you'd like to borrow any." She shoves a big box across the table toward me.

My eyes light up. "I love books," I tell her.

My brother and I both peek in the box. The love of books is one thing we've always shared.

I'm thumbing through them when my brother pulls one out. "Ah man, I had this book when I was a kid," he exclaims.

I don't pay much attention. Ash and I had the attic lined with books, so no doubt he's found something we've already read.

Kelsie takes it from him. "This one is special to me." I catch her hug it to her chest out the corner of my eye. "It saved my life."

This gets my full attention. When she holds it out in front of her, I pale.

Jackson's grip tightens around my waist.

She opens it up. "You see, I was trafficked by a family member. He always dropped me off at the same location in the desert."

I try to stand, but Jackson won't release me. My gaze bounces from Kelsie to my brother. They are staring at each other intently. He's fully invested in her story ... in *my* story.

"I saw a plastic bag sticking out from under this big rock near where I waited for the men who would pick me up. My uncle had dropped me off early, so I knew I had time to investigate. It was a book and when I flipped it open, this is what I found." Her eyes leave my brother's, her gaze falling to the page.

To whoever finds this,

This book belonged to the best brother in the whole world. Please treat it with care.

Also, I don't know if you need to hear this, but it will get better. It will. You are strong; you can overcome anything. I know because I lost my brother, and I'm still here.

Anyway, do whatever it takes to survive. Hopefully, this guide will help.

From the girl pretending to be a dragonfly.

When she raises her face, turning toward me, tears are streaming down her cheeks. My brother also turns to face me ... along with everyone else.

"It's why I ran. It's why I'm here. It's why I have a family. It's … it's why I'm alive," she cries.

She's looking at me like I'm her savior. Why is she looking at me like that? Why are they?

I start to squirm in Jackson's arms. "Shh, it's okay," he tries to soothe me.

"I need to go." I push away from him harshly, barreling out of his arms right into a set of ginormous ones.

"Billie Rose, I'm going to take Willow here up to your old room, if that's okay? She needs a minute to compose herself," Big Dan says.

"Of course," she says quickly.

Dan grabs me gently by my bicep and leads me inside the warehouse. He snaps his fingers on his free hand, beckoning Jackson. "You too, kid."

When we get inside, I try to pull away from him. "I need to go," I tell him, hoping my voice relays the urgency in the matter.

"Rule number one, no running. We've had enough of that in this club. So, I'm trying a more proactive approach," he tells me, unfazed by how I'm clawing at his hand.

"You don't understand," I tell him, my voice rising.

He rolls his eyes. "This isn't my first rodeo, doll. I understand just fine."

He drags me up the stairs as Jackson's boots thud behind us.

When he pulls me into a bedroom, I stomp on his foot as hard as I can. The man doesn't even wince. He just picks me up and tosses me on the bed. I bounce a few times before trying to catapult myself back off.

His hand lands in the center of my chest, and I find myself once again falling back against the soft mattress.

I stare up at the ceiling as the door clicks shut. My chest rapidly rises and falls, my breath coming out in loud, short bursts.

And then my head falls to the side, and I'm met with a beautiful mural of the sun setting.

"I listened to you in our meeting today. When you talked about the girls who were trafficked …" Dan pauses. "She was one of them, Willow. You fucking saved her."

"She saved herself," I say to the wall.

"Because your words gave her hope."

I sit up and glare at him. "It wasn't me. I wrote those words to make *me* feel better. He was making me give my only memento of Ash away. He did it to hurt me, and I wanted someone to know what that book meant to me."

"She ran because you told her to do whatever she could to survive. So, she ran, Willow. She got away from them."

I cross my arms over my chest.

"She ran and then she ended up in a treatment facility where she met Billie Rose," he continues.

He dips his head when I start to look away, holding my gaze hostage. "That's where Lily and I met her. Do you want to know how we knew we were meant to be her parents?"

I give him a tiny nod, curiosity getting the best of me.

"She told us her story and showed us the survival guide with your message written inside."

When my brows pull together in confusion, he reaches out and touches the dragonfly pendent resting on my chest. My gaze falls to the necklace.

"You signed the letter with *a girl pretending to be a dragonfly.*"

My eyes fall closed.

He drops his hand. "So, maybe you were right. It had to be you … she wouldn't be here if it wasn't for you. Thank you for the sacrifice you made so my daughter could find her way home."

The bed shifts, and I hear the door click open and then closed behind him.

"Jackson," I cry out.

And he's there, pulling me into his arms. He whispers sweet nothings into my ear while I weep in his arms. I don't know why they call them nothings because right now they're everything.

Eventually my tears run dry.

I wrap my fingers around the pendent hanging from my neck. "You said this necklace was bigger than you and me. You weren't lying."

Jackson smiles. "No, I wasn't lying. Let me tell you the story."

He pulls us to the window seat overlooking the lake. His family and what's left of mine are sitting around the fire pit.

"My dad gave that necklace to my biological mom when they were just teenagers. It was right before they ran away to become models. Someone tricked them into thinking they could get them into the business."

"Your dad was the friend who told her that dragonflies had two sets of wings so they could carry angels on their backs." I reach out and place my hand over his arm.

Avenging Skulls

He lays his hand over mine, narrowing his eyes. "Yes. She had it on when they were trafficked. Years later, she ended up at the home of a senator. He was Lily's father. And now mine, too. You get the gist he was a bad man."

I see guilt in his eyes that shouldn't be his to carry.

Shaking his head, he continues, "Anyway, my mother befriended Lily. She saved her life. She told her it was okay to run, to get away from the evil that resided in that house. That's how my sister ended up here. It's how she met Dan." He points to the necklace. "Big Dan did a dragonfly tattoo on her. She got it in memory of my mother."

My eyes widen. This is all so crazy. But if the senator is Jackson's father too, that means …

"He raped my mother. He's a monster," Jackson answers without me having to ask.

He drops his head, his face becoming flushed. I know that was hard for him to say out loud.

"Raffe recognized the necklace my mother had given Lily, and before long they put the pieces of the puzzle together. Shortly after, they figured out I was her brother. I guess the senator allowed my mother to pick the family who adopted me. She recognized her old friend, and that is how I came to be Raffe's son."

"Jackson, this is …"

"The magic of the dragonfly."

We both sit quietly for a few seconds, marveling at how our worlds have collided.

"We should probably get back downstairs. It's getting late," Jackson finally says.

I nod and slide off the bench.

He grabs me around the waist and pulls me close to him, his lips crashing against mine.

"I don't ever want to lose you," he mumbles as he kisses me, his tongue darting in and out of my mouth. "You're fucking perfect for me. Perfect, Willow."

My stomach flips, and suddenly I can't get close enough to him. My hands slide around to his back, frantically trying to pull him closer.

He picks me up, his hands resting under my butt as he carries me out of the room. "I'm going to figure out how to make this easier for you," he says. "I want to be with you so bad, but I'll wait as long as it takes, baby."

"I don't want to wait." I wrap my arms around his neck, sliding myself over the growing bulge in his pants. I can't believe I'm doing this. But it feels so good. I want him to wrap himself around me, all the way down to my heart.

He groans, setting me on my feet at the top of the stairs. "You're going to have to tell me something funny to get my mind off of you and him." He nods toward his crotch.

I giggle. And then I giggle again because I realize Jackson being aroused doesn't scare me. It excites me, pleases me even.

"Okay." I hold up my finger, trying not to look at his pants by staring at the ceiling. I really try to think of something that could take his mind off his dick, but I can't because that's all I'm thinking about, too.

God, I bet he looks amazing without his clothes on. All his tanned skin and tattoos on glorious display. I wonder how much ink he has in the places I haven't seen.

Avenging Skulls

Someone clears their throat, and we both turn toward the sound.

It's Jackson's dad and my brother. They're both staring up at us from the bottom of the stairs.

Raffe shakes his head. "Your brother needs to talk to you before he heads out."

Jackson whispers in my ear that he's going to use the restroom and then pushes me toward the stairs. I hesitate a moment, glancing back at him before heading down. He walks backward as he runs his hand down the front of his pants, winking at me.

Flustered, I turn and jog down the stairs.

Raffe places his hand on my shoulder when I reach the bottom. "I'm going to run your brother to the airport. There's a flight leaving in two hours."

"No," I groan. "I thought you were staying."

My brother holds my face in his hands. "Calm down. I'm just going home to get my things, Willow. I'm ready to get out of there. I don't want to wait. I can't ..." He glances away. "I can't stay there with her, knowing what she did to you."

"You'll come right back?"

"I'll come right back."

Raffe gently squeezes my shoulder. "You both are right where you belong. Your brother is going to stay here at the warehouse in Jackson's old room when he gets back. And then we'll go from there."

"I trust that you'll take care of my sister?" Ash asks Raffe.

"You know it."

"Don't go. Mom's going to convince you to stay there with her," I whimper.

"Willow," he says, holding up his old survival guide. "I believed you before, but this ..." He taps the book lightly against my forehead. "I'll never leave you again. Never."

Raffe runs his hand down my arm. "He'll be back."

Jackson finally joins us, and my brother fills him in.

"I'll take good care of her," he tells Ash as they shake hands.

My brother pulls me in for a hug. "I love you, Willow."

I nod against his chest, unable to speak.

He pushes me back and kisses my forehead. "I'll see you soon. I gave Raffe my number so you can call me anytime." He chucks me under the chin and then quickly makes a beeline for the door.

I watch as him and Raffe leave.

"He'll be back," a quiet voice says from around the corner.

Kelsie steps into the light. "I'm sorry if I upset you. I didn't mean to. I really did just run home to get you the books, but then my dad showed up and told me what you had said in your meeting."

"I'm sorry for my reaction," I tell her. "I was just a little shocked. I'm glad you found my message."

She perks up, realizing I'm not upset with her. "You saved me," she says quickly.

I school my face, not wanting to show her what I'm really feeling. While I might not believe I saved her, she clearly does.

"I gave it to Ash," she adds. "The book is back where it belongs."

"Thank you for taking such good care of it for me ... for him."

Her face turns serious as she turns to look at Jackson. "You'll help her like you did me?" she asks him.

"It's already in the works," he says confidently.

She nods, then darts away when her brothers call for her.

"We should get back to the farm and take care of the animals," Jackson tells me. "Let me go tell Dirk we're leaving."

I sit down on the step. "I'll wait right here."

He leans down and kisses me on the top of my head before walking away.

Lily steps out of the shadows when he disappears down the hall. "Are you okay?" she asks. "I told Dan I didn't think that was the best way to tell you about Kelsie."

"It's okay," I say, hugging my knees. "I don't know why it upset me so much. But I'm good. No worries."

She sits down beside me. "I know exactly how you were feeling. Did Jackson tell you about our father?"

"Yeah," I say on an exhale. "I'm sorry."

She chuckles sadly. "I blamed myself for the pain my father caused." She runs her hands back and forth over her jeans as she talks. "It still haunts me sometimes. But the blame doesn't lie with me ... just like it doesn't lie with you."

Chapter Thirty-Two

Jackson

Willow is quiet on the way back to the farm. Elijah and Dirk are guarding the house tonight. I'm not sure where they are, but I know they're out here somewhere.

Once we get the animals cared for and we're inside, the tension between the two of us begins anew.

She rocks back on her heels. "Well, I guess I'll go shower." Her dainty finger points to the stairs.

"Yeah, sure. There should be towels in the hallway closet," I tell her.

"Thank you. Billie Rose showed me where they were." She turns to go up the stairs.

I shove my hands in my pockets, watching her go.

She pauses on the bottom step. "Will you come to my room later?"

"Do you want me to?" I ask, my stomach somersaulting with nerves of my own.

Her hand drifts over the wood banister. "I … I want to try."

I know she can't make any promises. "Have you ever been with anyone besides him?"

"Just once."

The clip of her tone tells me it wasn't willingly.

"Okay," I tell her.

She proceeds up the stairs and shortly after, I hear the shower turn on.

I pick up my phone and hit the familiar number that called earlier. When she picks up, I apologize, "Sorry I missed your call. I was tied up."

She gets right to the point. "I got a lead on the guy you messaged me about the other day."

I roll my eyes. "I bet you do."

"What the fuck is that supposed to mean?"

"Look, I don't know where you're getting your information, but I'm taking heat for it." I go out to the kitchen and light up a cigarette, knowing Grandma Maggie will kick my ass if she finds out I'm smoking in her house.

"Don't know what to tell you, kid. I won't divulge my sources. Anyway, do you want the asshole when I end him so she can see he's gone? I know this one is close to you."

I sigh. "Of course, you do. Jesus, if someone's feeding you club information, they're eventually going to get caught. Dirk isn't stupid. He's going to find out."

"Humph. I care about that why?"

"Okay, whatever. Yeah, bring him to me, but I want this one alive."

"No can do, kid. You know the rules. I make sure they aren't breathing before I let them out of my sight."

"Fine. At least make it painful."

"Oh, it will be."

The phone goes dead as the water shuts off upstairs and Willow's feet pad across the hall to her room.

As I'm taking my shower, I get a sick feeling in my stomach. Anytime I think about being intimate with someone, all I can picture is waking up with Lanie sitting on top of me and the confusion that followed.

How the hell am I going to help Willow with this if I can't even help myself? As I'm drying off, an idea comes to me. I head to my room to get what I need before knocking on her door.

A hesitant "come in" sounds from the other side.

I swing the door open but remain in the hallway. She's sitting on the end of the bed in a t-shirt and a pair of shorts. I'm in nothing but sweatpants.

Her gaze roams over my bare chest. I smile when she visibly shivers.

She wrings her hands together. "Are you going to come in?" she asks.

"Only if you invite me." I dip my head, letting my hair fall over my eyes.

She nods.

"Say it out loud." She's going to have to ask for it every step of the way, no matter how uncomfortable it makes her.

Avenging Skulls

"Will you please come in?"

I bat my eyelashes at her dramatically, making her giggle. "I'd love to."

When I get close, I point to the spot beside her. "May I sit?"

"Yes." But she tenses as I begin to lower myself.

"You're sure?" I ask, my ass hovering over the mattress.

"Yes," she says with a tad bit more confidence.

I drop to the bed with a thud, and she bounces toward me, her hands landing on my thigh. We both look down at them.

"It's a bouncy bed," she squeaks, pulling away. She bites her lip. "I'm sorry. I'm a little nervous."

"Me too," I tell her honestly.

Slowly, she swivels toward me, her eyes roaming over my face. Her brows pull together. "Jackson, I want this so bad. I don't want to mess it up."

"We can't mess it up because there is no right or wrong. We do whatever feels right to us." I lean back and set a box on the mattress between us.

I reach into my pocket and pull out a dresser knob, tossing it in one hand a few times before dropping it in the box.

Willow stares at me for a second and then leans over to peek inside. "What is it?"

"It's the knob off a dresser I once made."

"What does it mean?" she whispers.

"I want you to go find something that reminds you of him."

She hops up and searches the house. I hear her opening and closing drawers and then hear her tiny feet run back up the stairs. She's breathing heavy when she reaches the end of the bed. She stares into the box, her fist hovering over it.

Her gaze meets mine before she drops it. "Someone hurt you the way he hurt me?" she asks.

I don't look away from her. It's time I admit to someone what happened to me. "Yes."

When she keeps her eyes trained on me, I continue. "She was Billie Rose's best friend. She always had a crush on me, but it was never going to happen. I just didn't see her that way. Then, one day, while the club was helping her move, I noticed she didn't have a dresser. So, I built her one."

Willow's gaze drops to the bright blue knob laying in the bottom of the box.

"A few months later, I bumped into her. I was having a bad day, so she invited me over to her apartment for a drink." I pause, swallowing hard. "I thought we were just two friends sharing our woes, but then I fell asleep and when I woke up she was …"

I glance away from her, unable to finish, nausea washing over me like it always does when I think about that night.

Willow drops something in the box. It's a business card for the local plumber.

"Bradley always had one," she says, staring at it.

She holds her hand over the box and moves her fingers, threading an imaginary card between them. "He would flip the card over and over and over again."

Willow focuses her gaze behind me.

"Each night I would rest my books against the wall of the van, so I could see them as I fell asleep. They were gifts to Ash and me from my father."

"Was one of them the book you gave me?"

She nods. "The other was the survival guide Kelsie found." She drops her head. "The first night he ..." She grimaces. "I looked at the dragonfly on the cover and thought I would just do what the female dragonfly did when she didn't want attention. I played dead."

It's like someone punches me right in the gut. This whole time I thought the dragonfly had some magical meaning for her like it had for me. But we've been looking at it differently.

"I don't want to play dead with you."

Her words pull me from my thoughts. "Willow," I whisper.

"Don't let me slip away," she begs, taking my hands in hers.

We stare into each other's eyes for a long time. Each of us letting the other see our insecurities.

"We can do this," I tell her. "But goddammit, you stop me if you don't like something."

A shy smile breaks out over her face, and she nods.

I stand up, taking the box with me and set it outside the door. "They stay out there, understand?"

She nods.

'Use your words, baby," I urge.

"Yes, I understand."

"Lights on or off?" I ask, my hand paused on the light switch.

"On."

Okay, I can do this. I can. I rub my hands together.

When I falter a few steps away from her, she takes the lead. Her fingers wrap around the bottom of her t-shirt and, slowly, she pulls it up and over her head.

Okay, that's all the encouragement I needed. Her tits are perfect. I want them in my hands. They reach out on their own accord, but I manage to stop myself.

She leans forward and takes my hand, pulling it to her chest. She presses my palm over her left breast, keeping her hand over mine.

"It's okay, Jackson. I'm not scared of you. I want you to see me; I want you to touch me."

Her hand falls away from mine and she reaches out again, her fingers dancing lightly along the waistband of my pants as she waits for permission.

"I want you to see me. I want you to touch me," I repeat back to her.

Gently, I squeeze her breast, reveling in the lines of her slender neck as her head falls back and she moans.

Jesus, my cock just turned rock hard from that sound alone.

She opens her green eyes just enough so that her long lashes flutter against the apples of her cheeks. Her hand dips inside my sweats, and her fingers hesitantly wrap around me. Her eyes widen.

Willow's reaction to my cock makes the corner of my mouth turn up. My personality is suddenly banging on my ribcage, begging to be let out so he can play. I lightly brush my fingers over her nipple before dragging my palm over her throat, tipping her head back. It continues its path, stopping at her mouth.

Her breath is coming out in tiny pants as I slowly slip my thumb between her lips. She closes her mouth and sucks hard, hollowing out her cheeks. Her hand continues to stroke me. And holy fuck, does it feel good. Too good. I reach down with my other hand to stop her.

"You first," I say quietly as I begin to push her back against the mattress.

I haven't been this turned on in ... well, in *ever*.

God, she's gorgeous.

Her hair fans out around her head as I crawl over the top of her, my eyes taking in every glorious inch of her body. When our gaze meets, I grab her cheeks in one hand and pull her up to me, pressing my lips against hers.

"You are mine, Willow," I say against them.

She nods, and then deepens our kiss. Her mouth is frantic, hungry, possessive. I match her lick for lick. When I release her, her head falls back against the bed with a tiny bounce. She struggles for air as my gaze roams over her body.

I slide my hand under her head as I roll to lie beside her. Threading my fingers through her hair, I grip it harshly. I watch closely as I tug on it, holding her hostage. Her pupils dilate, and she bites her bottom lip. I push her head down so that her chin rests on her chest, forcing her to watch my other hand slowly slide down her body. Her skin is flushed and sweaty. Her chest rises and falls fast as I close in on the promised land.

When my fingers tap over the light dusting of hair between her legs, she lets out a guttural moan, her eyes slowly rolling to mine. Her bottom lip pushes out, and she whimpers. She knows she's going to have to ask for it.

Eventually she gives in; my attention to her pussy is consistent but not enough to take her where she wants to go.

"Please, please give me more."

And that is all the permission I need before I'm sliding two fingers inside her at once. She lets out a satisfied groan, her eyes rolling into the back of her head.

I lean down, rubbing my nose against hers. "Is that what my baby needed?"

"Yessss," she hisses, her hips rising off the bed as I pull my fingers away.

When I push them back in, she closes her eyes.

"No. Open them." I demand, capturing her bottom lip between my teeth. I'm not giving that bastard any chance of slipping into her unconscious mind.

Her eyes fly open as I slip another finger inside her.

I release her lip with a pop, right before she begins to roll her head back and forth over the pillow.

"Jackson, oh my god."

"Come for me, Willow. Come all over my fingers," I order, my thumb pressing down on her clit, my fingers curling inside her as I continue to give her exactly what she needs.

Her eyes frantically seek mine. I see the panic on her face, but it's too late. She's coming.

She cries out as her body convulses against me. I take the opportunity to quickly slide a condom on while kicking my pants down, then I climb on top of her. I wait for her eyes to focus on me. I need some sort of permission here. But I need it fast; I need to be in her like I need to breathe.

Clarity returns to her seductive green gaze, and she gives me a tiny nod. Half a second later, I'm gently guiding myself inside her. I pause once I'm fully seated because she's coming again. She's squeezing my cock so goddamn hard it takes everything in me not to come myself.

"Oh, oh, oh god, Jackson," she screams. Fuck, I love how vocal she is.

I start to move and her nails claw at my back, her legs wrapping around me, feet digging into my ass, pulling me closer. "You feel so fucking good, baby," I tell her, my breath hot in her ear.

"Don't stop. Don't ever stop," she urges me on.

"Never," I whisper before raising up on my arms, her eyes shining with tears as I fuck her with everything that I have. "You are mine, Willow. Mine," I repeat as I pound into her.

Her mouth falls open in a silent scream as she clamps down on me. That's it; I'm a goner.

"Shit, shit, Willow. I'm never going to get enough of you," I say before the world tips on its axis. I spiral into a world of color, feeling a high that I've never experienced before. It's pure euphoria.

I fall on top of her, our bodies sticking together as we try to catch our breath. "Shit, I'm sorry," I say, feeling bad for resting all my weight on her but she pulls me back down.

"Don't. Please stay. Just for a moment," she says, hugging me to her. Her body is shaking. She's crying.

"Did I hurt you?" I ask into the crook of her neck, afraid to look into her eyes and see that I did.

She squeezes me tighter. "No. You set me free," she whispers brokenly.

I push up this time, needing to look at her. Her green eyes are swimming in tears, but she smiles at me. I lean over and run my tongue up her cheek, licking them away.

"I will absorb your pain," I tell her. "I'll take it all and come back for more."

She cries harder. "I think I love you," she rasps.

When our gaze meets, her cheeks turn pink.

"Don't. Don't be embarrassed. I think I love you, too."

Usually, I have a hard time holding eye contact with others. But it's not like that with her. I could stare into her eyes for days and find something new as each moment passes.

"We did it," I say, a flirty smirk pulling at the corner of my mouth.

She nods shyly in agreement. "Can we do it again?"

I raise an eyebrow at her request. "I've created a monster."

She runs her hand over the side of my face. "And I've found an angel."

Avenging Skulls

"I'm no angel," I tell her honestly. She watched me dump a dead man to the hogs. She knows this.

"Angels don't always have white feathers. Sometimes they wear black leather jackets." Her fingertips dance over my throat before she wraps them around my neck and pulls me to her, pressing her lips against mine. "Don't ever doubt that you're mine."

Chapter Thirty-Three

Willow

Jackson and I continued to stare at each other in the dark, both of us laughing from time to time because we kept making funny faces at each other.

I didn't think it could be like this. So comfortable. So good.

His fingers played across my skin like they do his cello. Although I don't make near as beautiful music. It was embarrassing, but I couldn't help how vocal I was. It felt so good. So good.

That was new, too. It felt like a wave, building and building, and just as I was about to stop him, it crashed against the sand, spreading out over my entire body. And then it wouldn't stop. Every time I tried to stand in the surf, another wave would knock me down.

It was wonderful but exhausting.

~~~~~

When I wake, I open my eyes to find him staring at me. He's so adorable with his big brown eyes and mischievous smile.

Avenging Skulls

"Good morning," he tells me.

"It is a good morning," I reply, rolling over and stretching, wiggling my toes under the sheets.

He pounces on top of me, tickling my ribs, and I laugh. My heart is so much lighter today. It had been heavy for so long. I want to enjoy every minute with him.

He hops off the bed like a ninja. "Come on; I'm starving." He pulls his sweats over his hips, tossing my undies and t-shirt to me.

I quickly put them on and follow him from the room, giggling into his back as he leads us down the stairs. When we round the corner to the kitchen, he stops dead in his tracks, making me bounce against him with a little umph. It's then I smell the bacon. He holds me behind his back, shielding me from whomever it is.

"'Bout time you two sleepy heads got up," Grandma Maggie says.

"Oh," I squeak, running for the stairs.

Dirk and Elijah both start laughing, and I hear Billie Rose scold them. Oh no. They all know. What must they think?

Jackson jogs up the stairs behind me. "Willow. Willow, stop. It's okay." He grabs me around the waist and swings me into his chest. He grabs my chin, forcing me to look at him. "If you think any of those people down there think any less of you because we might have enjoyed some time together, you are wrong."

I blink up at him, swallowing back tears. "But ..."

"But nothing. You deserve to be happy, Willow. Just because someone hurt you doesn't mean you're not entitled to intimacy."

"We just met." A tear slips down my cheek.

He swipes it away with his thumb. "That's the best part. We didn't waste any time. I don't want a second to slip by that doesn't involve me loving you."

I wrap my arms around him and bury my face into his bare chest. "You always know the right thing to say."

"I don't. I really don't." He pushes me back and stares down at me with those warm brown eyes of his. "But I will be straight with you, Willow. I'll never play games with your heart."

I believe every word he says.

"Now, let's go get some real clothes on and then go back down and eat. I'm not missing a chance at Grandma Maggie's cooking. If we don't hurry, Elijah will eat it all."

"Okay," I agree, wiping my eyes.

As I get dressed, I think about what Jackson said to me. I do deserve to be happy. I'm a grown woman; I can be with whomever I choose. Bradley would be winning if I denied myself pleasure from the man I'm quickly falling in love with. And I'm done letting him win. In fact, I'm done playing his games altogether. This is my life. It doesn't belong to anyone but me.

When we get back downstairs, the other men are gone and it's just Grandma Maggie. She's sitting at the table, buttering toast.

"Sit, sit," she says, pointing at the chairs with her butter knife.

"Sorry we weren't dressed for the table, Grandma. We thought we were alone," Jackson says as he slides my chair in for me. Then he takes a seat across the table.

Avenging Skulls

"No worries. The others went out to start on the chores. Billie Rose picked me up this morning so we could come help Willow with the garden."

Jackson shoves an entire piece of bacon in his mouth, nodding.

"I've got a few garden tricks up my sleeve," she continues, reaching over and nudging my plate toward me. "Eat. We've got a lot of work to do today."

I give her a small smile, my cheeks heating to an alarming degree, but she doesn't mention that her grandson and I slept in the same room. She just continues on about the garden.

"The food at Gladstone is shit," she says, and Jackson chokes on his food.

He pounds on his chest. "Grandma, did you just curse?"

She rolls her eyes. "Shit is shit, boy. And that is exactly what the food is there. I'm hoping maybe we can get a good amount of produce from the garden, and we can donate it to them. Vegetables shouldn't come from a can, Son."

He laughs. "Just take some of the jars from the cellar that you've already done up."

"Well, I plan on it. But we have to keep things going, and now that we have help, I think we can do that."

A squeal of delight rings from the yard. I take a bowl of strawberries and walk over to the screen door, watching as Billie Rose runs with her daughter through the sprinkler. Her husband, Elijah, is leaning on a garden hoe, his face filled with love for his little family.

Jackson slides up behind me and rests his chin on my shoulder. "Billie Rose was hurt too; would you want her to deny herself the pleasure of that little girl?"

I turn my face so we are nose to nose. "No," I whisper.

My gaze goes back to them as I pop another strawberry in my mouth, absentmindedly holding one up for Jackson. He bites it in half, and I put the rest of it in my mouth. We do this for several minutes, just watching the little girl toddle through the sprinkler, the sun glinting off the water like she's running through a spray of tiny jewels.

When the bowl is empty, we both turn around to find Grandma Maggie with tears in her eyes. I glance at Jackson. "I'm going to go help outside," I tell him.

He nods, holding the door open for me before walking over to comfort his grandmother.

Before I take the first step down the stairs, I hear her say, "Your mama sent that girl to us. There's a reason she's here."

"I know, Grandma. I know," he replies.

Chapter Thirty-Four

Willow

Her words stay on my mind the rest of the day. She made it sound like I'm here to do something for them, but it's the other way around. They're going to help me get justice for the girls that Bradley and his organization have hurt.

People have come and gone all day, each seeming to know what their job is when they get here. And Grandma Maggie has kept an endless amount of food coming out of the kitchen. I stand up and wipe my brow as the sun slides behind the trees. It's wonderful; here I feel like I'm a part of something bigger than myself.

Billie Rose and I take Aurelia upstairs to get clean. She's going to give Grandma a ride home. I head into my room to grab some clothes while she takes her daughter into the bathroom across the hall. When I come back out, Raffe is standing with a box in his hands. He reaches in and pulls out the business card.

He looks up at me. "What's this?" he asks.

I tug on my shirt, hesitant to answer but I can't lie to him. "The card reminds me of Bradley." I shake my head nervously. "It was something

Jackson came up with to help me keep Bradley out here and not in …" I shyly point to the bedroom.

Raffe drops the card back in the box like it burnt him. But then he picks up the blue dresser knob. "This came off Lanie's …" He sets the box on the floor where he found it before spinning in a circle. He presses his fingers into his forehead. "No. No."

His beautiful blue eyes stop on me, pleading for me to tell him whatever he's thinking isn't true.

Jackson jogs up the stairs, and his brows pull together when he notices the distress on his father's face.

"Dad?"

Raffe spins around. "Did Lanie?" He jerks his head toward the box on the floor.

Jackson sighs loudly. "She drugged me," is all he says.

In two forceful steps, Raffe has his son wrapped in his arms, patting him on the back. "I'm sorry, Son."

Jackson and I lock eyes, neither of us flinching. Is this hard? Yes, but we are both committed to healing. No matter how uncomfortable that is. We both need to face things head on so we can move forward.

The bathroom door opens the same time Raffe says, "Does Billie Rose know?"

"Know what?" she asks, but then she notices the look on all our faces.

"No, she doesn't know," Jackson answers.

Raffe drops his head. "Shit, I'm sorry."

Avenging Skulls

Billie Rose's gaze bounces from one man to the other, worry beginning to pull at her features. "What is it? What's wrong?"

Jackson walks over to her and puts his arm around her shoulders. "Nothing is wrong. Why don't you go get Grandma dropped off, and I'll meet you at your place after I shower."

She looks down at her daughter who is tugging at her hand, ready to go. She's played hard all day. I smile as she rubs at her eyes; she is so cute.

"Okay, yeah, I'll see you soon." She rises up on her tippy toes and gently places a kiss to his cheek, then she's off, jogging down the stairs.

"I'm sorry," Raffe apologizes again.

"No worries, Dad. I was going to tell her anyway. Willow is making me want to face a few things." He grabs my hand and brings it to his mouth, kissing it gently.

"Is this why you've been so distant?" Raffe asks.

"Yeah, I … I feel guilty for not speaking up. If I would have, maybe Billie Rose wouldn't have gotten hurt."

Raffe's shoulders fall. "You are not to blame for that."

I'm a little confused, but I get the gist. This Lanie person doesn't sound like she was a very good friend to Billie Rose.

"Can I go with you?" Raffe asks.

"Yeah," Jackson says, running his fingers through his unruly brown hair. "Just let me shower, and I'll meet you downstairs. That is if you'll be okay?" he directs his question to me.

"Sure, I'll be fine. I could use a little quiet time," I tell him. "That big bookshelf downstairs has been calling to me."

He presses a kiss to my forehead and then notices the clothes in my hand. His mouth tips up on one side, and he winks at me. "Go get the water going, babe. I'll be there in a minute."

He pushes me toward the bathroom and then smacks me on the butt. My mouth falls open as I rub my hand over my ass.

His dad starts laughing. "That's my cue to go. If you kill him for that, I don't want to be an accessory to the crime."

I narrow my eyes at Jackson. His grin just gets wider.

"I don't think you quite know what you've gotten yourself into, Willow," Raffe hollers up the stairs as he makes his way down them.

But when we're alone, I allow my smile to come out. "You're terrible," I scold.

"And you love it." Jackson grabs a towel out of the closet and tosses it over his shoulder.

"You like to make people smile, don't you?" I ask, leaning against the door jamb.

"I get it from my dad." His gaze wanders to the stairwell. "I don't want him feeling bad over this shit. He's a great old man. He doesn't deserve to feel one ounce of guilt over any of this."

"I feel the same about my brother." Stepping back, I begin to close the bathroom door.

He points at me. "Don't you dare lock that door. I wasn't kidding, I'll be there in two seconds."

He doesn't lie. Soon enough he is slipping in behind me, his big hands roaming over my body. I drop my head back against his chest and sigh. "Why am I so comfortable with you?" I ask.

Avenging Skulls

"Because you already know me. We're soulmates."

I turn in his arms.

"Don't ever lose me again," I whisper.

He dips his head and captures my mouth against his. "You found me. You're strong, Willow. Have faith you will find me for all eternity."

We finish washing, knowing his dad is waiting for him downstairs.

While we're drying off, he shakes his head. "You know what? Why don't you just come with me. I don't like the thought of leaving you here alone."

"I'm hardly alone. Fred is here, and I'm sure there are at least two Skull men outside."

He tosses his towel in the hamper. "Dan and JD are on tonight, but that's not the point. I don't want to leave you."

"That is a *you* problem, not a *me* problem," I tell him. "I'll be fine. Like I said, my head is a jumbled mess. It won't hurt me to have some time to reflect on all that's happened."

"Way to put me in my place," he jokes, rubbing his hand over his heart like I wounded him.

I flick my towel at his butt. "You had a life before me, Jackson. I know how important this conversation with your cousin is."

After they finally leave, I settle down in front of the bookcase, rifling through all the old books. I get lost in the words of a curled-up paperback. It looks like it's been well-loved, and those are usually the best stories.

The back door opens, and Big Dan fills the frame. "Hey, Raffe asked me to come in and let you use my phone to call your brother back."

I place the book on the footstool and wave him in. "Thank you. I hope he made it okay. I miss him already."

He sets his big body in the chair next to me. He pushes a few buttons before handing his cell over.

My brother picks up on the first ring. "Thank god," he says. "Willow, listen. I'll be fine. Don't …"

And then it's not his voice any longer. The man on the other end rattles off a number. 'Call that number as soon as you're alone. Got it?" he asks.

"Yeah, yeah," I say, glancing at the old landline phone hanging on the wall in the kitchen.

Big Dan's eyes never leave me.

"I'm glad you made it," I manage to say.

"Don't fuck with me, Willow," Bradley's grandfather says in my ear.

"Yeah, I'm tired too. I was just getting ready to head to bed."

"I mean it, Willow. You have no idea how far my reach goes," he warns.

"I'll talk to you soon. Get some sleep." I can hear my brother struggling on the other end of the line.

"Love you," I force out and then disconnect the call. I stare at the phone for a second, forgetting Dan is beside me.

"Everything okay?" he asks.

"Yeah." I hand him his cell, standing up. "He made it." I yawn and stretch. "He was pooped. Me too, but I'm glad he called. I'll sleep better."

Avenging Skulls

Big Dan doesn't move. He just watches me head to my room.

"Thanks for letting me talk to him. Goodnight," I say, then turn and calmly walk up the stairs, even though my heart is beating as if I had just run up them.

I pause to listen at the top and when I hear him leave, I rush into my room. I stumble over the phone cord as I pull it onto the bed. My fingers shake as I dial the number. Is this right? God, please have let me remember it correctly. It rings a few times before someone picks up.

"What do you want?" I ask the minute I know he's there.

He remains silent. Shit. I want to cry out in frustration. He's the master of the game. He's the one who started it all.

"Hello, this is Willow. I'm returning your call," I try again, my voice trembling.

"Much better," he says simply.

"How can I help you?" I grit out, hating every minute of this but he has my brother.

"Perhaps you know where I could locate my grandson?"

My heart stops. "No," I say quietly.

"No? Well, you see that's a problem. Because the people you are with have him."

"I don't know, I swear. Please don't hurt my brother," I beg, choking back a sob.

"You've always been such a good girl, Willow. You want to continue that, don't you?" His voice filters through my head. That warm feeling of pleasing them floods my system.

"Yes," I whisper.

"Good. Then this is what you're going to do. You are going to come to me."

I glance around the room. "Why?"

"I want my grandson back, Willow."

"You ... you think they'll trade Bradley for me?" I ask in disbelief.

"I know that's what they'll do." His voice is full of arrogance. "You figured out how to escape Bradley; I'm sure you'll have no problem escaping them. I'll be at the last place we met, same time. I suggest you hurry."

Click. The phone goes dead.

I place it on the bedside table and walk over to the window. I'll have to take the train and then either hitch a ride or walk. He's not far ... it was the last place we met up with him. A place I'd like to forget.

Masculine voices filter up the stairs; Jackson must be home. Quickly, I shove my things in my backpack, pausing to look at the bug catcher Jackson gave me. I press my finger over one of his prints.

"I'm sorry," I whisper.

When I hear his boots thud up the stairs, I rush under the covers and pretend to be asleep.

I listen as he shuffles around the room and then slides in next to me. He doesn't wake me, and I breathe a small sigh of relief for that. But I know this was just the first hurdle. I still have to get past him and the two men guarding the farm.

I wait for what feels like forever before I slide out from underneath the blanket, tiptoeing to my bag. Standing at the foot of the bed, I pray

I'll find my way back to him. But I can't let my brother die for me. He was resurrected once; I don't know how many more times that can happen.

After creeping downstairs and out of the house, I get to the edge of the trees and glance around. So far so good. Maybe this will be easier than I thought. I slow my steps and quietly make my way into the forest. Just as I'm about to cross the stream, a twig snaps behind me. I freeze.

"Tsk. Tsk. Tsk," Jackson ticks off behind me. "This is one game I won't allow you to win."

My shoulders drop. "Jackson, this isn't a game. I have to go."

"Not happening, sweetheart," he says, stepping out into the light of the moon.

I take a step back. "Jackson, he has my brother. I can't lose him again," I beg.

"Willow, Dan listened in on the call you made. He heard everything. He knew something was up." Jackson pauses, running his hands through his hair. "Did you know your brother made me, made us, promise we would look after you?"

Elijah jumps out of a nearby tree, making me jump a foot, giving Jackson just enough time to grab me. He holds my hands behind my back, speaking into my ear.

"Listen to me. We will get your brother back, but we need to be smart about this. I'm not risking you. I'm just not."

Several Skull men step out from the shadows.

I try to pull away from him. "I'll be fine. He just wants to use me as a trade. He wants Bradley back." The more I squirm, the tighter his grip becomes.

Dirk's boots thud loudly as he makes his way through the trees. He stops when he spots us. "Get her inside." He whistles sharply and everybody moves.

Jackson flips me around and heaves me over his shoulder. My hands press against his muscular back as I try to get my balance. *Jesus, what is happening?*

When we get inside, I'm dumped into a chair as the men crowd the kitchen. This is much more intimidating than the meeting I had with them at the warehouse. Tonight, they are agitated and restless.

Dirk slams a pint of ice cream down in front of me, then takes the seat beside me. Jackson takes the other side and hands me a spoon.

I'm so confused that I stop fighting. I glance back and forth between the two men.

Dirk takes the lid off, and I watch his large, tattooed hands as he speaks. "How old were you when he took you?"

"Fifteen," I answer quietly.

He takes the spoon from me and sticks it in the container. "You didn't have any family around to protect you then. But you do now."

"But my brother," I hiccup, wiping my eyes.

"Your brother has spent the last five years beating himself up for not being there for you. And when he found out you had been kidnapped and didn't just run off like your mother wanted him to believe, it just about killed him."

I take the spoon filled with ice cream. "Strawberry is my favorite," I tell them, feeling a bit awkward with them all watching me eat.

"I know. Grandma Maggie brought it for you this morning," Jackson says, running his hand over my back.

Slowly, I set the spoon down. When Bradley's grandfather called me, my mind instantly went back to telling me I was alone. He so easily persuaded me right back into being the girl in the van.

I don't even know his name. I've always just called him Bradley's grandfather in my head. I've never had any reason to address him as anything other than that.

Until now.

"Can we feed him to the hogs?"

Raffe barks out a laugh, pushing away from the countertop he was leaning against. "At least she didn't ask to set him on fire." He slaps Dirk across the back.

Dirk raises an eyebrow but doesn't look at him. "Who is he?"

"He's the man who runs it all. He's Bradley's grandfather." I shove another spoonful of ice cream in my mouth, suddenly feeling better. There's no reason whatsoever that I have to keep any of this quiet. Well, except for my brother. My stomach turns, wondering what is happening to him.

Dirk runs his hand over the stubble on his face as he watches emotions play over mine. "Your brother was in the military. Don't doubt his abilities."

He's right; my brother is a survivor. We both are. "Well, what are we going to do?" I ask them.

Jackson turns my face toward him. "We're going to go with you … and then you're going to get your wish."

Bradley's grandfather is my punishment for pretending like the female dragonfly. Bradley is always kind and gentle with me; for some reason I'm his soft spot. But he wants me to look at him when he is intimate with me; he wants me to love him.

But I would rather die than open my eyes.

It's the one thing I can save for my soulmate. Not that I'll ever find them. But even the female dragonfly quits playing dead at some point. When she finds the dragonfly she wants.

Maybe I'll never get away. Maybe Bradley is the only man I'll ever know.

Pain radiates down my back as his grandfather presses his boot against it. "Maybe I should keep you for myself." He leans over, his finger trailing down my spine. "You would be so much fun to break. You're a tough one, aren't you?"

I keep my eyes shut tight.

He crouches over me. His fingers run through my tangled hair. "I've been in this business a long time, and I've only seen one other girl have as much gumption as you. She was one of the first girls I ever took."

He yanks my hair, pulling my head back. "It's okay." He runs his hand over my face, smearing tears down it. "You can keep your eyes closed; I don't mind."

Jackson takes the spoon from my hand and scoops another bite, shoving it in his mouth. His gaze scans my face as he goes in for another spoonful, bringing it to my mouth.

"Tell us everything you know, and we'll watch your back."

I accept the ice cream and think about what he's saying. They aren't asking me to stay behind; they're letting me save myself.

"Like I said, he wants to trade me for Bradley. So, he's going to expect to take me."

"No can do," Big Dan says. "We can't let her out of our sight."

Avenging Skulls

"We don't even have Bradley yet, so no, we can't let it get that far," Jackson agrees.

"But ... he said you guys had him."

Dirk leans back and folds his arms across his chest. "Petey is working on it. We'll find him."

I'm nervous. Is Bradley really missing like his grandfather thinks, or is this all a big scheme to get me back? Either way, it has to play out. I have to get Ash back.

"I'm going to need another map," I tell them.

A man standing off to the side takes a seat at the table and opens his laptop. "Resident computer geek here. My name is Travis. What do you need, hun?" His fingers are clicking away before I even speak.

"I'll put the coffee on," Big Dan says.

"None of this leaves the room," Dirk's voice booms across the space. His eyes turn dark as he runs them over each of his men.

They all nod in unison.

Chapter Thirty-Five

Willow

We got the call right before we arrived at the rendezvous point that my brother escaped. Raffe had to talk him down over the phone when he relayed our plan to him. I don't know how the call ended because I had to get in position quickly. We didn't want Bradley's grandfather to know I had found out that my brother had gotten away.

The plan has to continue. It's just changed from a rescue mission to an assassination. When I handed over my maps to the Skulls, I had hoped they would catch Bradley's grandfather in the process of rounding up the traffickers. But he is a bit trickier. He only comes out at certain times and rarely, if ever, do his own people even know when he's on the move.

I run my hands down my jeans, a bead of sweat trickling down my spine as the sun beats down on me. Their eyes are on me, but I'm still nervous.

One of his hired men steps out from the trees first. I didn't think he would come alone. Not this time.

My gaze stays focused on my shoes as he walks around the trees, his boots heavy with authority. "It's all clear boss," he says into his collar.

The minute Bradley's grandfather steps out, a cold breeze blows across the lake, making me shiver.

He sits down beside me, his arm draped lazily across the back of the bench. "It's a beautiful day, isn't it, Willow?" he asks.

"Yes, sir," I reply, my eyes still trained in front of me.

"High noon. You remembered," he jokes.

That was when we met for my punishment. I'm assuming the plan is the same as it was then; he'll take me back to his home hidden in the mountains. The thought makes me whimper out loud.

This seems to please him. He places his palm against my cheek and turns my face toward him. "Maybe we can see about getting you to keep your beautiful green eyes open this time." His thumb rubs over my face. "They *are* so beautiful filled with tears."

I begin to tremble, my bravado dissipating with every second that passes. What if the guys aren't really here? I don't know where they are. I can't see them.

No. Don't think that way. They're close. Jackson won't let me down. I have to trust them … him.

Bradley's grandfather smiles before his gaze roams down my face, pausing on my neck. His forehead wrinkles, his normally handsome face changing right before my eyes. His finger traces over the silver dragonfly resting against my skin.

He jerks his hand back as if it burned him. His eyes meet mine.

A shot echoes across the lake, and his hired man drops to the ground with a thud. Bradley's grandfather jumps up. "What the …"

I stand slowly.

"Where did you get that?" He points to my neck, his eyes frantically searching the area for the shooter.

Skull men begin to filter in around us.

Bradley's grandfather starts to back away, but he stumbles right into Jackson. Jackson brings his knife up to the old man's neck, holding him securely in place. Then, he turns his brown eyes my way, tossing me a quick wink.

Bradley let this man hurt me. Jackson, well, Jackson's going to kill him for it. And I hate to admit it, but I've never seen anything sexier.

Dirk whistles across the lake, and I see my brother stand from the weeds, a rifle in his hands.

I double over with relief at seeing him.

"Willow?" the old man rasps in disbelief.

I straighten to my full height, hearing my name fall from his lips. "What? You didn't think I was capable of deceiving you?"

He clenches his jaw, pulling his head back, trying to escape Jackson's blade. "Where did you get that necklace?"

My fingers dance over it, confused as to why he's so focused on my jewelry.

"She got it from me," Raffe breaks the silence, stepping up behind me.

He reaches around me and cups the little dragonfly in his hand. He stares at it a long time before letting his stare roam over to the old man.

Avenging Skulls

"Does it look familiar to you?" He tips his hand, letting it fall softly against my skin before stepping around me.

Bradley's grandfather pushes back against Jackson as Raffe approaches them.

"Because you look awfully familiar to me," Raffe says, his eyes roaming over the man's face. "You've aged well."

What the fuck is happening?

Dirk cracks his knuckles loudly, making the old man whimper. I watch in fascination as Dirk and Raffe begin to circle him.

Jackson's eyes widen as the realization hits him. "Is this ...?" He shoves the man to his knees before stepping away.

"It's the man who handed your mother a business card at the mall and convinced her he could make her a star," Raffe answers Jackson, flicking his finger out in front of him for effect. Venom drips from his tongue as he crouches down in front of Bradley's grandfather.

Jackson spins in a circle, his fingers combing through his hair. "Fuck. Fuck. Fuck!"

Dirk glares at the old man. "Oh, we've been looking for you for a very long time." He cracks his knuckles again. "Seems a little dragonfly dropped you right in our lap." He looks over his shoulder at me.

I'm stunned, frozen, blinking like a doe in headlights. Is Bradley's grandfather the man who tricked Miss Maggie's daughter, Jackson's mother?

"I'm not giving you any information about my business, so you may as well kill me now," he says, trying to sound stoic but even I detect the fear in his voice.

Raffe laughs harshly. "Oh, I don't want your information. I want you." He shoves him in the chest with a finger, making the old man topple over onto his ass. "Tie him up and take him to the truck," he orders.

Everyone moves on Dirk's whistle.

"No, wait. Kill me here," the old man pleads.

Dan and Elijah drag the man away. His wail fades as they make their way through the trees.

Jackson rests his hand against the side of my face. "Are you okay?" he asks.

"What just happened?" I whisper.

"We can talk about it on the road. We should get going." He urges me toward the path.

"Wait. I forgot to ask about how your conversation with Billie Rose went."

"It went fine. No worries about that right now. My only concern is you."

I allow him to pull me along, glancing over my shoulder, catching Dirk and Raffe in an embrace. Raffe's head is buried in Dirk's chest. The scene makes my heart hurt.

My mind is fried by the time we reach the vehicle. My brother jogs across the field and bowls me over, picking me clean up off my feet.

"I'm so glad you didn't come alone."

When he sets me on the ground, I put my hands on my hips. "I didn't have much choice."

Avenging Skulls

He exchanges a look with Jackson, and then my brother reaches out and shakes his hand, pulling him in for a hug. "I owe you, man. I was so worried she would listen to that bastard and take off by herself."

"Oh, she tried."

My brother gives me a scolding swat on the butt before shoving me toward the truck. He slides in next to me as Jackson comes around and takes the driver's seat.

On the way back to the warehouse, I lean against my brother, enjoying the warmth of his arms. He hugs me tight. "Sleep, Willow. I'll wake you when we get home."

"Home." That sounds nice. A sleepy smile tugs at my mouth. Before my eyes drop closed, Jackson wraps his hand around mine.

I've never felt more safe.

"My grandfather taught me everything he knew. It's really not that hard to spot a good one," Bradley says, his eyes perusing over the girls on the beach. *"It's the quiet ones. Those are the ones you want."*

I keep my eyes on the page, trying to focus on the sound of waves breaking against the beach.

"The ones who don't know how pretty they are."

I brush sand off my hands and sit up. My gaze roams over the group of friends who are unknowingly being stalked.

"Then you dangle a business card in front of her, just like a worm on a hook. You'll catch one every time just by playing off their insecurities."

He flips the card through his fingers, over and over as he searches for his next victim.

I know the minute he spots her because the card stops. He dusts sand from his shorts and stands. "Don't move," he orders and then jogs over to the group of girls, giving them a view of his perfect body and killer white smile.

Giggles waft on the wind as I watch him approach the shy girl. The one who still has her t-shirt on over her bikini. She takes the card from his hand, her cheeks turning bright pink. Her friends all turn away, not interested now that they are not the center of his attention.

When he comes back and plops down beside me, he tips his sunglasses down his nose. "See how easy that was?" He laughs cruelly as he talks about how surprised she'll be when she shows up at the address on the card.

The one that's forever changing.

Chapter Thirty-Six

Raffe

I glance in the rearview mirror, watching the old fucker tug at his binds. He isn't going anywhere.

When I spied him through the binoculars, the scared fourteen-year-old boy I thought I'd left behind came back. I didn't have time to wrap my head around the fact that the man I'd been searching for most of my life was right in front of me.

Then I saw the look on his face when he saw the necklace Lily had given Willow. The very one I'd given to Jackson's biological mother before we were trafficked. I didn't have time to ponder the extreme coincidence of it all. I just knew I didn't have much time, so I gave the signal to Willow's brother to take out the bodyguard.

Thank god Ash escaped when he did. I picked him up on the side of the road and dropped him off across the lake with a weapon. The kid proved himself today. I think he would do anything for his sister. That's just the type of guy we need in the club. I'm going to talk to Dirk about having him prospect.

"You okay, man?" Dirk asks.

My gaze leaves the road, meeting his briefly. "I don't fucking know."

He lays his head against the seat. "This might be an even bigger mind fuck than finding out Lily was Jackson's sister."

Dan is crammed in the back, his eyes focused on the man in the bed of the truck. "Lily isn't going to believe this. We've looked for this asshole for twenty plus years. And then Willow just falls in our lap. We were messed up over her connection to Kelsie, but this …" He pauses before meeting my eyes in the mirror.

We all sit quietly and then Dirk starts to laugh. "Fuck! Fuck!" He hits the dashboard. "We finally got him!"

I nod slowly, reality finally hitting me. "We got him." I shake my head in disbelief.

"Shit, I can fucking retire now," Dirk says.

Dan and I exchange a glance. "Fuck that," I tell him.

"No, I'm serious. I'm ready to take a back seat and enjoy my girls. You don't know what it's like being married to someone who is sixteen years younger than you."

Dan snorts. "Fuck, I can keep up just fine with my woman. Is Jesse getting the best of you?"

Dirk's eyebrow climbs up his face. "I keep up just fine."

"Then what do you mean?" I ask him.

"It's just I'm not getting any younger. I want to enjoy my time with my family without the pressure of running the club."

"Have you talked to Jesse about this?" I roll my window down and light up a cigarette.

Avenging Skulls

"She knows. But we hadn't given up hope. We wanted to find him first." He nods toward the back of the truck.

I flick my cigarette out the window, avoiding his gaze. "You two ... Jesus, you guys don't owe me anything. You should have quit when you wanted. But we've found him now, so I guess you can pass the gavel on."

We all sit quietly for a few minutes.

"Well, I ain't taking the fucking job," Big Dan bitches from the backseat, breaking the awkward silence.

Dirk and I both laugh. "I agree," I add. "I just want to ride. I'm getting too old for this shit."

"You think it's time to pass things down to the next generation?" Dirk smirks. "You guys think they can handle it?"

"We did, and we had no idea what the fuck we were doing. I don't expect much more than that."

We all chuckle.

"It's been a hell of a ride, brothers," Dan says, placing a hand on each of our shoulders.

When we get back to town, I tell Dirk to text Brody. "Have him stop by and pick up Grandma Maggie. She gets the first swing."

Dirk chuckles darkly. "Don't be surprised if the old woman ends him before any of us get a chance. I've seen that woman wield a fly swatter."

Again, we laugh, and it feels good. Man, the club has needed a win like this.

Jenny, we got him. The angel you sent led us right to him.

Chapter Thirty-Seven

Willow

Grandma Maggie has Jackson place a chair directly in front of Bradley's grandfather. I still don't know his name. I think I like it that way.

She sits and stares at him for a long time. So long, it begins to get under his skin. When he starts to tug against his binds, she motions for me to join her. Jackson steps behind us.

She takes my hand in hers and squeezes. "Thank you," she says quietly.

I begin to tell her it wasn't me, but she clicks her tongue. "Don't say it," she scolds, then her eyes narrow on Bradley's grandfather. "Did you hurt this young woman?" she asks him.

He doesn't respond.

Like lightning, she stands and slaps him across the face. "That was for my daughter." Her hands shake as fury rushes through her body. She rears back and slaps him again. "And that one was for my new granddaughter, Willow."

Blood trickles out of the corner of his mouth.

"May you rot in hell for eternity," she spits. Then, she hobbles away from him, patting me on the arm on her way past.

But the old man refuses to let her get the last word. He smirks at me. "Both were so worth it."

Suddenly Raffe appears; he pulls a knife out of his boot and, without missing a step, walks up to Bradley's grandfather and presses it against his neck.

"You're going to die tonight. The only question is how."

The forest is quiet except for a flock of birds that rush out of the trees above us. Blackbirds, hundreds of them, circle in the sky.

Jesse wraps her arm around Raffe's neck. "We should set him on fire."

Raffe's chest heaves as he holds the knife to the old man's throat, his hand trembling.

Dirk walks up to join them. "Your call, man."

"Let the bonfire begin!" Raffe yells, raising his fist.

He backs away after spitting in Bradley's grandfather's face. His eyes remain locked on the man who trafficked him all those years ago as the club members gather wood.

Dan walks up and hands Raffe a can of gas. "This should help things along."

The old man begins to plead with Raffe for mercy, but there's none to be had.

After he's doused with gas, Raffe lights up a cigarette and tosses it at the old man's feet. I turn in Jackson's arms, burying my face in his chest as the fire erupts.

"Do you want to leave?" he whispers.

"No. I just can't watch," I say as screams ring through the night.

When they stop several minutes later, I let out a shuddery breath.

"It's over, baby," Jackson says.

I look over to find Dirk and Jesse on each side of Raffe, hugging and comforting him. My eyes slide over the remaining members of the club, most slipping through the trees, headed back to the warehouse. Big Dan hugs Lily to his chest as she cries.

That feeling of being a part of something bigger than myself bubbles in my gut. While I just witnessed something horrific, I still feel safer than I ever have before.

Jackson takes Grandma Maggie's hand after passing me off to my brother, and the four of us begin to make our way back up the path.

"Grandma, do you want to stay with us tonight?" Jackson asks her.

"I think I'll go home with Dan and Lily," she says, patting his arm. "Your sister wears her heart on her sleeve. I'd like to be there for her."

He kisses the old woman on the cheek and tells us to help ourselves to the bar. He's going to help her out to Dan's truck.

"Why don't you both stay here at the warehouse tonight?" my brother suggests, helping me onto a stool then walking around to make us both a drink.

I stare into the brown liquid after he pushes it in front of me. "I've never had a drink," I tell him. "Well, I had part of a beer once," I chuckle sadly to myself.

Ash sits across from me and sighs. "You've missed out on so much."

I pull the glass to my lips, reveling in the burn as liquor flows down my throat.

"I'm sorry about shooting that guy in front of you today. And for everything you saw tonight." He looks away, guilt pulling at his brows. "I haven't done a very good job at protecting you from much of anything."

"If you allow yourself to feel guilty, he wins. Besides, it's not the first time I've seen someone killed."

"It doesn't ever leave you," he groans, ghosts from days gone by appearing in the lines on his face.

The military changed him.

Jackson comes back inside, joining us. "You okay, baby?" he asks.

"I'm ready to go home," I answer, setting my glass down on the bar.

"You're not staying?" My brother pouts.

I shake my head. "No. I'd like to sleep in my own bed tonight."

"Okay," he says sadly.

Jackson pulls me to my feet. "Why don't you come with us?" he asks my brother. "You can have my room."

Ash still sees me as a child. Not enough time has passed for him to see me as a woman. He opens his mouth but then snaps it shut. "That's okay, man."

"You sure? We'll be right across the hall."

He shakes his head and waves us off, bringing the glass to his lips.

Ash is still struggling when we walk away. I'd like to make this easier for him, but I need to take care of me first. Tonight, I need Jackson. I need him wrapped around my heart and my body. It's the only place in this world I feel completely safe.

Before we walk out the door, my brother rushes over and gives me a tight hug. "I love you, Willow."

"I love you too, Ash."

"I'll see you tomorrow."

I nod, giving him one last hug before leaving him behind at the warehouse. As the door closes, I catch Dirk and Raffe waving my brother back over to the bar.

Maybe Ash needs these bikers as much as I do.

On the way home, I fight back tears. I can't believe Bradley's grandfather is gone and it's over. Well, Bradley is still out there, but without his grandfather the business is dead. At least for now.

The Skulls have men all over the United States watching the pickup locations I've given them. Unfortunately, there are so many people involved, some will no doubt slip by. A new master of the game will lay down his board, and the trafficking will continue.

"Watcha thinking about?" Jackson asks, his sharp features standing out against the dash lights.

"Nothing." I swallow, focusing my attention back to the road.

"You know we're going to get Bradley, too. It's just a matter of time. Petey won't stop until he finds him."

The farmhouse comes into view as we round the bend, and I breathe a sigh of relief. Yesterday, when I tried to take off alone, I worried I may never see it again.

"Your grandmother is the strongest woman I've ever met. She's the best thing that's ever happened to me," I tell him, remembering the first time I saw her.

Jackson shuts his truck off and stares up at the house. "She is," he simply says. And then he turns his warm autumn eyes my way. "You remind me a lot of her."

I pull my head back and chuckle lightly. "Wait. You're serious?"

He lays his hand on the side of my neck and gently tugs me close. His minty breath whispers over my face. "I wish you could see yourself as we all do."

"And I wish the same for you," I return, running my fingers through his short beard. "You're beautiful," I tell him.

He laughs.

I'm sure he's been told this before, so I add the most important part. "And you're even more beautiful here." I move my hand from his face and place it over his heart.

This makes him drop his head.

"I know you don't believe it, but it's true, Jackson. The men in your club respect you ... they're loyal to you. Petey and Brody, especially. I think you've been selling yourself short."

"Not anymore," he says, suddenly pressing his lips to mine.

I tip my head back as he licks and bites his way from my mouth down the side of my neck.

"God, I love you, Willow. You're the best goddamn little woodland fairy."

This makes me smile at the ceiling of his truck. "Will you be my fae king?" I ask him.

His mouth stills, his breath hot on my skin. "What are you asking me?"

"I don't know how any of this happened. It's all crazy, but the one thing I do know is how I feel when I'm with you."

He lifts his face as I drop mine, our gaze locking.

"I never want to lose you."

He sits back in his seat. At first I think I've said something wrong, but then he smirks. "Oh, did you think you had an option?"

A warm sensation starts to build low in my gut. "What do you mean?"

Jackson's pupils dilate, and his tongue runs across his bottom lip, his piercing catching the light of the moon. A shiver courses down my body.

"I'm never letting you go, Willow. You could run to the other side of the world, and I will follow. You could pass into the next life, and I will be right on your heels."

I gasp and place my hand over my chest, pretending to be shocked by what he said. I thought I was tired of playing games, but maybe not. Jackson is a fun opponent, *and* he lets me win. Maybe we can both win this flirty duel.

I know what some people might think of this. They might wonder how I could fall so fast for him after what I've been through. Well, it's because Jackson is not Bradley. Not in the slightest. Yes, he has staked a claim on me, but he doesn't want to keep me under his thumb. No, he wants me to stand by his side, not two steps behind him.

Avenging Skulls

Bradley pretended to be the boy next door. With his charm, polo shirt, and white smile, he could set anyone at ease. He made it easy to think he was someone you could trust. But Jackson ... Jackson is all dark ink, piercings, and a wicked grin that makes you doubt your ability to think straight. You know he's dangerous, but not to me or anyone else he loves. And even though we're playing cat and mouse right now, I know the minute I wave my white flag, he'll stop. He won't change the rules on me.

"Awfully quiet over there," he says as my gaze skitters over the yard. I wonder who is on watch tonight? Are they wondering why it's taking us so long to get out of the truck?

"But what if I want to leave this place?" I ask, tipping my head and pressing my hand over the latch on the door. "What if I don't want you to follow me?"

He raises an eyebrow, leaning forward. "Then I will tie you to my bed."

Zing! His gravelly voice zips down my spine, making a beeline for my crotch. When I squeeze my legs together and wiggle in my seat, I begin to doubt myself. This is wrong. After what happened to me, I shouldn't feel this way. I shouldn't be turned on by the idea of being trapped.

Jackson pinches my chin between his finger and thumb, tilting my face. "Don't you dare feel guilty about us. We're only playing. There's nothing wrong with that." He slides his thumb into my mouth before pulling it out slowly. "Don't let him steal anything else from you."

"How did you know what I was thinking?"

"Because I understand. I felt it too, but I'm not letting that bitch take one more thing from me. And I'm especially not going to let her take anything away from you."

How in world did fate guide me to this man, to this place in the trees that I've come to love so much? No other man would have ever been able to understand me the way he does. We share the same pain.

"Well," I say haughtily, slipping back into character, "you can't just go tying me to your bed."

The smile that pulls across his face flips my stomach ... in a good way.

He tilts his head to the side. "Well, then you better not be thinking about leaving me."

He pulls his phone out of his pocket and begins to type, the glow from it lighting his face. There's a sexy orneriness painted across it.

"What are you doing?" I ask, biting my nail.

His gaze meets mine briefly before going back to his phone. He shrugs his shoulders. "Eh, just texting the guys to let them know if you run to let you go."

My head snaps back. "You're just going to let me run away?"

He chuckles darkly. "I said *they* won't stop you."

Oh. *Ohhhh.*

I squeeze my thighs together again, trying to ease the ache that's burning there. It's not so much the thought of the chase that's turning me on, it's the thought of being caught ... by him.

Him.

The dark god sitting across from me.

As he slips his phone back in his pocket, I hit the latch and swing my door open, not bothering to close it. I run for the trees. I'm not going to make this easy for him.

When I duck into the forest, my heart rate picks up but my feet slow as I try to quiet my steps. I make my way toward the stream, quickly darting across it, knowing just where to skip across on stones to avoid getting wet.

Clouds slide over the moon, darkening my surroundings. A noise makes me jump and hide. It's Brody; he looks down at his phone and shakes his head.

"Jesus Christ," he mutters under his breath. His gaze scans the area, but he doesn't see me.

But I sense someone does.

Jackson pushes me against a tree, grabbing my hair and tugging my head back. "Shh," he whispers in my ear, the hard length of him grinding against my ass. "Let him go."

Brody heads back toward the house as Jackson pulls my head to the side and begins feasting on my neck. His tongue piercing rakes over my sensitive skin, and I let out a long, drawn-out moan. It feels so good.

"Are you two for real?" Brody bellows from the darkness. I don't know where he is, and I don't care.

Jackson is licking and sucking and biting. Oh, god. He tightens his grip in my hair, holding me still. He takes a moment to yell a quick "fuck off" to his friend.

Brody's chuckle follows him into the night as he continues on his way.

"You've been a bad girl, haven't you, Willow?" Jackson's deep voice vibrates against me.

"No," I squeak, denying everything.

He tuts, grinding against me. His tongue goes back to my neck, licking from my shoulder blade all the way to my ear. When he reaches my lobe, he bites it.

"Maybe I should punish you right here for running away from me," he threatens, one hand braced on the tree by my face, the other still in my hair.

The whine that leaves my mouth makes him release a low growl. "You like the sound of that, don't you? You know I'm the only one who can make you feel like this."

"Please," I whisper, pressing my hands against the bark of the tree, shoving back against him.

"Or …" he pauses. "I could make good on that promise and tie you to my bed."

"I can't wait that long," I beg.

He tips my head all the way back, so I'm staring up into his brown eyes. He looks absolutely terrifying right now, and I love it.

"I'm going to push you, Willow."

I swear my panties just soaked clean through. It's going to be embarrassing when he finds out just how wet I am over all this.

When I don't respond, his gaze bounces over my face. He leans down and kisses me, his mouth hot and hungry. His piercing scrapes across my tongue and all I can think about is how I want him to consume me. I want him to fill me up with everything that is him, leaving no room for anyone else.

He breaks away, his eyes narrowing, as he runs his palm gently over my throat. "Just tell me to stop if you don't like something."

I give him a tiny nod, my stomach jumping for joy that he's not afraid to treat me like this. Rough and possessive. It's nothing like …

Avenging Skulls

He shoves my head down, pushing me to my knees, and all thoughts of Bradley flutter away.

Blinking up at him, I balance myself with my palms on his thighs. He stares down at me, waiting for my response.

I don't know what he wants me to do. I've never experienced anything like this. Will I be good enough for him? He's a biker. I'm sure he's been with plenty of girls. I've only been with Bradley, and he was always gentle.

Chewing on my bottom lip, I dig my fingers into the denim covering his legs. The corners of his eyes soften as he realizes my plight.

"Do you want me to stick my cock down your throat?" he asks.

Oh, that's what he wants. Is it what I want? I don't know; I've never ...

He brushes his hand over the back of my head, and suddenly his dick being in my mouth is everything I crave.

"Yes," I breathe out, knowing he will talk me through this. Jackson reads me as if I were a novel penned solely for him.

With shaky hands, I fumble with his zipper. Then, I take a deep breath and slowly shove his pants down along with his boxers, pushing them to the top of his thighs.

My eyes flick up to his, finding the encouragement I need. I run my fingertips lightly over the length of him, teasing him a bit before leaning forward. When the tip of my tongue touches his silky skin, he instantly threads his fingers through my hair, releasing a low moan from the back of his throat. It sends a thousand butterflies fluttering in my stomach.

I can do this. Excitement courses through my veins when his stomach muscles tighten. His hips pitch forward as I take him fully in my mouth.

This kind of intimacy is new to me. I've seen a lot in the last five years, yet I've been sheltered. Bradley decided what I read, and I didn't get to watch movies or popular TV shows.

"Eyes." He snaps his fingers, sensing my mind wandering from the here and now.

When my eyes meet his, he begins to take over the pace. I gag as he hits the back of my throat, but I don't have time to be embarrassed because his pupils dilate, letting me know how much he liked it. He does it again, his fingers tightening in my hair.

"Do you want me to come down that pretty throat of yours?" he asks, his fingers massaging over my neck.

Tears run down my cheeks when I nod.

"Don't you dare take your eyes off me," he warns.

And then he fucks my mouth with abandon.

I want to please him, so I don't blink. I don't move. It feels so good because I'm the one choosing this. He isn't taking anything from me … not even his pleasure. It all belongs to me.

"You're such a good girl," he says as his warm cum floods my mouth. His head falls back as I struggle to swallow everything he's giving me. "Jesus, Willow." He braces his hand against the tree to steady himself.

When he pulls out of my mouth, I remain where I'm at with my eyes fully on him. He's beautiful inside and out. Other people might not see it. They look at him and only see a man covered in skulls and devils. I'm sure it frightens them, but if they would only look closer, they would see what they really mean.

Jackson is a good man, a man who I know will protect me at all costs.

I want to be his ... for eternity.

Chapter Thirty-Eight

Willow

Chirping birds pull me from my slumber. I blink my eyes open to find Jackson sitting in front of the window with the bug catcher perched on the sill in front of his face. He's still naked, so I quietly allow my gaze to roam over the ink on his skin.

"Good morning," he says, turning to look at me over his shoulder.

Busted. Heat floods my cheeks as I yawn and stretch, pretending to just wake up.

He laughs, grabbing the bug catcher and jumping on the bed. I squeal as he jumps a few times before flopping himself down on the mattress beside me.

"Didn't your mom teach you to not jump on the bed?" I giggle.

"No, she jumped on it with me," he answers, putting the bug catcher between our faces so we have to look at each other through the screen.

I run my finger over it. "I can't wait to meet her."

"She's going to love you," he says.

A smile tugs at the corner of my mouth.

"So, were you allowed to jump on the bed?" he asks.

I think about it for a minute. "I don't remember ever jumping on the bed. After my dad passed, Ash and I moved up to the attic and we slept on the floor."

Jackson's face falls into a frown.

"Don't be sad," I tell him. "I loved it up there. We lined the walls with books. It reminded me of a treehouse."

Jackson sits up. "That's it!" he exclaims.

I laugh as he stands over me. He doesn't have a care in the world that he's naked. He reaches for my hands, pulling me to my feet.

Jackson grabs me around the waist until I get my balance. Then, he takes my hands in his and starts jumping. "Come on. I know you can do it."

"We're naked," I giggle.

"Makes it even more fun." He laughs.

Cautiously, I bounce a few times on the balls of my feet.

"No. Jump," he orders.

So, I do. Soon we are jumping, our hands still clasped together. His hair falls over his eyes and something tugs at my chest. It's love. I love Jackson. I love him more than I've loved anything in my entire life.

"We should build a treehouse out back," he says.

I laugh, but he's serious. "For real?"

"Yeah, an adult treehouse. I mean, our kids can play in it, too. But right now, it will just be for the two of us."

My feet pause as he continues to jump.

I've never thought about having a family. I'm not sure I want kids. The world is dangerous and ugly.

He stops and presses his palms to my face. "Hey, I was just talking out of my ass. If you're not ready for that kind of conversation, I'll shut up."

"No, it's not that. I just … I've never allowed myself to think that far ahead." My gaze falls to the bug catcher on the bed.

Jackson plops down on the mattress and pulls me onto his lap. He reaches forward and grabs the tiny cage. "You and I are like them." He points to the little black and red bugs climbing around on the leaves. "They've become so accustomed to their life inside here, they aren't even concerned with all of the possibilities beyond this screen."

He shifts so he can rest his chin on my shoulder. "I've been trapped too, Willow. Unable to let my thoughts stray any farther than the walls I put up around me. I don't want to do that anymore. I want to dream with you. I'm not saying I want or even need kids. Right now, I just want to imagine all the possibilities."

"You're right. I'm free to dream again."

"You are, and maybe that involves kids, maybe it doesn't. We'll figure out what's best for us along the way."

"It definitely involves goats, though," I tell him seriously.

He laughs, flipping me on my back. "As long as it involves me, I'm okay with it."

Avenging Skulls

I brush my fingers over his forehead, pushing his hair back. "We should let the ladybugs go."

We both turn toward the bug catcher.

"You're right. We should," he agrees.

Hurrying, we get dressed and jog down the stairs. Brody is at the table, scarfing down a pile of pancakes. Elijah is standing at the stove in Grandma Maggie's pink apron.

"Want some pancakes?" he asks, waving a spatula over the pan.

"Sure," Jackson says, handing me the bug catcher. He fills his arms with peanut butter and jelly, then takes a plate piled high with pancakes. "Come on," he says, nodding his head toward the door.

Brody grimaces, his eyebrows pulling together as he studies me.

"I'll meet you out there. I'm going to grab us something to drink," I say, walking over to the refrigerator.

"See you at the rock." He juggles two apples in one hand before the screen door bangs closed behind him.

Brody stands and takes me gently by the arm, steering me out of the kitchen. Elijah pretends not to notice, concentrating on his next batch of pancakes.

"Are you okay?" he asks as soon as we are out of earshot.

I feel heat rise up my neck. "I'm fine," I say, my gaze falling to the floor.

He tips my chin with the pad of his finger. "I don't mean to embarrass you, I just ..." He glances over his shoulder to make sure we're still alone. "I wanted to make sure you're okay after last night." He shrugs his shoulders. "You are part of this club, and it's my job as Jackson's best friend to make sure his girl is okay. Even if it's him who might have hurt you."

The warmth that was occupying my cheeks floods down to my chest. It builds and builds as I take in the concern pulling at his features. Brody is worried about me.

I reach out and lay my hand over his bearded cheek. "Brody, I'm fine. Jackson and I were only playing. It was …" I turn away from him, embarrassed. "I know I'm safe here. You don't have to worry about me."

"Well, it's a little late for that. I'll always worry about you."

I don't know what to say. So, I simply answer with an "okay."

"Seriously. I know my brother, and sometimes he can be a little reckless."

He loves Jackson. I can see that some of his concern is for his friend, too.

"I love him, Brody."

His eyes widen, and he runs his fingers through his hair. "That was …"

"Fast," I giggle.

Instantly his shoulders fall, and a smile breaks over his handsomely rugged face. "You two are quite the pair."

I nod, holding out the bug catcher. "We're letting our ladybugs go," I tell him.

He looks at it. "Okay, let me rephrase that. You two are weird," he says, rolling his eyes as he steps around me to go back to the table.

Avenging Skulls

I follow behind, grabbing two bottles of juice from the fridge. "Someday you're going to do crazy things for a girl, too," I tease.

Elijah laughs, tossing the pink apron aside as he sits down to eat. "She's right. You'll turn into a straight up weirdo when you meet the right girl. We all do."

Brody drops into his chair. "No, thank you. I'm never going to lose my mind over a female. No offense." He points at me with his fork.

"None taken."

I leave the men to their discussion about the opposite sex and head out to the forest.

Jackson has a blanket laid out with the plate of pancakes sitting in the middle of it. "What took so long?" he asks, dusting his hands off on his pants.

"Brody thinks we're weird," I say, sitting down beside him, facing the stream.

"We are weird," he agrees without missing a beat.

I laugh. "Yeah. Being weird is fun."

"Way better than being normal." He picks up a pancake and spreads peanut butter and jelly over it before rolling it up and handing it to me.

"What's this?" I ask, bringing it up to my mouth to lick a drop of jelly from the side.

He blinks at me, his gaze fixated on my tongue. "The Jackson Special," he answers mindlessly.

I hum behind my lips. "This is good."

We eat several of his *specials* before we get around to releasing the ladybugs.

Jackson sets the leaf they're perched on beside us. We watch as one after the other finally show their wings and fly away.

"Sometimes I forget they can fly," Jackson says.

I take in my surroundings, remembering how happy I felt when I found this place. It's even better now that he's here with me. Bringing my foot up to the rock, I hug my leg, resting my chin on my knee.

"This might be the most relaxing place on the planet," I sigh dreamily.

He runs his hand over my back. "Willow, I wanted to talk to you about last night."

I close my eyes. He's upset with me because I told him no. When we got back to the room, he wanted to return the favor I had given him.

"Did you enjoy flirting with waiter tonight?" Bradley asks, typing away at his laptop.

"I ... I wasn't flirting," I try to explain.

"You were."

Closing my book, I attempt to slip under the blankets. Bradley is angry at me.

"Go shower," he snaps, cracking his neck from side to side.

My eyes flick toward the window. It's dark outside, and we're parked at least a mile from the showers.

"Now," he barks.

I jump, scrambling to grab clothes. I just showered before we went into town for supper. That was only a few hours ago.

Avenging Skulls

When I slide past him, he grabs my wrist. "I'm not sleeping in the same bed with you when I can smell your arousal for another man."

My head snaps back in shock.

I wasn't ...

His eyes narrow as he reads my thoughts. He knows I'm arguing with him, even if it's only in my mind.

"You stink." He snaps his gum and turns back to his computer, releasing my arm.

I slide the door open and hop out, leaving him behind.

I'm terrified the entire walk to the showers as the shadows play tricks with me. When I get inside the shower house and flick the light on, I feel somewhat better.

I glance down at my shorts, confused by what Bradley said. The waiter didn't arouse me. He told me I had pretty eyes. I smiled and said thank you, flattered by his sweet words, but I wasn't ...

Jackson snaps in front of my face. My eyes fly open.

"Hey, I lost you there for a minute." He rubs his thumb over my cheek. "We don't have to talk about it. It's okay. Whenever you don't want to do something that is where we leave it. I just ... your mood shifted so quickly. I was worried you let Bradley get in your head."

Last night, when we finally made our way back to the house and undressed, I suddenly got very self-conscious. I'd been so turned on by our little chase that I worried ... I hadn't showered all day and Bradley told me he could ...

"I'm sorry," I whisper, pulling my face out of his hand. I pick up a rock and toss it into the stream. It lands with a plop.

"Willow, there's nothing to be sorry for. You said no and that's fine. I'll never question your reason for not wanting to do something; I just want you to know that if you ever want to discuss something we've done or haven't done, you can come to me. I don't want you to be embarrassed."

My gaze bounces over his face. I've regretted my decision since last night. The thought of looking down and seeing his devilishly handsome face between my thighs would be, well, I think it would be as close to Heaven as one could get in life.

I cover my face with my hands and throw my self-preservation right over a cliff. "I hadn't showered."

He clicks his tongue. "Shit, that didn't matter to me."

I peek at him through my fingers. Okay, that wasn't so bad. Maybe I can go a little further. "I ... I didn't want you to ... well, I didn't want you to smell how turned on I was. Bradley told me ..." I can't finish.

Jackson's stare is heavy on my face as I hide behind my hands again. Oh my god, why did I say that? But that *is* why I turned him down last night. And he deserves to know it wasn't because of anything he did. He deserves to know what another man ruined for him.

"*Or maybe saved him from,*" my self-doubt chimes in.

He pulls my hands away from my face. "Eyes," he orders.

Slowly, I open them, sure I'm going to die of embarrassment right here on this rock.

His brown gaze is calm and clear as he speaks to me. "Willow, he was fucking with your head." He pulls me close to him and kisses me on the cheek. "God, I just fell in love with you all over again. Thank you for sharing that with me. I know it was hard for you. But now I know just how much you trust me."

Avenging Skulls

This is a side of Jackson I don't think many people see. They see the scattered, high-strung Jackson. But I get the "light house" version of him. The tower that stands strong and still, that calls to me through the storm of my thoughts and feelings. He is my beacon of light.

"You're not alone in these type of insecurities. Everyone has them. Even me," he says, pulling my head close to his chest, sheltering me from my mortification. "I'm sure he used many of your fears against you."

His chest vibrates as he speaks; the low rumble of his voice calms me. It makes me snuggle closer to him.

"You're not mad I turned you down last night?" I ask.

"No, I'm not mad. I never want you to do something you're not comfortable with."

"Maybe we could try again." I rub my face over his soft t-shirt, afraid to look at him.

He stills. "You want to give it a go?"

I nod against him.

Jackson pushes me back, giving me a once over. "You're not doing this just because you feel bad for stopping me last night, are you?"

"No. I regretted my decision," I admit, staring at the stream. "In my heart I knew I was being silly, but in my head ... well, sometimes he's still there."

"Close your eyes," he says, brushing his hand over my face. "Do you see the box outside our bedroom door?"

Instantly, the box appears in mind. The blue knob and the business card are resting in the bottom, slowly collecting dust. I smile at the thought. "Yes," I whisper.

"That's where they stay, okay?"

Slowly I open my eyes. "Okay."

He pushes me back against the blanket until I'm staring up at the trees, the leaves rustling above us in the wind. The sun peaks between them, dancing over my face. I shield my eyes and focus down my torso as Jackson's fingers make quick work of my jeans. He tugs them down my legs, leaving my panties in place.

When he crawls over me, he drags his nose right on over them, inhaling deeply. My breath catches, frozen in my lungs as I fight the sting of embarrassment.

"You smell divine," he growls, his voice vibrating against my quickly dampening panties.

His thumbs hook under the soft material above my hips before dragging them down my legs and over my toes. Then, he presses his palms against the inside of my knees and gently spreads me open for him. His gaze holds mine hostage the entire time.

"I'm going to devour you, Willow."

My hips raise on their own accord, responding like a string on his cello when his fingers play over them. His warm autumn eyes abandon mine, roaming down my body and leaving a trail of goose pimples in their wake.

A shiver ripples through me, and he chuckles. "I'm so glad we waited," he lulls me. "Your green eyes are so fucking beautiful in the sun."

His big hand lands in the center of my chest, his other teasing over my thigh, coming closer and closer to where I need him to touch me.

My moan begs him to keep going but he pulls away, then he lowers his hand down to my pubic bone, his face joining it there, his breath warming my skin. A whimper escapes me as I stare at the leaves above us. When the tip of his tongue touches me, I yip loudly, making him laugh.

"You're so sensitive, baby."

He slides lower and wraps his arms around my thighs, pulling me gruffly down to him, the backs of my thighs coming to rest against his shoulders. Then, he buries his face between my legs.

"Oh, oh god." I try to squirm away. This is too intense, but when I think I can take no more, he lets up, replacing his fingers where he was just filling me with his tongue. An embarrassing grunt leaves me as I try to slide closer to him, wanting to impale myself on his hand.

He chuckles wickedly. "Oh, you're going to be fun," he taunts.

I direct my stare down my body, his teasing brown eyes focused on mine. "I ... oh."

My eyes widen as he slides a third finger inside me at the same time flicking his piercing over my swollen clit.

"Jesus," I hiss, trying not to move. A move in either direction, and I'm going to come. I don't want to come yet; I want to see what he's going to do next.

"Jackson," he corrects. "But I'll answer to either." He presses his fingers against the walls inside me, his other hand splayed over my pubic bone, holding me down.

My mouth falls open. *Oh, oh no.*

"Do you trust me?"

He presses and presses, and I can't answer; I can't even think clearly. His teeth nip at my clit lightly, and I have to squint to keep from coming, tears trickling out the corners of my eyes.

"I ... yes, yes," my voice rises.

God, just seeing the confidence sparkling in his eyes is enough to get me there. A slow smile spreads over his face, and then he does exactly what he promised as his gaze holds mine.

My soul combusts into nothing but star dust.

The wind carries the particles above us, scattering them amongst the heavens. The blue sky suddenly looks bluer, the leaves more sharp. My ears ring as I smile at the sky, my chest heaving with each breath I suck into my lungs.

Jackson slides up my body, his face blocking my view. He brushes hair away from my cheeks. "I love you, Willow. Your wings are so beautiful. Thank you for showing them to me."

He kisses me, and I taste myself on his lips. It's strange and intimate. No matter what I do with him, he never makes me feel less. He builds me up. I'm trusting in that more and more as time passes here amongst the trees.

But the roar of motorcycles interrupts us.

He pulls away, shaking his head. "Having a big family is a pain in the ass sometimes," he jokes.

I pull him back to me, my lips whispering over his. "I love you, Jackson."

"I love you, too." He smiles, pulling me to my feet.

When we step into the yard, we smile at each other. Jackson stops and looks up at the treetops, my gaze following his. "I took a walk in the woods and ..."

"Came out taller than the trees," I finish for him.

Avenging Skulls

When we turn to head to the house, I spy Grandma Maggie watching us from her chair, a look of contentment resting on her soft face. I give her a small wave and she returns one. I look back at Jackson.

"Everything I went through was worth it to be here with you." I lace my fingers in his.

He squeezes my hand. "I don't know if I'm worthy of your praise, but I'm greedy, so I'm going to take it." He laughs, kissing me on the tip of my nose.

Billie Rose is pulling weeds in the garden, and she waves us over to her. "Mom says we're having the party here."

Jackson reaches down to scoop Aurelia into his arms.

I sit in the grass and stare up at them. He looks so natural with a child in his arms. This morning he made it sound like he wanted children. I'm not sure what to think about that. I've never wanted to be a mother; I'm too afraid I'd turn out like my own.

She shoves a dandelion in his face and almost up his nose. He fakes an exaggerated sneeze, making the little girl giggle. He leans forward, pretending to almost drop her.

When he rights himself, he takes the weed from her and holds it in front of her mouth. "Okay, we need to blow on it and make a wish."

I'm not sure if she's old enough to understand, but she giggles when he puffs out his cheeks. She copies him and soon they are blowing on it, the seeds breaking off and floating in the breeze.

"Make a wish," he tells her, closing his eyes. She does the same.

I catch him peek at her with one eye before quickly closing his again.

After a few seconds she opens her eyes and pats his face. "Did you make a wish?" he asks.

She just giggles and rubs her face tiredly over his, her little hands digging into her eyes.

Billie Rose stands up. "I'm going to go put her down for a nap in the living room while I run home and shower. Can you watch her?" she asks Jackson.

"Sure," he says.

"I'll be right back. Mom is bringing the food over in about an hour," she adds looking at her watch.

"What's the party for?" he asks.

"Your mom got back from her trip today."

"Jesus," Jackson says, rubbing the back of his neck.

"You know how my mom is; she throws a party for everything. But she didn't want Willow to have to go to the warehouse." Her gaze meets mine briefly.

Jesse changed her plans for me. All of these people have altered their lives in some way or another to make room for me. My own mother never once changed anything to make my life easier ... not for me anyway. Maybe for herself.

I offer to sit inside with Aurelia as everyone else does the chores and gets ready for the party. My brother joins me when he arrives.

"Hey," he says quietly, staring down at the little girl still asleep in her playpen.

"Hey," I whisper back.

He walks over and sits down beside me on the couch. "How are you doing?" he asks.

"Fine. You?"

"I'm good, baby sis." He laughs harshly. "I talked to Mom this morning," he continues, resting his head back against the cushions.

"Oh yeah?"

"She said she was going into treatment. Seems someone's offered to pay for it."

Jesse walks in and sets a bag of groceries on the table, her gaze lingering over my brother and me.

"It was the club, wasn't it?" I ask.

He lets out a long, drawn-out sigh. "Couldn't say, but that would be my guess. These people are something else."

"In a good way, right?"

Aurelia giggles in her sleep, and both of our gazes go to the playpen.

"Yeah, in a good way." He places his hand on my shoulder. "They've asked me to prospect for them."

My brows pull together.

"Do you know what that is?" he asks.

I shake my head.

"It's like trying out for the team."

"Do you want to join their club?" I ask, envisioning him in a black leather jacket.

"I've been lost without my brothers in service, so yeah, I like it at the warehouse. It feels good having someone at my back again."

Kelsie pops her head around the doorway, blushing when she realizes she interrupted us. "I'm sorry," she squeaks before ducking back around the corner.

The little girl in the playpen peeks her eyes open.

"No! Wait, Kelsie. She's waking up." I point to Aurelia as she pushes herself up on all fours, swaying slightly.

Kelsie smiles big. "She's not as scary as she looks," she teases, picking up the small child and coming to sit between my brother and me.

My brother naturally coos over Aurelia, shaking her tiny little hand in his. "Well, aren't you a pretty girl," he says in a voice I haven't heard since we were children.

"I'm going to go help outside," I tell them, scooting off the couch, not sure they even heard me.

Chapter Thirty-Nine

Jackson

When I introduce my mom and Willow, it's like the final piece of the puzzle clicks into place. My mother hugs her so tight, I'm not sure Willow can breathe.

"Mom. Mom. Mom," I say louder. "You're smothering her."

My mom steps back. "Oh, I'm sorry. I just ... it's so nice to finally meet you. Raffe's been filling me in over the last few weeks. I've been away at a conference."

"Yes. Isn't it interesting you were gone a week longer than you thought you'd be?" Dirk asks, narrowing his eyes at his sister.

She pats her hands down her hair. "Yes, well, like I told Raffe, I ran into some friends from college while there."

"Is that so?" Dirk kicks his feet up on the picnic table beside us, his elbows resting on the table behind him.

I run my hands down my jeans, still nervous over Petey's text this morning. It just said he had found Bradley, and they were close. I'm sure that's why they moved the party here. I'm itching for Petey to get him to the warehouse so I can murder the bastard.

I know I always said that victims need to see their abuser before we get rid of them, but I'm not sure I want Willow to ever have to lay eyes on him again. I'm debating doing this without her. Is that wrong? After this morning, I realize just how much the asshole has fucked with her head.

She's strong, but he's changed her. None of us will ever know the woman she would have been had she not met him. Not even her.

Willow takes us all in with a small smile on her face. She seems at ease with my mom; she's leaning into her like a real daughter would her own mother. That's a good sign, right?

Jesse waves for the girls to help her inside. "Elijah says the steaks are about done. Could you ladies help me with the salads and chips?" she asks.

Dirk's eyebrow crawls up his face as he watches the women disappear inside. "Who's been sharing information with their woman?"

Everyone holds up their hands in surrender. A chorus of boisterous banter erupts.

Dirk stands up and whistles. "Why haven't we thought of this before? It has to be one of the women. But why? Why would they tip off the assholes we're trying to eliminate? It doesn't make sense."

My dad taps his lighter on the table. "Maybe they aren't tipping them off, maybe they're …"

He doesn't finish because Dan jumps up from his seat, suddenly understanding where they are going with this.

"You think they're killing the assholes themselves?"

Oh, shit. This isn't good.

Maybe that's where she's been getting her information ... the club wives. It makes perfect sense.

Just then, my phone dings. I pull it out of my pocket and inwardly groan.

I've got him. I decided to be nice and let you play with this one. He's alive.

Oh, shit, shit, shit, shit, shit.

Be there in a few.

No, crap, no. Everyone is parked on the side of the barn. She's not going to see that they're here.

I'm trying to type out a response when the girls come back outside. Billie Rose jumps on my back, and my phone falls from my hands.

"Goddammit, Rosie," I curse, bending over to retrieve it.

She laughs as my gaze scans the yard for Willow. Jesus Christ. I focus back on my screen, opening up my messages to try again. I have to stop her from bringing Bradley here.

A commotion rings out from the side of the house. A man and a woman are cursing at each other. Everyone looks that way as Petey steps around the corner, struggling to drag a man away from a petite woman with her long brown hair tied back in a braid.

"He's fucking mine," she grunts, tugging at the man's tied up arms.

"The fuck he is," Petey snarls.

"Aunt Katie?" Billie Rose says, her mouth falling open.

Jesse walks out of the house, and the bowl in her hands falls to the ground with a loud crash. Katie and Petey turn in unison, their eyes widening when they notice all of us.

Jesse rushes down the steps but stops short of her sister when she notices the man kneeling on the ground between them.

"Katie?" she asks, shaking her head, confused as to what is going on.

"Oh, shit." Brody whistles.

Petey looks at me. "You all know her?" he asks, his gaze roaming over his brothers.

Dirk stands up. "This is Jesse's little sister. She's supposed to be in Florida."

Katie glares at him before turning toward Petey. "I'm not *supposed* to be anywhere. And this asshole is mine, so let go," she grates through clenched teeth.

She jerks Bradley toward her, but he doesn't seem interested in anything going on. His gaze is searching the group for Willow.

"Have you been tipping off our marks?" Petey accuses.

Katie leans her head back and laughs. "Tipping them off? Oh, I've been giving them the tip of something." She pulls a knife out of her boot and points it at him.

It's quiet as we all stare at each other. No one knows what to do next.

And then the back door bangs shut.

Bradley's eyes change from terrified to hopeful. He starts to crawl on his knees, trying to move closer.

I turn slowly to find Willow frozen on the top step.

Avenging Skulls

"Willow," Bradley manages to get out before Katie grabs the back of his head, ordering him to shut up.

Willow continues to stare at him, her shoulders slowly crawling up to her ears. "Um, I forgot the napkins," she says, then calmly opens the door and disappears inside.

Jesse whistles. "Ladies, get your families on home. The party is over."

Everyone instantly listens. This is not the first time a party has come to an end abruptly. We're all used to club life. I rush inside, finding the house empty. I search the entire place, opening the front door to find Brody positioned just outside.

"Did she come this way?" I ask.

"No. She's in there somewhere," he says.

"Jesus." I slam the door shut, turn, and bump right into Ash. "Fuck, man, you scared me."

"She's in the attic," he says sadly, leaning against the wall. "When things went south at home, that was always her safe place."

I slide past him as the house begins to fill with club members who are all trying to figure out what the fuck is going on.

Big Dan steps in front of me. "Move," I tell him.

He crosses his arms over his chest. "Have you been helping Katie?" he asks.

"Fuck, this isn't the time, man. I need to find Willow." I try to sidestep him, but he isn't having it.

I take a deep breath. "Dan, so help me god, I'm going to drop you to your motherfucking knees if you don't move."

My grandmother pats him on the arm. "It was me, you big bully," she scolds.

Every mouth in the room falls open.

"Oh, don't you all look at me that way. I wanted the man who took my daughter. Katie offered to help. And he ..." she waves her hand out toward me, "he just disposed of the bodies. He didn't divulge your secrets. Now get on, boy." She waves me up the stairs.

Dan steps aside, and I run past him, taking the steps two at a time. When I get up to the attic, I find her sitting in the window staring down into the backyard.

I scoot up beside her.

And that's when she begins to cry.

"Hey, shhh." I wrap my arm around her, pulling her between my legs. ' He can't hurt you."

She swipes angrily at her tears. "I know. I'm just ..." She presses her hand against the dusty glass. "He's going to die tonight."

I don't know whether she's asking or telling.

"Do you want him to?"

She sits back against me, curling into a little ball. "I don't know what I want."

"Okay, let's talk about it. There's no hurry."

When she remains quiet, I give her the option I hope she doesn't choose.

"We could call the police and turn him over to them. I'm sure there's enough evidence we could have him put away for a long time."

Avenging Skulls

She tips her head and blinks up at me as tears fall softly onto the apple of her cheeks. I brush them away, cradling her face in my hands. "We don't have to kill him," I hear myself say, hating every word.

Her gaze goes back to the window. "I wasn't prepared to see him," she admits quietly.

"I know. I'm sorry about that." I rub my hands down her arms, pulling her as close as I can.

We sit quietly for several minutes, watching Petey and Katie wave their hands at each other in a heated discussion. Bradley is sitting in the grass between them, calmly looking up at us.

"I want to talk to him."

"Willow," I say on an exhale.

She turns in my arms, climbing up on my lap. Her lips brush up the side of my neck. "I want to see him." Her tongue snakes up to my earlobe, where she pauses to nibble on it with her teeth. "Please," she begs and it's in this moment, I realize just how much of a Skull she really is.

"Okay," I find myself answering. Shit, who am I kidding? I'd give this woman any goddamn thing she asks for.

She slides off my lap. "I need to freshen up. I'll be down in a minute."

I stand, pulling her with me. "You're mine. Don't forget that." I nudge her chin, and she smiles.

"I won't forget."

Then she climbs down the stairs and goes to her room, closing the door softly behind her.

When I get downstairs, I start barking orders. Dirk watches me from the corner of the room with his arms across his chest.

"Take him to the barn," I order Brody.

He turns on his heel, not hesitating for even a second.

"This is between her and him. Whatever Willow decides goes. Even if that means calling the law."

"You're letting her confront him?" Dan asks as my dad joins us.

"It's what she wants."

"He's going to try and manipulate her," my dad argues.

My grandmother is sitting in her rocker, quietly rocking back and forth with her fingers steepled in front of her. "She won't let him sway her," she answers on my behalf.

"How can you be so sure?" my dad groans. He's truly worried for her, and this time it has nothing to do with me.

She drops her hands in her lap. "I can't be. But because of that girl, we were able to avenge Jenny. We need to trust she will do the same for herself."

Billie Rose and Kelsie both quietly slide past us, heading for the stairs. Grandma watches them go.

"The women in this family are strong. And this too shall pass."

She stands, following the girls upstairs.

Chapter Forty

Willow

I stare at myself in the mirror, running my hand over the smooth wood frame. Jackson's hands built this. His hands are slowly helping to repair me, too.

A light knock on the door interrupts my thoughts. "Come in," I answer, hoping it's not someone coming to try and talk me out of this.

Billie Rose sticks her head in. "Do you want some company?" she asks.

"Sure," I say, smoothing my bright green sundress over my legs.

Kelsie walks in behind her. "Wow. You look beautiful in that. It makes your eyes look even more green," she says, sitting down on my bed.

I walk over and sit down at the vanity. "Thank you," I say quietly.

Grandma Maggie steps in, and her eyes meet mine. "Here, let me help you with your hair," she says, hobbling over to me.

I watch as she runs her fingers through my tangled locks. The touch instantly soothes my soul. Her bony fingers expertly thread my hair together as she begins to braid.

"I used to braid my Jenny's hair every morning before school," she reminiscences, a smile pulling at her soft cheeks.

More women filter into the room. Lily and Rachel join the girls on the bed. Jesse and a woman I haven't met sit together in the window seat. Jesse wraps her arm around her, and the younger woman lays her head on Jesse's shoulder.

My gaze goes back to Grandma Maggie. "Will you tell me about her?"

This makes her smile widen. "Oh, my Jenny was a sweet girl, but her head was always in the clouds. Just like Jackson. She wore her heart on her sleeve. I think that's why he picked her."

Her hands pause on my hair as we stare at each other. Lily let's out a little sob, remembering her friend.

"She was a kind girl. Just like you," she says, her eyes going back to her task. "Now, I'm going to say the unpopular thing here. The thing no one wants to talk about. The man sitting out in that barn served a purpose. Men like him are what brought this family together. Everyone in this room has seen their fair share of evil men, but they are what made it so easy for us to recognize the good men downstairs ... even though they look like sin themselves."

We all chuckle at that.

"He brought you here, Willow. So, if your heart feels some sort of love for him, place it there. Love him for bringing you to us. Love him, forgive him, and then let him go," she finishes as she wraps a tiny band around the end of my braid.

Avenging Skulls

She grabs my shoulders and then spins me to look directly in my eyes. "This club stands behind you one hundred percent however you decide it goes down."

I nod because I believe her. They will have my back.

"We could paint her face," Jesse says from across the room.

Billie Rose laughs. "Yeah, do you want us to paint your face like a skeleton? That's what we did when we faced our abusers." She waves a finger between her and her mother. "I couldn't do it as myself, but I could as someone else."

I think about it for a second. It would be nice to have something to hide behind, but I've been doing that for the past five years.

"That's okay. I think I'd like him to see me."

The woman sitting by Jesse stands up, holding her hand out to me. "Hey, I'm Katie. No one's introduced us yet, but I'm Jesse's little sister. It's nice to finally meet you."

My eyes bounce over the woman. She has rich brown hair. Her grip is firm as she shakes my hand.

"I just want you to know I got to Bradley before Petey did. Don't give that asshole any of the credit."

She holds my hand hostage waiting for me to respond with a serious scowl on her face. Then, she bursts out laughing. "Just kidding. We all know, Petey comes up short every time."

She shakes her head and goes back to sit by her sister. Jesse shoves her playfully as she sits down.

"Petey is going to beat your ass if you keep talking about him like that," Jesse scolds.

"Pffft." Katie rolls her eyes. "He'd have to catch me first."

"Okay, that's enough you two," Grandma waves a hand over the sisters.

She pulls me to my feet. "Go on, honey. It's time."

Every single woman gives me a hug before I leave the room. And each one felt real.

Just as we are about to leave the room, the vibration hits me. My eyes fall closed as Jackson's music wraps around my soul. My feet carry me effortlessly down the stairs with the women following behind.

The music stops when he sees me, and he stands slowly. His mouth kicks up on one side. "You look fucking hot," he says, waving me toward him with the bow of his cello.

He sits down and pulls me between his legs, placing the cello in front of us. He begins to play, keeping me cocooned between him and the instrument. My eyes fall closed as I listen, *no,* feel the music he's playing. He's filling me up, coating every cell of my being with his message of love.

He loves me enough to show the world who he really is.

When the song ends, he's breathing heavily against me. "I love you, Willow," he whispers, his lip piercing brushing the shell of my ear.

A shiver courses through me, and he smiles against my neck, snuggling into me. "I'll take that as an I love you too," he teases.

Raffe clears his throat.

We both jump. Oh shit. I forgot we weren't alone.

My eyes dart around the room. Everyone is staring at us. When my gaze lands on Elijah, he winks at me.

"Shit, brother, you're making me want to learn to play an instrument. That was fucking hot."

Billie Rose shoves him in the arm, making him stumble. "The only instrument you need to be concerned about is me."

Dirk whistles loudly, effectively silencing the chatter.

He cocks an eyebrow my way. "You ready, sweetheart?"

"I'm ready."

But when we get to the barn, I wonder if I am. I've only been away from Bradley for a short time. Maybe he will wear me down. Maybe I'm destined to continuously lose to him.

Brody is leaning against the barn door, smoking a cigarette. He doesn't move to let me in. He just drops his hand and knocks on the wood.

"Dammit," I hear my brother curse from the other side.

"What's going on?" I ask, trying to shove him away so I can enter.

He pushes me back with one hand to the center of my chest. "Hold on, baby girl. Just giving your brother a chance to work out a little frustration."

The door starts to push open, so Brody steps aside. Ash walks out, his face red and sweaty. "He's all yours, sis," he says, walking past me without stopping.

I open my mouth, but Jackson reaches for my hand. "Let him go. He has his own demons to work through. It's time to face yours."

I turn back to the barn door, staring at it.

"Ready?" Brody asks.

I give him a short nod.

When I step inside, I find Petey sitting up on Jackson's work bench clipping his nails. Bradley is tied to a chair, his eye slowly swelling shut, his face bloody and bruised.

Jesus.

Petey jumps off the work bench startling Bradley, making him jerk in his binds. Petey laughs. "Don't worry, asshole. I'll only hit you if she asks me to. She's in charge from here on out." He bows to me as he passes. "And for the record, I hope she does," he adds before closing the door behind him.

Jackson touches the small of my back as Bradley and I stare at each other. "I'll get you a chair," he says. He steps around the corner briefly before coming back and placing a chair directly in front of Bradley.

I sit down.

Bradley's jaw clenches when Jackson leans down to place a soft kiss on my cheek. Quickly, I turn my head, and Jackson's surprised lips find mine. We both stare at each other with our eyes wide open. I feel his hand at my neck, and my soft skin dimples as his fingers dig into my flesh, pulling me close. He begins to kiss me possessively, our eyes never leaving the others.

I bite his lip, making him groan with pleasure into my mouth.

As he slowly pulls away, an unspoken promise passes between us. He trusts me and I him. We both want each other to win. Neither of us are going to lose this time around.

"I'll see you in a bit, yeah?" he asks, rising to his full height above me.

My head tips back to stare up at him. He slowly slides his thumb in my mouth, leaving it there until I give him a firm nod.

"Okay, baby."

He backs away, and my eyes follow him. When he disappears behind the door, I take a deep breath before facing Bradley.

"Are you trying to make me jealous?" Bradley asks as I turn around.

His face looks like shit.

I get up to grab some paper towels, wetting them in the sink in the corner of the room. When I go back, I pause a step away from him. He smirks, and all I can think is how weird it is that he doesn't have any gum in his mouth.

Hastily, I take the final step and begin wiping blood from his face. He stares at me with his glacial blue eyes, but I keep mine focused on my task.

"I asked you a question," he says sternly.

Without thought, I answer. "I wasn't trying to make you jealous." As soon as the words leave my mouth, I realize what is happening.

"Look at me, Willow," he demands calmly, softly even.

Hesitantly, I let my eyes slide over to his. When we connect, he smiles. "There's my girl," he rasps.

I've heard him say it a thousand times, and it's never sounded more wrong than it does right now.

I'm not his girl. I'm Jackson's. I always have been. Jackson puts me first. The only time he hasn't was when he put me on the back of his bike. A spot I'll gladly accept.

I finish cleaning his face and then sit down across from him. My knee bounces as I try to figure out what to say. I'm not sure what I want to happen here.

"I forgive you," he says, pulling me from my thoughts.

Wait. Did this motherfucker just say what I thought he said?

It takes everything in me not to react. He's still playing games.

"All you have to do is tell them you want to leave with me. You heard them. Whatever you say goes." He narrows his eyes. "You have the chance to do the right thing here, Willow. You know I've always taken care of you and will continue to do so. I love you."

I stare at him. His jaw clenches as his patience wanes, but he forces a smile on his face. "Come on, baby. Untie me, and I'll help you talk to them. They'll understand you were confused."

"Confused?" I ask, leaning forward.

He leans back. "Come on, Willow. You know I didn't take you. Your mom gave me permission."

I scratch my head. "Did she give you permission? Or did she sell me?"

"Does it matter?" he asks flippantly.

"No, I suppose not. So, the men from the Army, they were in on it too?"

His eyebrows rise, and he shrugs. "He thought it would be easier for you."

"He?"

"The man for whom you were intended. You caught the eye of a very evil man, Willow. You should be thanking me. I saved you from a life of pain, however long that would have been. It was his idea to make you believe your brother was dead." He tips his head back and stares at the beams above him. "He didn't want you to have any connections left to the outside world."

"So, this man was powerful enough to get two very convincing military men to lie to me, and then he just let you have me?"

"Oh," Bradley says on a sigh, stretching his back over the chair. "I wouldn't say he let me."

"You killed him?"

He drops his chin to his chest, chilling me to the bone with the look in his eyes. "Don't you see, Willow? I would do anything for you. Anything."

"That's not true," I accuse.

He blinks at me. "Name it. What do you want?"

"Let me go," I whisper.

His face falls, but he changes tactics quickly. "Do you think he's willing to do the same?" He nods his head toward the barn door.

I answer him honestly. "No, he will never let me go."

Bradley raises his eyebrows like he's won this debate, but we're not done.

"I don't want him to let me go. I want *you* to."

He narrows those fucking cold blue eyes my way. "Willow, I've had enough. You're being a brat. Fucking untie me right now," he growls, tugging at his binds, his patience coming to an end.

"Why did you never kiss me?" I lean forward and ask, my dragonfly necklace dangling from my neck. I wrap my fingers around it, drawing strength from the women who've worn it.

He keeps his gaze focused on me but doesn't respond.

"It's okay. I know there were a lot of things that were hard for you," I continue. "It must have been terrible being raised in the cruel world your grandfather carved out for you. The chaos, the noise, the insanity of it all. I understand why you wanted me. I was the opposite of him. I was what you craved. The silence. The calm."

"Willow," he warns.

"It's okay. He can't hurt you anymore."

He chews on the inside of his mouth as his foot taps rapidly against the barn floor. "What are you talking about?"

"Your grandfather. He's dead."

His eyes widen, and his mouth falls open. "What did you do?"

"No." I hold up my finger. "It's what he did. He's ruined thousands of lives. But his reign of terror is over. His victims have been avenged."

He starts pulling at his binds. "That's not what I wanted. I didn't want him dead."

"I know it's not what you wanted. That life was all you'd ever known. You couldn't see it any other way."

Slowly, I stand up.

"Does that mean you're letting me go?" he asks, both anger and hope pulling at his face.

"Yes. I'm letting you go."

He breathes a sigh of relief. "Thank you. Oh god, Willow, I love you."

I close the distance between us.

Avenging Skulls

Leaning down, I bring us nose to nose. His eyes dart between mine, and then I lean forward and press my lips to his, keeping my eyes open.

His widen in surprise, but when he tries to deepen the kiss, I pull away.

"This is the first time I haven't been afraid of you."

"I've never hurt you. I love you," he says sincerely.

"What you did to me isn't love, Bradley."

"No. No. Willow, listen, I do love you," he pleads.

I put my fingers to my mouth and whistle loudly. Instantly, the door opens, and Jackson is behind me.

Bradley's gaze darts between the two of us as I lean back against Jackson. He wraps his arms around my waist, resting his chin on my shoulder.

I raise my hand and softly caress his scruffy face, looking down at the man who kidnapped me. "If I asked you to let him go, what would you say?" I ask Jackson.

He looks down at Bradley and sneers. "I'd say you were nuts, but I'd cut his binds myself if that's what you want. I'd give my girl anything."

I let a slow smile stretch across my face. I pull away from Jackson and peruse the room, running my finger playfully over the workbench. "I was thinking we could build a library up there." I point to the loft, hopping up on the work bench.

Jackson grabs my chair and spins it around, giving me his full attention. "Abso-fucking-lutely. Then we can be together while I work."

"A daybed up there would be nice too, you know, so I can relax while I read."

The smirk Jackson gives me makes my stomach flip. "If there's a bed up there, ain't neither of us getting any rest."

"Enough, Willow," Bradley barks.

Jackson ignores him but stands up, grabbing some duct tape from a drawer beside me. "How many shelves do you want up there?" he asks as he walks over, grabbing Bradley by the hair and slapping a piece of tape over his mouth.

Bradley mumbles profusely behind it, but we pretend he's not here and continue our discussion.

"Four, no five." I tap my finger on my chin. "We'll have to have room for the kid's books."

Jackson stops, the smirk falling from his face.

I keep going. "But first we should work on that treehouse, don't you think?"

He bites his bottom lip, and my stomach flips clean over. He presses his hand over the growing bulge in his pants. "You're making me hard, baby."

I smile at that. "You going to fill me with your babies?"

"Fuck yeah, I am."

Bradley is so fucking mad at this point that I think his head might explode. So, I turn to give him my full attention.

"Do you see this?" I motion between Jackson and me. "This is what love is. Sharing your dreams, letting each other run wild with the possibilities." I hop of the counter, walk over, and wrap my arms around Jackson's waist, resting my cheek over his heart.

Avenging Skulls

I look directly at Bradley. "Thank you for helping me find someone who will allow me to dream."

I give Jackson a big squeeze, rise up on my tiptoes, and place a kiss on his scruffy face. When my heels drop to the ground, I back away, keeping my gaze trained on the man I love.

"He's all yours."

And then I turn and walk out as Bradley's muffled scream follows me out of the barn.

As soon as the door closes behind me there's a loud thud, and I know Jackson has begun. The thought sends a sick shiver of delight down my spine.

"You good?" Brody asks.

All I can do is nod as I hurry past him, needing some distance between me and the barn. Everyone is sitting around a fire. Raffe rushes toward me.

I hold my hand out. "I ... I need a moment. I'm ..." I glance over my shoulder at the barn, the moonlight illuminating the dragonfly mural. "I'm not running. I just need ... I'll be back."

He nods once, and then I run. I run. I run. I run.

And no one chases me.

I'm free.

I'm finally fucking free.

Jackson is cutting my binds as we speak.

I kick my shoes off, holding them tight to my chest as I run barefoot through the forest. I'm breathing heavy when I get to the cemetery. I run toward the little glowing dragonfly on Jenny's grave and drop to my knees when I reach it. I press my palm over her name.

"Thank you," I cry. "Thank you. Thank you," I chant, lying on the cold ground above her, rolling over to stare up at the stars.

I wrap my fingers around the dragonfly pendent. The tears fall freely, pooling in my ears. "I don't know if you felt guilty for trusting Bradley's grandfather, but I've felt so guilty for putting myself in the position I did."

The wind chime blows in the wind, breaking the silence of the night.

My heart begins to slow down as a peace washes over me. "What we went through was all worth it though, wasn't it? If I hadn't met Bradley, I would never have met your son." I swipe at my eyes. "He's kind, funny, and a bit ornery, but I'm sure you already know that. He's everything I could have dreamed of and more."

It's nice to talk to her. I feel close to her even though we've never met. Hours pass as I unburden my soul.

My eyes fall closed, the chimes lulling me to a dreamy state. "I promise I'll be careful with his heart," I whisper before drifting off to sleep.

The signature sound of a Harley pulls me from my dreams as I blink up at the stars. Soon after Jackson is stepping right over the top of me, a boot on each side of my waist. He's showered and changed. His wet hair drips in my face as he towers over me. He chuckles, shaking his head like a dog.

"Stop," I laugh, wiping at my face while sitting up.

He gives me a hand, pulling me to my feet and right into his chest. Neither of us say anything as he holds me.

"I packed us a bag," he says after several minutes of silence.

Avenging Skulls

"Where are we going?" I ask.

"I noticed that out of all the maps you had, you didn't have one for Sequoia National Park."

A grin tugs at my mouth.

He places his hand on the side of my face. "Let's go. The club will look after the farm for a few days."

"I don't know. Maybe it's too soon."

"Come on. I know you want to see those gigantic fucking trees they got there."

"Okay, but you're sure the club won't mind taking care of the animals and the garden and …"

He cuts me off by picking me up and tossing me over his shoulder. As he walks away, he hollers behind him. "Bye, Ma! Thanks for looking after my girl."

I watch as the little glowing dragonfly gets smaller and smaller as we walk away. He sets me on my feet when we get to his bike and shoves a helmet in my chest. When he opens the saddlebags, to grab me a jacket, I spy my butterfly bag.

He notices me eyeing it as a tear slips down my cheek.

"It's all there. The girls grabbed you some clothes and other stuff; it's in my bag. This tiny thing doesn't hold much," he says as he hands it to me.

The tears come faster when I unzip it and find my giant book of bugs right beside my brother's survival guide.

"Ash wouldn't let me leave without it," Jackson says, taking the bag from me and gently placing it back in his saddlebag.

'Grandma also said I better have you back in a week or she's going to beat me with the flyswatter." He shudders, making me laugh.

"Well then, we better get going."

He tosses his leg over his bike and then holds out his hand to me. I take it but pause beside him.

"He's really gone?"

He nods. "The hogs have been fed."

An embarrassingly loud sob escapes me.

Immediately, he cradles my head in his hands, bringing our faces together. "You are safe, Willow."

He gives me all the time I need to pull myself together, and then he helps me onto the bike behind him. I wrap my arms around his waist, hugging him tight.

"Let's get out of here and see some trees, baby," he soothes, patting my leg.

Chapter Forty-One

Jackson

I've never done anything as gruesome as what I did to the man who hurt my girl. I ripped him limb from limb while the men of the club stood at my back. None of them even flinched at the barbaric way I went off on him.

Most of it was for her, but a small part was for me. His grandfather took my mother. I have no doubt he would have carried on his legacy had we let him live.

I knew Willow would make the right choice. She didn't come all this way to let him go. She wanted vengeance just as much as the rest of us. He was too dangerous to send back out into the world, and she knew that.

It was my father who suggested I take her away for a few days. He told me if I didn't, she would throw herself into the farm and not take the time needed to process all that had happened. The first few days of our trip, I thought I had made a terrible mistake bringing her here. She cried non-stop.

Then ... it just ended. Her smile returned.

We're getting ready to leave now. She's saying goodbye to her favorite tree

Fuck all if she ain't the most beautiful girl in the world. She stands up and hugs the thing. Well, as much as she can; the trunk is gigantic. It's not the tallest or the prettiest ... but she has claimed it as her own. She's spent a lot of time sitting beside it. I'm not sure what horrors or joys she's laid at its roots. But whatever they were, they must have been heavy, because I've never seen her stand taller.

Myself, well, I've never felt smaller in my entire life. But maybe there's a lesson in that. I'd like to say I've done some deep thinking while here, but that would be a lie. I've spent my days watching her. Her beauty outshines anything in this forest.

She makes my heart beat faster while at the same time slower, if that makes any sense. Willow just accepts me as I am.

Her green eyes sparkle when she turns from the giant sequoia tree to smile at me. I've never felt closer to another human being. Not even my parents.

We spent our nights sharing our fears, dreams, and our everythings. Some of those conversations were hard, but we had them. Since Bradley took her at such a young age, she's worried she's been delayed socially and academically. So, we talked about ways to help with those things.

She promised she would lean on me for those awkward moments. And fuck if I don't want her to. I'm so fucking excited to watch Willow grow now that she's free. In return, I promised I would tell her when I'm feeling restless.

And we both agreed to be honest when Lanie or Bradley are fucking with our heads. I don't think they will ever go away entirely, but together we will help each other cast them out when they surface.

"I'm ready," she says when she reaches me. "Sammy told me to tell you goodbye," she jokes.

"Oh, he did, did he?" I reach out and pull her close to me.

"He did," she laughs.

Willow rests her head against my chest. "Thank you for bringing me here. My dad always talked about coming here someday. He would be grateful to you for sharing this with me."

"Um, before we go, I wanted to let you know that Jesse called. Your mom is doing well in treatment."

Willow stands up straight. "I'm happy for that, but I don't think I'll ever be able to let her back into my life."

I run my thumb over her cheek. "That's okay, baby. Don't feel guilty about it."

"It's funny how it's been easier to forgive Bradley than it has my mom."

"She was someone you should have been able to trust. Don't be so hard on yourself."

We stand there, listening to the birds, and I wonder if she's struggling to leave. But then she breaks the silence.

"Take me home, Jackson," she says, pulling her shoulders back and holding her head high.

"Fuck yeah." I toss my leg over my bike and hold my hand out for her. This will never get old.

Never.

It's dark by the time we get to the farm, and all I want to do is make love to my girl, but it looks like our family has different plans.

Willow screeches in my ear, "Goats! We have goats!"

She barely waits for me to shut off the bike before she's running toward my grandmother and throwing herself in her arms.

"Willow, oh girl, I've missed you so," my grandmother shushes her, patting her back. "Did you see the goats?"

"Yes, I'm so happy to be home."

Everyone takes their turn hugging Willow. My dad walks over and gives me a hug of my own.

"Missed you, boy," he rasps, holding me tight. "Let's go inside and have some pie. Then we need to let these kids get some sleep. They've had a long day on the road."

Petey lags behind, offering to round up the animals.

Willow wraps her hand around my arm. "I would like to help Petey so I can see the new goats. Go on; I'll be right behind you."

I watch her walk toward the scary motherfucker. She's already come such a long way since I found her. Or, I guess I should say, my grandmother found her.

I know she wants to thank him for helping to find Bradley.

Chapter Forty-Two

Willow

"That fucking woman thinks she found him first, but I was hot on both their tails the entire time," Petey tells me as I pet one of the goats before we lock them in for the night.

I laugh and shake my head. "Well, I just wanted to let you know how much I appreciate your help."

"Yeah, yeah, the pleasure was all mine. Fuck that bastard."

My eyes flit briefly to the hog pen, but I quickly look away.

Petey notices and wraps his arm around my shoulder, giving me a light squeeze. "Let's go get some of that fucking pie before it's all gone," he says.

As we're heading toward the house, a woman storms around the side of it, dragging a small child beside her. She stops when she sees Petey and drops a bag to the ground.

"She's all yours," she says, pointing to Petey. "She's done nothing but cry for you."

Then, the woman takes off the way she came, leaving the little girl behind. The child must be around four years old.

Petey starts cursing and chasing after her. The little girl reaches for him as he passes, but he doesn't notice.

"Wait, goddammit, Susan! You know she's better off with you. You're her aunt; you can't just leave her like this."

"And you're her father!" she yells back.

They continue to scream at each other as the girl and I stand there staring.

Suddenly, it hits me. This is Petey's daughter. She looks just like him with long black hair and eyes so dark they reflect the moon.

"Do you like pie?" I ask her.

She sniffles, looking over her shoulder, but she gives me a tiny nod when she returns her focus back to me.

I hold my hand out to her, and she slowly takes a few steps toward me. When her little hand is in mine, I give it a gentle squeeze. "Let's go inside. I'm sure your dad will join us soon."

This makes her perk up a bit. I get the feeling she's missed him. I'm not sure what in the heck is going on, but I can see this girl could use a little kindness.

When I open the door, everyone stops and stares at us. The child instantly wraps her tiny frame around my leg.

"Uh, this is Petey's daughter. Someone might want to go out and check on him. He seemed a little surprised to see her."

Brody stands up, cursing. "She's been staying with his sister-in-law. I'll go see what's going on."

"Do you like books?" I ask, peeling her from my leg and then guiding her through the house to the living room where Jackson placed our bags.

Again, she nods. So, I sit down, pulling her onto my lap. She runs her finger over the little butterflies on my bag.

"Do you like butterflies?"

Another nod.

When I pull out my big book of bugs, her eyes light up. Together we sit and look at the pictures.

Brody storms back inside. "They're gone."

Katie hops up. "I'll find him," she says, pushing her way out of the house.

Jackson snaps his fingers. "Brody, go back to the warehouse in case he shows up there."

"Good idea," Brody says, rushing out.

The little girl blinks up at me as tears pool in her eyes. "He'll be back," I tell her. "No worries. You are safe here."

Jesse and Rachel begin discussing a place for the child to stay.

"She could stay with Billie Rose, but Aurelia's been running a fever," Jesse says.

"She could stay here," I suggest. "I mean, I don't know how to take care of a child, but maybe Grandma Maggie would be willing to help."

Grandma Maggie claps her hands together. "That sounds like a wonderful plan, Willow. I'll go bake some cookies. Do you like cookies?" she asks the little girl.

"Yes, ma'am," the child answers.

'Such good manners you have. Well then, that's settled. Why doesn't everyone go take care of business, and we will make sure she's cared for."

'My name's Willow," I tell her. "What's yours?"

She bites her little lip before answering me. "Charlotte," she answers quietly.

"That's a beautiful name."

"What is your favorite bug?" I draw her attention back to the book and away from the discussion about her runaway father.

"I like the butterflies best," she says, flipping to the page with a bright blue one.

There is hustle and bustle around us, but I keep her focused on the book. Before long the room turns quiet, and only the sounds of Grandma Maggie banging around in the kitchen remain.

I glance up to find Jackson standing in the doorway, staring at us. He mouths a 'thank you' to me. Without thought, I place a kiss on the girl's soft hair. He smiles at this. I can't explain why, but I feel like I need to protect her, like Petey did me. This is how I can repay him.

I know none of these people expect me to trade for anything they do for me, but old habits die hard.

"How about a game of Candyland?" he asks us.

Charlotte closes the book and jumps up to stand beside him as he digs it out of the closet. She bounces on the balls of her feet, clapping her hands.

"You seem pretty eager to play this game. You're going to beat us, aren't you?" he teases.

Avenging Skulls

She nods, plopping right down beside him as he sets up the board game. She leans her elbow on his leg as she picks out a yellow gingerbread man as her playing piece.

I've seen Jackson with Aurelia, but it just now hits me how good he is with children. Maybe because he's never really grown up. I like that. I really like that. He's serious when he needs to be, but he's not afraid to act goofy. He's not afraid someone might laugh at him. He's unapologetically him.

Grandma comes out to watch us play, setting a plate of cookies and glasses of milk beside us on the coffee table. Then, she lowers herself in her rocker, contentment settling over her face. When her gaze meets mine, she tilts her head and smiles.

Charlotte jumps up, clapping and squealing.

"Well, you little turkey. You beat us," Jackson says, raising his hand to give her a high five. He starts to chase her around the living room, picking her up and tossing her gently on the couch.

"Okay, that's enough. Time for bed," Grandma tells us.

As I'm helping Grandma clean up, I tell her she can have her old room with Charlotte, and I'll stay in Jackson's room with him. She agrees before kissing me on the cheek. Then, all four of us climb the stairs.

We say our goodnights in the hallway. Soon after, I'm pressed against Jackson's warm body, his arm draped across my stomach.

"That wasn't quite the night I had in mind," he teases, pressing his hard length against my bottom.

"I'm sorry," I whisper. "I had to help her. She looked so confused by Petey's reaction. I'm sure he didn't mean to hurt her, but I think he did."

'I love that you jumped right in. You're a true Skull, baby. Don't apologize for helping her. That is what we do. Everyone was quite impressed by how you handled the situation."

He kisses my neck, brushing his lips over my collar bone. "Let me make love to you," he whispers, lifting my thigh and draping it over his.

My eyes fall closed when his hand roams low across my belly, his fingers leaving goosebumps in their wake. I reach behind me and wrap my hand around his cock, making him groan quietly in my ear.

"This is going to be a challenge," he says, pushing my hand away.

I giggle, but it's short lived because he's slowly entering me. "Oh," I moan into my pillow.

"I love you, Willow."

His thrusts are strong and sure and hitting me in a place that makes me see stars.

"Jackson, I … shit, I'm going to be too loud," I whisper, trying as hard as I can to keep quiet.

He reaches around and places his hand over my mouth as he whispers dirty words into my ear. "Are you going to come for me, baby?"

I nod frantically. Yes, yes, yes.

And then it's like a bomb goes off in my head. I can't hear anything. I'm floating in bliss. Sheer, beautiful, endless bliss.

His beard scratches over my shoulder as he places gentle kisses there, waiting for me to come back to earth.

When I do, I turn my head so we are nose to nose. "I love you, Jackson."

Avenging Skulls

He wraps himself around me and snuggles in. "Sleep tight, baby. I have a feeling tomorrow is going to be another crazy day."

I sigh dreamily. "It might be crazy, but it's nice to know we all have each other."

He hums in agreement, sleep stealing him away from me.

I lie quietly until his breathing evens out, and then I slowly slide out of his arms. After putting on a t-shirt and pair of shorts, I slip from the room, taking a quick peek at Grandma and Charlotte. They both seem to be sleeping peacefully; I hear a light snore from the old woman.

When I get outside, I take a deep breath and make my way to the hog pen. I dig my toes into the grass as I stare at the mud. Is there really no trace of him left behind?

The guilt comes in one giant wave, knocking me to the ground. *I ordered someone's death.* How could I? He took care of me when there was no one else. I betrayed him.

Through my blurry gaze, I catch sight of the dragonfly on the side of the barn.

I swipe at my eyes angrily. He would have hurt others. I couldn't let that happen. He hurt so many already.

A tiny hand wraps around my shoulder. "Are you crying?" Charlotte asks.

Startled, I turn. "Yes, but I'm okay," I say, patting the spot beside me on the grass.

She sits down, her black eyes bouncing over my face.

"Why aren't you sleeping?" I ask her.

"Sometimes I have bad dreams," she tells me.

Her words make me pause and remember I'm not the only one with problems. I was lucky that the dragonfly brought me an angel. Maybe it's time I become one for someone else. Grandma Maggie brought me comfort when I needed it most. I need to do the same.

Pushing Bradley out of my mind, I focus on Charlotte. This beautiful girl deserves my full attention. "Do you want to tell me about it?"

She shakes her head no. Then, she notices the dragonfly painted on the side of the barn. "It's just like the one on the book you showed me."

"It is. Did you know that dragonflies have two sets of wings so they can carry angels on their backs?"

She looks at me out the corner of her eye like I'm crazy.

"It's true. One brought me Grandma Maggie."

Charlotte plucks at the grass. "She's really nice. I like her, and she makes good cookies."

I laugh. "They're the best."

"I don't have a grandma or a mama. The bad man killed mine. She's in Heaven now."

My heart cracks clean down the middle. "I'm sorry," I tell her. "I don't have any grandparents either, and my daddy is in Heaven."

She blinks at me. "Is your mama in Heaven?"

"No, but she's sick. I don't get to see her much."

She hugs her knees to her chest and stares at the barn. "Maybe a dragonfly will bring me an angel someday."

"I bet one will." I wrap my fingers around my necklace.

Avenging Skulls

"Do you think my daddy is mad at me?" She changes the subject, her tiny voice cracking.

I'm not sure what this girl has been through, but I can see how smart and strong she is.

"I don't think he's mad at you." I mirror her, hugging my legs to my chest. "I think he's scared."

"Of me?"

"No, honey. I think he's scared he's going to fail you in some way. But he'll be back. I promise you. He's a good man, and I'm sure he's a good daddy, too."

She smiles and wow, it lights up her whole face. "He's the best." But just as quickly, her face falls. "I miss him."

"I have an idea. Let's make a wish to the dragonfly. I'm sure she'll bring him back to you."

She shrugs, not really interested in making wishes she knows might never come true. But I know in my heart that Petey is a good guy. He'll be back.

I reach behind my neck. "You know, there is a trick to it. You have to wear this. I don't need it anymore because I already got my wish. It can't hurt to try, can it?"

She peeks into the palm of my hand when I hold it out to her. She draws her tiny finger over the pendent. "It's so pretty."

"It is. It belonged to Jackson's mommy. She's in Heaven, too. But this … this necklace has granted so many wishes. I know it will work for you. But you have to promise me you'll keep it safe and someday, when you find someone who needs it, you'll pass it on. Okay?"

She nods her head enthusiastically.

"Here. Hold up your hair, and I'll fasten it."

When it's in place, she drops her hair and immediately wraps her tiny hand around it.

"Okay, close your eyes and make a wish."

As her eyes fall closed, I turn around and stare at the man hiding in the shadows.

When she opens them, she smiles at me. "How long does it take to work?" she asks.

"I don't know, sweetie," I tell her.

And then Petey shows me he is indeed the man I thought he was. He steps out of the shadows and coughs quietly, trying not to startle her.

Charlotte's eyes widen, and she jumps to her feet. "Daddy!" she cries, running to him.

I stand slowly, watching him scoop her into his arms. He hugs her to his chest with his hand braced on the back of her head.

"Hey, baby. I'm sorry I left. I'm here now. I'm here now," he soothes.

She leans back and places her hands on his scruffy face. "The dragonfly made my wish come true," she tells him. "I wished for you and poof, you're here. It worked. It really worked."

He laughs at that. "I'm here. Do you want to go see our new home?" he asks her.

"Yes!" she squeals.

"Go on; go get your helmet on. It's hanging on the bike," he tells her.

Avenging Skulls

She rushes to do as she's told but stops and runs back, wrapping her arms around my legs. "Thank you," she squeals and hurries to the front of the house where Petey's bike is parked.

He walks over and grabs my wrist, pulling me to him. "Thank you, Willow. You are an angel."

"I didn't ..."

"You did," he cuts me off. He places a kiss on my temple and walks away.

When I hear his bike roar to life, I slowly make my way back to the house. Jackson opens the backdoor as I take a step up.

I pause, waiting for him to say something.

"I'm ... I'm sorry I gave your mother's necklace away," I tell him when he doesn't say anything. I should have checked with him, but Charlotte was just so sad. It broke my heart.

He stares down at me, his hair messy and his face serious. "You told her you got your wish. Is that true?"

My shoulders fall. He heard everything. "Yes."

His gaze roams over the farm, stopping on the dragonfly. "Then it was time for it to move on." He jerks his head. "Get your fine little fairy ass in this house."

"Shhh, Grandma will hear you," I warn, stopping on the top step.

"That's fine. That old woman was the one who started all this." He motions between the two of us.

"So, you're not mad about the necklace?" I ask again.

He reaches out and wraps his hands around my waist, dragging me close to him. "Listen to me. I will never be mad at you for helping someone. I'm not him, Willow."

Then, he remembers I left the bed to come out here. He steps forward, letting the door close behind him. He takes my hand and pulls me to sit with him.

My first instinct is to apologize, but that's not what he wants. He wants an explanation.

"I don't know why I came out here," I tell him honestly.

"Maybe I should have let you see he was gone. I've always done that for the others. I'm sorry I didn't do it for you."

"No. I didn't want to see him. I just … I don't know, Jackson. I feel guilty. Like, who am I to say whether someone should live or die?"

"You're someone who wanted to end the suffering. It was all he'd known. He would never have stopped."

"My head knows all that, but my heart is having a harder time accepting it."

Jackson just nods. I love that he accepts how I'm feeling. He doesn't tell me I'm wrong or that I'm just being stupid. He lets me feel how I feel.

Bradley used people's weaknesses against them.

My mom's addiction.

My teenage insecurities. My loneliness.

"You let Charlotte win tonight."

He raises an eyebrow. "No. I didn't," he denies.

"You did. I saw you switch the pieces when she wasn't looking."

Jackson is a person who also sees other's insecurities, but instead of using them against someone, he tries to ease them.

"She was sad. I wanted to give her something to be happy about." He shrugs.

I think back to the first time I saw Jackson. If I would have let that first impression guide my heart, I wouldn't be here with him. And god, what a beautiful soul I would have let slip between my fingers.

"What are you thinking about?" he asks.

"I'm thinking about how all of it was worth it, for this one moment, here with you. I wouldn't want to be anywhere else."

He drops his head. It's still hard for him to accept his worth.

When he raises his face, there are tears in his eyes. "I never thought I'd find someone who would see past my devilishly good looks," he jokes, pressing his thumbs under his eyes. "You've made me feel like a man again, Willow."

"Will you play your cello for me?" I ask.

He jumps up and seconds later, his cello is between his legs and his bow is in his hand. When he begins to play, I stand and jump off the steps, making him laugh.

"Play something happy," I tell him, spinning in a circle in the yard.

So he does.

The deep reverberating notes awaken every part of my soul.

And then I let go. Truly let go.

LM Terry

I dance, barefoot and free.

The dragonfly steadily watches over us as we begin something new ...

Something beautiful.

Epilogue

Willow ~ six months later

Kelsie stands by her dad, watching as he puts the finishing touch on my tattoo. "It's beautiful," she tells me.

"You don't think he'll think it's stupid?" I ask them for the hundredth time today.

Big Dan pauses and wheels his chair so he can look me in the eye. "If that kid tells you it's stupid, you let me know and I'll kick his ass."

This makes me giggle. I love Dan. Actually, I love them all. I feel like I've known them forever.

He goes back to work. "I thought your brothers were picking you up from the farm?"

"Well, they were late," Kelsie says. "So, I decided since Ash was giving Willow a ride here, I would tag along."

Big Dan grunts at this.

I know my brother has been having some issues. None of them have really talked to me about it, but I'm not blind. He's been drinking. A lot. He's prospecting for the club, but I would be lying if I wasn't worried about him messing it up. I don't know how many chances Jackson is willing to give him.

It's been especially hard on Ash that my mother was unsuccessful at rehab. Jesse told me she had arranged for my mom to go to treatment for me, not my mother. She wanted me to know in my heart that we had tried everything. It's on her now.

That's another thing about the club. Each member has their own strengths and weaknesses. It makes it easy to find someone to talk to. Jesse has been a godsend when it comes to helping me deal with my feelings about my mother. It's one thing we have in common.

Katie, too. But she's been busy with Petey. Or I should say, she's been busy trying to avoid him. Those two are something else. They can't be in a room for two seconds without going at each other. I think the only reason Katie hasn't left town is because Charlotte has taken a liking to her, much to Petey's distress.

The door to the shop bangs open, and in storm Carson and Cole.

Cole starts right in. "Kelsie, what the fuck? We were supposed to pick you up at the farm. Why didn't you wait for us?"

Dan snaps his fingers, making even me jump. "Boys, that's enough. Don't talk to your sister that way."

"Thanks, Daddy," she says, batting her lashes at him as he goes back to work.

I glance over my shoulder, catching her stick her tongue out at the boys.

"Dad, she can't be running amuck," Carson says.

Avenging Skulls

"Do you even know what that word means?" Dan laughs.

"Fine. Whatever. Let's go, Kels. Mom's waiting for us."

Kelsie hugs her dad. He pats her arm and gives her a quick kiss on the cheek. "Be good for your brothers."

"Of course."

Carson and Cole both mumble under their breath as they head out.

When the door closes behind them, Dan shakes his head. "I think Kelsie is being a brat to them because it's her way of distancing herself before they head back to college."

The boys have been back on break, and Kelsie has been a bit standoffish toward them, but I think something else is going on. She just hasn't been herself lately.

"There, all done," Dan says, pulling off his gloves and rolling his chair back. "I'll step out while you put your shirt back on."

I stand in front of the long mirror and hold up the little one he left for me. A huge smile breaks over my face. It's perfect. Quickly, I slip my t-shirt over my head.

"Well, what do you think?" Big Dan asks when I step around the privacy curtain.

"It's perfect!" I squeal, rushing toward him and wrapping my arms around him.

He leans down and kisses the top of my head. "I'm glad you like it."

"I don't like it. I love it," I tell him.

When I release him, I swear he's blushing. "If Jackson gives you any gruff, you remember to tell him to come find me. I don't care that he's been elevated to president of this club. I'll still kick his ass."

I just bounce on my toes, clapping my hands which makes him laugh.

"Somedays you remind me so much of my wife."

I grab my bag and head for the door. "That's a compliment," I sing song as I walk out.

His rich chuckle follows me as I step outside.

I rush across the street at the same time Jackson steps out of Junkyard Treasures, turning to lock the door behind him. When I wrap my arms around him from behind, he laughs.

"Did you have fun hanging out at the tattoo shop with Kelsie today?"

"Yep."

"Good. I'm anxious to get home. I've got a surprise for you."

I pull my head back. "A surprise?"

"That's what I said." He thumps me on the end of my nose before pushing me toward his bike.

On the ride back to the farm, I take everything in. It's something I do now. I allow myself to enjoy every single thing. The sun, the smell of his leather cut, the hard feel of his abs under his soft t-shirt, and we can't forget the trees, always the trees. But I also enjoy the sting of my new tattoo. I allow myself to feel it all. The good, the bad, and the in-between.

Life is precious, and I'm not going to waste one second of it.

Fred greets us as we climb off the bike. I lean down and pat his head. "How's my good boy?" I ask him.

He gives me a little gruff bark.

Grandma Maggie says that even Fred is happier with me here. I don't know if that's true. But I'm happy I can give him a little extra love during his golden years.

Jackson takes my hand and leads me to the barn. The minute I step inside, I notice white lights hanging in the loft. He nods his head toward the stairs. "Go on."

He's made me a library!

But when I get up the stairs, I see it's so much more. I quickly finish the climb and spin in the middle of the newly polished wooden floors.

"What is this?" I ask, not quite sure what I'm seeing.

"Well, Jesse and Lily have been working with their foundation to bring your idea to life. You are now the CEO of Willow's Words."

When I told Jackson I wished I could provide books to kids in need, I didn't think he was really listening. He was busy sanding a piece of furniture. But I should have known he heard me. Even though he's always on the move, he listens.

"They've already contacted some child advocate centers who are excited to work with you. And look …" He runs his hand over the desk I saw him working on just last week. "You have a computer and a shipping printer." He points to the items lining the desk.

"Jackson," I rasp, spinning in a circle.

"Oh, and this is the best part." He rushes to the loft door to show me his newest creation. "Look, it's a lift, so you don't have to lug the books up and down the stairs. I tried to think of everything you might need."

"It's too much," I cry.

Slowly, he walks toward me. "Willow," he warns.

I fan my face, trying to halt the tears. Okay, we've talked about this. About me thinking I have to trade for everything that's given to me. So, I change my thoughts and look at it for what it is. No one expects anything in return. This is a gift for me … for all the kids who will benefit from it.

When he stands in front of me, he places his hand on the side of my neck, his warm brown eyes grounding me.

"Thank you," I rush out. "It's amazing."

The side of his mouth kicks up in a grin. "That's better," he says. "You're going to do great things, Willow. This is just the beginning."

"Oh, I have a little surprise for you too," I tell him.

I start to take off my shirt, but he pushes me to the corner of the room.

"I don't want someone to walk in," he says, his brows pulling together in question as to what I'm going to show him.

When he's satisfied I'm not within eye shot from below, he releases me.

Slowly, I pull my shirt over my head. He groans, biting his lip piercing, his eyes roaming over my breasts. "I like this surprise," he says, running his finger over my lacey new bra.

I smack his hand away playfully. "That's not it." Then, I turn around.

His breath hitches. When he doesn't say anything, I turn around to face him, but he stops me by placing his hands at my waist. Then, his finger trails alongside my spine, careful not to touch the new ink.

"You tattooed my fingerprints on you," he whispers in disbelief.

"You don't think it's silly?" I ask, worried he won't like all the little bugs now crawling up my spine.

"I think it's the best thing I've ever seen. I love it." He presses his lips to my shoulder, making me shiver.

I turn in his arms and wrap my arms around his neck. "I wanted your prints on me forever," I whisper. "But right now, I could use the real thing. How about we give that daybed over in the corner a try. It looks comfy."

He laughs but then turns serious. "Oh, that's very tempting. But no, because I have one more surprise for you."

Jackson helps me with my shirt, then heads down the ladder before me. My gaze roams over all the shelves filled with books, my heart swelling to double its size for him and his family.

"Come on, but be careful," he hollers up to me.

When my feet are firmly on the ground, I turn around, finding him on one knee with a tiny black box in his hand.

My mouth falls open.

"Marry me, Willow," he says, his brown eyes sparkling with mischief and mayhem.

"Yes," I answer, dropping to my knees, bringing us eye to eye.

He tenderly places the ring on my finger. "It was my grandmother's," he says quietly.

Okay. I've held it together pretty good up until now, but I can't … I just can't. The tears begin to fall, and I cannot stop them.

"Baby, baby, baby," he soothes, placing kisses all over my face.

I stare at him through tear filled eyes. "I'd almost given up. But then I found this place, and I felt this familiar tug at my heart. I think it was your soul calling to mine. They were finally close enough to feel each other."

His eyes bounce over me. "Let's get married here on the farm," he says. "I can't wait. Let's do it tomorrow."

I start laughing, wiping my eyes. I love Jackson's personality. And though I probably shouldn't feed into it like I do, I can't help it. I love his enthusiasm. "Let's do it."

Dirk starts yelling from outside the barn. "Did she say fucking yes or not?"

Jackson rolls his eyes, making me laugh even harder.

"She said yes," Jackson yells back.

Cheers erupt from outside the barn.

"They thought they all needed to be here. There may or may not be a party waiting for us outside."

I lean forward and kiss him with my eyes wide open. I have nothing to fear from him, nothing to hide, but everything to gain.

When we step out, everyone cheers again. Then the hugging begins.

"We're having the wedding right here tomorrow," Jackson announces.

Jesse rolls her eyes but smiles. "See, I told you all. Dan, you owe me twenty bucks."

"Goddammit, kid. Who proposes and then gets married the next day?" Dan grumbles.

"That's what Jesse and I did," Dirk smarts off.

"Don't worry, baby. I'm on this shit. It's already planned," Jesse tells Jackson, patting him on the arm.

"Thanks, Aunt Jesse," he says, wrapping her up in a big hug.

Jesse is the glue that holds this club together. Everyone would be lost without her.

Lily pulls me aside. "Can I see it?" she asks.

I think she's talking about the ring, so I give her my hand.

"No, your tattoo," she says quietly.

I turn and pull my shirt up so she can take a peek.

"Aw hell," Dan says, wrapping his arm around her. "Don't cry, baby. I hate it when you cry."

"It's just ... god, I never knew how wonderful my life would turn out to be when I was standing on that bridge."

I drop my shirt and turn around. "Thank you for helping shape Jackson into the man he is today."

She waves her hand at me. "He's always been a wonderful human. I can't take any credit for that." Dan rests his chin on her head. "Life is funny, isn't it?" she says, patting at her cheeks.

"It is," I agree.

Jackson grabs me around the waist, making me squeal as he picks me up off my feet.

"Come on, my mom hired a photographer. She wants pictures of us in front of the barn."

Raffe and Rachel stand beside the photographer as she snaps away. They look so proud of their son, it makes me tear up. Jackson dips me back, nipping at my nose.

"No more tears," he whispers.

Jackson has a way of making everything fun. Even taking pictures. When he pulls me upright, I let my gaze roam over all of the people here today. I'm sure there will be even more tomorrow.

Look at this, Dad. A life amongst the trees. It's as beautiful as you always promised it would be.

But it's not the trees that make it so special ... it's the people.

"Hold hands, so I can see the ring," the photographer says.

Jackson shoots his grandmother a thankful smile before wrapping his hand around mine. The woman steps forward with the camera to her face, zooming in on the ring. Just then, an unexpected guest decides to get in on the photo. A dragonfly zips between us and lands right on our entwined hands.

Both of us freeze, our breath catching as we stare down at it. Jackson and I both slowly raise our eyes, smiling at each other.

"It was all worth it," he says quietly.

"It was all worth it," I agree.

May you touch dragonflies and stars, dance with fairies, and talk to the moon ~ unknown

Other Books by LM Terry

Rebel Skulls MC Series

Sugar and Skulls

Watercolor Skulls

Roses and Skulls

Avenging Skulls

The Hidden Series

Finding Anna

Saving Addy

Discovering Danielle

Stand-alone

The Dirt Road Home

All Your Firsts Without Me

About the Author

LM Terry is simply a crazy Gemini, writing stories that contain both light and dark elements. Her novels will take you on an emotional roller coaster. But when you get off, she promises it will be with a happy ever after. LM Terry lives in a small town in the heart of the United States. She is a wife, mother, and book lover. You will find her most days with her head in the clouds.

If you would like to stay up on new releases and promos, please visit her website or Facebook page.

Facebook: https://www.facebook.com/lmterryauthor/

Website: https://www.lmterryauthor